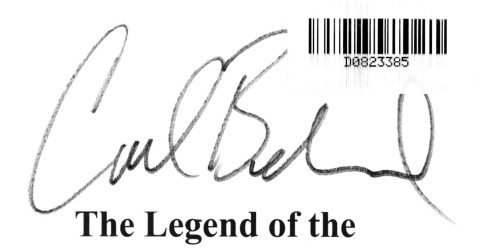

The Legend of the

Christmas Ship

The Legend of the

Christmas Ship

A novel by CARL BEHREND

Cover Design

Tom O'Connell

Boomerang Marketing

Cover photos courtesy of Chicago Historical Society

Cover Artist

Dietmar Krumery

Read more about the artist on the back of the book.

ISBN Soft Cover 0-9728212-8-7

ISBN Hard Cover 0-9728212-9-5

Second Edition, May 15, 2006

Acknowledgements

I'd like to thank my family, especially my wife, Dori, for making our home an enjoyable place to write, and all those who have made the story of the Christmas Ship come alive for me. Marylin Fischer, of whom I can truly say first aroused my interest in Great Lakes history, at first as a singer-songwriter, then as an author. To Don Hermanson of Keweenaw Video Productions for giving me my first "big break" by using one of my songs on his video. Also thanks to the many others who have shared their knowledge of the Christmas Ship. Rochelle Pennington for her exhaustive work on the book, *The Historic Christmas Ship*. Photographs and background information from *Lumberjack – Inside an Era in the Upper Peninsula of Michigan 3rd Edition*, by Wm. S. Crowe, are used by permission of North Country Publishing and co-editors Lynn M. Emerick and Ann M. Weller. To Wayne and Miles Stanley for the use of photos and stories they have told me of Thompson. Jack Deo of Superior View Photos, Bob Epson for use of underwater photos, and Alex Miron for her book *A History of Thompson*. All of the Great Lakes authors who have written about the subject and to all who have purchased my recordings through the years. Thank you for helping to inspire me to write this book. Now, this story is for you to enjoy.
Thank you, Carl Behrend

Old Country Books and Records
E7099 Maple Grove Road
Munising, Michigan 49862
www.greatlakeslegends.com
(906) 387-2331

Foreword

The story of the Christmas Tree Ship has become a legend in Great Lakes folklore. Authors have written books and poets and songwriters have been inspired by the story. Plays based on the tale are performed in schools and theaters. But for me, growing up in Manistique, Michigan, the story of the Christmas Tree Ship was often spoken of in local lore and written about in newspaper articles, especially at Christmastime. These stories eventually inspired me to write the song, *The Christmas Ship*, a song that became a regular part of my musical repertoire at my performances. Therefore I told and retold the story, and over the course of time, learned more about the Christmas Tree Ship, eventually becoming quite knowledgeable on the subject.

This story is not meant to be an actual account of every detail, but rather to give the reader a feeling of what it was like to be there, living in that exciting time period.

Although nearly all of the characters in the story really did exist, and many similar events actually did take place, the book is an accumulation of several stories from that time period portraying pictures history has painted for us of the kind of people and situations that Captain Schuenemann and his family were likely to encounter.

Longfellow, in his epic poem *Song of Hiawatha,* made use of a collection of Native American legends that had been meticulously compiled by Henry Schoolcaft in his book, *Hiawatha Legends.* Longfellow used those stories and legends, weaving them together into one interesting and beautiful account of the life of Hiawatha.

It is my desire as the author, not so much to record these legends in their every detail, as Schoolcraft has done, but rather as Longfellow, to use these legends to bring the reader on a journey into the past by joining these often forgotten pieces of our history into one beautiful tapestry for the reader to enjoy, thereby making the true history of these legends more relevant, that each of these characters from our past will live on in our imagination, and in that way will never be forgotten.

Carl Behrend
September, 2005

CHAPTER ONE – THE CAPTAIN

Chicago 1911

The Chicago River extends inland from Lake Michigan for about one-half mile, then dividing into the north and south, giving the city of Chicago 38 miles of riverfront, in addition to the Lake Michigan shoreline. After the destruction of the larger part of this city by the Great Chicago Fire in 1871, the city was rebuilt with the style and splendor that made it a marvel of the modern age.

One of Chicago's most striking and picturesque features is its riverfront, winding through its very heart, lined with warehouses, filled with vessels of every description, and crossed with bridges. Ships and hurrying boats along its bustling shores, and thronged drawbridges present an ever-changing picture.

There are 33 of these draw bridges. It is to one of these bridges that a young immigrant mother and her two young children are making their way. Through the busy streets they hurry on, with as much determination as a woman with two young children can have. The children's young minds are easily distracted by the sights and sounds of Chicago preparing itself for the Christmas holidays. There are horses and buggies "clip-clopping" along, the chugging of an occasional automobile, and the ringing of streetcar bells as they rumble along on their tracks.

"Come along, now, Annie! Come along now, Jimmy!" says Mother, in her heavy Irish accent. "Do you want to see the big ship with all the Christmas trees?"

"Oh, yes!" he replies excitedly. "How big is the ship?" asks little Jimmy in his innocent little voice.

"It's big," said Mother, opening her eyes wide and raising her hand heavenward. "Taller than the trees!"

"Look at all the ships," says Annie.

As they walk along the river, they see steamships, tugboats pulling sailing schooners, and numerous smaller boats, all busily heading in different directions.

"This is the best place!" exclaims little Jimmy.

"We're almost there," encourages Mother. "There it is— the Clark Street Bridge. That's where the Christmas tree ship is docked. I do hope they have some trees left," says Mother. "I've seen so many people carrying trees home. And I do hope we can afford to buy a tree. We only have a dime left that we can spend. Maybe they will have a wee, small one."

Finally, they arrive at the bridge and make their way down to the dock.

"There's the ship," Mother says excitedly.

"Oh, Mama!" cries Jimmy. "It is taller than the trees. It must be the biggest thing in the world," he says with wonder, as he looks at the ship's tall masts reaching heavenward.

"Look, Mama," points Annie. "There's a Christmas tree at the top of the ship! Oh Mama, this is wonderful!"

As they approach the ship, Captain Schuenemann slowly walks down the gangplank with a couple of Christmas trees in his hands and sets them along side the ship, amidst a group of other trees. The ship is decorated with wreaths and garland. A hand-painted sign hangs on the side of the ship that reads, "The Christmas Tree Ship. My prices are the lowest."

"Is that the captain?" Annie asks quietly.

"I think he is. He looks like a captain," says Mother.

Captain Schuenemann looks up from his work as the small group timidly approaches. His rosy cheeks and warm smile quickly dispel any fears they may have had.

"Merry Christmas," he says in a cheery voice.

"Are you really the captain of the ship?" says little Jimmy, in a voice beyond his years.

"Yes, I am," says the Captain. "And who are you, young man?"

"I'm Jimmy O'Malley, and this is my mother, and my sister Annie, and we're looking for a Christmas tree," he says boldly.

The Captain appears amused by the brave little lad. He leans over and takes him in his arms and holds him up, resting him against his hip.

"Can we go look at your ship?" Jimmy asks.

"Oh Jimmy," Mother says.

"That's all right," the Captain smiles. The Captain seems delighted. "You sure can," he says, and begins to walk up the gangplank of the ship. Annie and Mother follow close behind.

"This is the biggest ship I've ever seen," says Jimmy, looking up at the tall masts.

"What are these?" asks Annie, pointing to the ship's stays.

"Those are the stays. They keep the ship's masts from tipping over," the captain explains.

"Watch your step," says Mother, as she follows close behind.

"Do girls ever work on the ships?" asks Annie.

"Oh, yes," the captain replies.

"I want to be captain of the ship, when I get big!" Jimmy exclaims.

The Captain gives them all a short tour of the ship, stopping at various points of interest and explaining the task performed at each part of the ship. All the while, the Captain is kept amused by Jimmy's boisterous comments.

Eventually, they make their way back down the gangplank. During their visit, the Captain has noticed how poorly the family is dressed, and the mother's heavy Irish accent, and guesses that they have not been in America very long.

"So, you need a Christmas tree?" the captain asks.

"Maybe you've got a wee, small one," says Mother, looking a little embarrassed. "This is all we've got is this dime."

"Let me see," says the captain, as he sorts through some trees near the front of the ship. "Here's one that I've been saving just for you."

The tree is about four and a half feet tall. The Captain holds the tree up for them to look at.

"It looks wonderful!" the children shout.

"It's lovely," says Mother, holding out her hand with the dime. The Captain reaches out and closes her hand.

"There'll be no charge for your tree this year, and I want you and your family to have a very merry Christmas."

"Oh, thank you Captain. Yer too kind."

"No, thank you; for bringing your children, and making my day so much happier. Now, you take this tree home, and have a merry Christmas. But I want you to promise me one thing--that you'll come back and see me again next year."

"We will," they answered happily.

"It's the greatest tree in the whole world," says little Jimmy.

Mother and Annie each grab an end of the tree, and begin carrying it toward the street. Little Jimmy toddles behind them.

"Goodbye, Captain Santa," they shout through the tree branches.

"Goodbye," he says, waving back at them.

Just then, some richly dressed Chicagoans approach the ship in a fancy horse-drawn carriage. The elegant-looking couple climbed down from the carriage and began shopping around through the selection of trees along the ship. The Captain engages them in conversation while they look over the beautiful trees from the Captain's fine assortment.

"Merry Christmas," he greets them.

"Merry Christmas to you, Captain. What a fine selection of trees you have again this year," compliments the elegant-looking young woman.

"Fresh cut in Northern Michigan, not more than a couple of weeks ago," says the Captain proudly. His bushy handlebar mustache and bright blue eyes accentuate his rosy cheeks and beaming smile. Somehow he seems to inspire everyone coming to the ship with a festive holiday spirit.

"We've been buying our tree from you every year since we've been married," the husband tells him.

"And how many wonderful years has that been?"

"Six," he answers, taking his wife's hand in his.

"You're a lucky man, I can see that."

The woman smiles modestly. "Oh, Captain!"

"Well, since you're such good customers, I want to find you a special tree. What size tree would you like?"

"A medium size," the wife tells him, looking at her

The Legend of the Christmas Ship

husband. He nods in agreement.

"I've got just the one for you, right here." He leads them over and shows them a tree.

"That one is just lovely," she says. "We'll take it!"

"I'll let this one go for a dollar."

The gentleman reaches for his billfold. "It's a deal!" he says, handing him the money.

"Here, let me help you load this on your carriage."

The two men easily lift the tree into the back of the carriage.

"Thank you, Captain!"

Then the husband helps his wife up onto the seat and he climbs on, grabbing the reins.

"You have a merry Christmas, now," the Captain smiles. "And do come again next year!"

"Oh, we will, Captain," he says, as he slaps the reins to his horse. "Buying a tree from you is part of our Christmas tradition. We wouldn't buy from anyone else!" The horse quickly responds with a clip-clop of his hooves, and the little carriage jostles off with the happy couple smiling and waving proudly with their newly purchased Christmas tree bouncing along behind.

CHAPTER TWO - FRIENDS

The following day finds Captain Schuenemann and several men from his crew busy doing what they like best, selling Christmas trees, talking with friends and old customers who stop by the ship, and just plain enjoying all the preparations for the holiday season. An old friend stops by to say hello, and purchase a Christmas tree.

"Captain Schuenemann! How's old Captain Santa doing?" he says with a familiar smile.

Captain Schuenemann turns and looks up from his work. "Captain Holmes, you old sea dog!" Captain Schuenemann reaches out his hand, and the two men heartily shake hands.

"Well, it's good to see you, Captain Santa," he says, laughing.

The two captains both have smiles from ear to ear, and are both dressed nearly the same, in dark blue Navy pea coats and leather-brimmed caps. Captain Holmes appears slightly older, and a bit stockier. They both wear a mustache; the only difference is that Holmes' mustache is met by his broad sideburns.

Not only are the two men sea captains, but they're also neighbors. The Clark Street neighborhood being close to the waterfront, the Mariners Hall, and ship's chandlery make it an ideal location for these freshwater sea captains.

"How's yer lovely wife and daughters?" Captain Holmes asks.

"Oh, just as wonderful as ever. Barbara and Elsie are both working on making wreaths in the cabin I had built here on the ship. They have 15 women working for them making wreaths and garlands."

"Fifteen women!" snorts Captain Holmes. "How many wreaths do you sell here, anyway?" he asks in a tone of total disbelief.

"I've got a contract with Mayor Carter Harrison to supply the whole city of Chicago with the wreaths and garland for the holiday. He wants over 400 this year."

"Four hundred," spouts Captain Holmes. "That's incredible!"

"Yeah, and he wants them done by tomorrow evening."

"Tomorrow evening," Holmes repeats again.

"Well, you know, they're decorating the whole downtown district this year, and hanging wreaths on all the lampposts," Captain Schuenemann explained.

"Wow, You've got a regular factory here then, don't you?"

"I guess I do," he smiles. "We've delivered over half of them already, and it looks like the ladies will have the rest of them all ready by tomorrow evening, and maybe a few more to sell besides."

"That's amazing," Holmes responds. "How about the twins? How old are they now?"

"They just turned 12 a few days ago."

"Twelve years old!" Captain Holmes lifts the brim of his hat. "It's hard to believe they're that old already. And hard to believe it's been that long since your brother, August, has been gone."

"Yes, it is," says Captain Schuenemann, looking down and shaking his head a little.

"You probably wouldn't be around either, if it wasn't for them girls being born at this time of year, or you would have been with him when the *S. Thal* went down with a load of trees."

"Yeah, you're right about that," agrees Captain Schuenemann.

"So the twins are a blessing for you in more ways than one, aren't they?"

"Yes, they are, and they should be coming home from school now at any time. Oh! Speaking of time…" the Captain says, quickly pulling out his pocket watch. "I promised to let Barbara and the ladies know when it was three-thirty. They're all going to some kind of rally this afternoon."

"Rally! What kind of rally is that?" asks Captain Holmes.

"Oh, some kind of political rally about voting, and women's

rights," Captain Schuenemann says in a slightly mocking tone of voice.

"Voting and women's rights!" Captain Holmes bellows. "What do women know about voting and politics? It is a proven scientific fact that a woman's brain doesn't have the same abilities to understand and reason as a man's. Why, if we let them start voting, next thing you know we'll have women running for government offices! Now, wouldn't that be a big mess!" he says, shaking his head slowly as though totally disgusted.

Captain Schuenemann smiles. "If it makes Barbara happy to go to this rally, then I figure that it's fine with me."

"Yeah, well, I'm sure you've heard what's been happening with that Carry Nation and her crazy bunch, smashing up the taverns and all. If we let them have their way, we'll all be a bunch of tee totaling…" he stumbles for words a moment... "Milk toasts!" he blurts out angrily.

"I know," Captain Schuenemann says mildly. "But if it makes them happy to go to this rally, that's okay with me."

"Yeah, well, I don't like it," Captain Holmes says, shaking his head. "Women ought to stick with their God-given place, and that is bearing and raising children, with the man being the Head of the House. Getting involved in politics! What is this world coming to?" he says, with a look of disbelief.

"Anyway, I want a nice Christmas tree for my house," he

says, calming down a bit.

"We can fix you up with that," Captain Schuenemann tells him. "But let me tell Barbara and the other ladies what time it is, first."

"Have you seen this room that I added on to my ship?" asks Captain Schuenemann, walking up the gangplank.

"No, I haven't," says Captain Holmes. "But it looks like a pretty nice setup for you."

"Yes, it is. I put it on here every year. It really makes a nice workshop. And it's real convenient, because everything's all in one place here. The evergreens, a place to make wreaths, and a place to sell them, all in one location."

"Yeah, that makes a lot of sense," Holmes agrees.

Captain Schuenemann opens the door, and the two men step inside. Captain Holmes pauses for a moment and looks around, taking in the myriad activities going on around him. There are women sorting stacks of evergreens, others fitting evergreens onto wire hoops, some sitting at sewing machines, all working together like bees in a hive.

"Ah, this is amazing," Holmes gasps. "You've got a Christmas wreath factory here, is what you've got."

"Yeah, well, Barbara and Elsie are really the ones in charge of this part of the operation, so that's all I have to worry about it is selling Christmas trees. They take care of all this," says Captain

Schuenemann.

Barbara looks up from her work with a big smile.

"Hello, Captain Holmes! How are you?"

"Just fine," he answers, tipping his hat. "It looks like you ladies run a pretty tight ship around here. Nice and warm in here, too," he says, glancing at the wood stove.

Barbara smiles and nods in agreement.

"Elsie! What a beautiful woman you've become."

"Captain Holmes," Elsie says, dropping her work and hurrying over to give Captain Holmes a big, cheery hug.

"Oh my, what a lovely young lady you've become! How old are you now?"

"I'll be 20 soon," she says proudly.

"I'll bet that you have to beat the young men off with a stick," Captain Holmes teases.

"No," Elsie blushes a bit and smiles, "But I have been seeing someone. His name is Edward Harkness."

"Edward Harkness," bellows Captain Holmes, raising his eyebrows. "Now, there's a family with some money. Don't they own half the county, now?"

"Oh, I don't know about that," says Elsie modestly, trying to downplay the conversation. "Edward and I have been seeing each other since this summer, and are making plans to marry when he's through with law school at Harvard."

"You do have them falling at your feet." says Holmes, with a look of approval.

"I would imagine he's coming and going for the holidays," says Captain Schuenemann.

"Well, no," she says quietly, with a touch of sadness in her voice. "I just got a letter from him today saying that he won't be able to make it back home for Christmas. He's very busy with his studies and all, and he said that he's not going to be able to make it back home to Chicago for Christmas this year."

"That's too bad," says Captain Schuenemann. "I know how you've been looking forward to it." All of a sudden Captain Schuenemann changes his tone. "Hey, I promised your mother I would tell her and the ladies when it was three-thirty, and now it's past that time already," he says, pulling out his watch again.

"Oh dear! We better get going, ladies," says Barbara. "We don't want to be late." They all scramble to put down what they're doing and get ready to go.

"Well, it was nice seeing you again, Elsie, and you too, Barbara."

"Same to you, Captain Holmes. Do stop by for the Christmas party tomorrow evening, and don't forget to bring Louise," Barbara tells him as she grabs her coat and joins the others on their way out the door.

"Oh, I wouldn't miss it for all the tea in China. It's the social event of the year," says Captain Holmes.

CHAPTER THREE- NEW FRIENDS

Captain Schuenemann again busies himself organizing his stock of Christmas trees. Two of his crewmen are hauling trees off the ship and standing them in bunches out on the dock. Christmas trees are everywhere! Big trees, little trees, spruce trees, balsam trees, pine trees—hundreds of them, all spread out on the dock around the ship.

The Captain's twin daughters are just coming home from school. They come running when they see their father. "Daddy!"

"How are you, my little darlings?" He reaches out and picks them up, one in each arm. They both plant a kiss on each of his big rosy cheeks. "How was school today," he asks.

"It was wonderful. But we missed you," says Pearl.

"Can we stay and help you?" asks Hazel.

"Yes, you may," says Father. "Maybe you can go into the cabin and do your homework first."

"Oh, all right."

"Mother will be coming with some supper for us, too."

Just then a dappled gray horse pulling a delivery wagon comes to a stop near the dock. The wagon has an enclosed back, with the roof extending out over the driver's seat. At the front of the wagon, there's a well-groomed, middle-aged man with his young son riding together.

Captain Schuenemann watches the father lift his son down from the wagon onto the ground. Both of them are wearing the same style wool cap, but the young boy's cap is still far too big for him, causing his ears to stick out from his little head. The tall wooden sides of the wagon are attractively painted like a large billboard sign saying "Philip A. Sanders & Co., Groceries, Meats, and Produce." The green painted background and neatly painted, gold lettering on the sign give the wagon an attractive look, and also make for a clever form of advertising.

The father approaches, holding onto the little lad's hand. Captain Schuenemann watches with some amusement. The child's expression and manner look so determined, but with the over-sized cap and protruding ears, Captain Schuenemann can't help but laugh to himself a little.

"Guten tag, Captain. Werg gheust du?" (Hello, Captain. How are you?) Mr. Sanders says in German.

The Captain returns the answer, "Ser-goot, danke." (Very good, thank you.) Captain Schuenemann reaches out and heartily shakes his hand. The two men converse in German for a while.

"So how long has it been since you came here from the old country?" Captain Schuenemann asks.

"I came here eight years ago from Bremer Haven, on the North Sea."

"Bremer Haven!" Captain Schuenemann exclaims. "That's where my father was from! In fact, his brother's family still lives there. They are all fishermen."

"Oh, really?" Mr. Sanders answers. "Do you mean Arthur Schuenemann?"

"Yes!" says the Captain, with a look of surprise.

"My father would always buy fish from him for his market there and I went to school with his boys, Alfred and David."

"Those are my cousins!"

"I knew them quite well. They're all still fishing there."

"Won't Barbara be surprised when I tell her about this!"

The two men hit it off right away together and formed an instant friendship.

"From the looks of your wagon, I would guess you're in the grocery business too."

"Yes. We got that wagon this summer for hauling groceries and supplies. So if you ever need provisions for your crew, all you need to do is make a call on the telephone and give an order to the store. We can deliver everything right here to your ship."

"I hadn't thought of that!" said Captain Schuenemann, with a look of amazement. "I never thought of ordering provisions on the telephone. How long have you done that?"

"I've had a telephone for almost six months now," Sanders

answers. "And it has really worked out well. Word is getting out along the water front, and a large part of my business now is delivering provisions to the ships that are coming and going here to our fine city."

"And who's this fine young gentlemen with you here?"

"This is my son, Philip. He'll be five soon and he would like to help me find a Christmas tree."

"Come on aboard, and I'll give you a tour of the ship first. Do you think you would like to come up and see the ship," Captain Schuenemann asks, kneeling down to get a better look at the little guy. With wide eyes, little Philip nods quietly and then looks up at his dad.

"Well, come on board and I'll show you around."

Little Philip holds on to his father's hand while Captain Schuenemann gives them a tour of the ship.

The Captain leads them into the cabin. "Pearl, Hazel, come here. I would like you to meet Herr (Mr. In German) Sanders, and this is his son, Philip."

"Pleased to meet you," they both say cheerfully. "Oh, how cute!" They both fuss over little Philip.

"Why don't you girls set him at the table and give him something to eat."

"All right." They help him to the table and feed him a little lunch.

"It sure is warm in here, with that wood stove blazing," comments Mr. Sanders.

Captain Schuenemann and Mr. Sanders have a drink together and talk, while Pearl and Hazel fuss over little Philip. They are all having a wonderful time together.

"You know," says the Captain, "Barbara and I are having our Christmas party tomorrow evening. Why don't you come over and join us. We'll be having dinner at six. There will be some games for the children, and then we'll all sing Christmas carols around the Christmas tree, just like in the old country."

"That sounds wonderful," says Mr. Sanders. "Do you think you would like that, Philip?"

"Yes!" He nods his head vigorously and smiles.

"It's all set then. Six o'clock at 1638 Clark Street," says Captain Schuenemann.

"That would be wonderful!"

Mr. Sanders and Little Philip look at each other in approval.

"Now! We've got to find you a Christmas tree. How tall is the ceiling in your house?"

"It's twelve feet high," he answers.

"Oh, good!" he answers. "Then we can find a nice tall one. I know just the one!" he says, leading them out of the ship's cabin toward the back of the ship. It seems as though the Captain knows each tree as intimately as a shepherd knows his flock of sheep. "This one, right here," he says with his face beaming.

Standing up along one of the ship's stanchions is a beauty of a tree. The Captain, with his cheeks rosy red from working in the cool outdoors all day, in addition to his naturally jolly manner, makes it easy for young Philip to imagine that there really is a Santa Claus.

"Ya, yer right Captain," Mr. Sanders agrees. "It is a beautiful tree. I think my wife is going to just love it. How much is it?"

The Captain looks it over. "For a tree this size, I usually get $1.50 or even $2 for a perfect one like this. But because you're my friends, one dollar."

"Thank you, Captain!" says Mr. Sanders.

"Here, let me give you a hand," he says, grabbing hold of the tree. "I don't think little Philip here is big enough to carry the other end yet. Are you, Philip?" the Captain laughs.

Little Philip shakes his head no with a shy little grin. The two men each grab hold of the tree and walk it to the other end of the ship.

"Come now, Philip." Pearl and Hazel each grab one of Philip's hands and walk with him to the gangplank. The two men struggle to keep their balance carrying the tree, followed by Pearl and Hazel guiding little Philip by the hand.

Together they carefully make their way down the gangplank onto the dock. The two men load the tree into the back of the wagon.

The dapple gray horse standing patiently at the front of the wagon turns its big head to watch, apparently amused at the sight of the two men awkwardly struggling with their bulky load.

"There we go," the Captain smiles. "That should decorate your house just right for the holidays!"

Mr. Sanders pays for the tree and the two men shake hands again. "Thank you so much, Captain Schuenemann. It's been a pleasure meeting you, and a pleasure meeting your wonderful daughters." The proud father lifts little Philip up onto the seat. "And I'm sure Philip has enjoyed our visit too."

The boy nods his head very positively, with a big smile running from ear to ear.

"We're looking forward to your Christmas party, too. I'm sure it will be wonderful."

"We'll be expecting you," says the Captain with a smile. "And bring your wife, too!"

Pearl and Hazel stand next to their father, waving and smiling sweetly. "Goodbye, Philip," they say, waving to him.

Mr. Sanders climbs up onto the wagon and gives the reins a little snap and the old horse strides off, pulling the wagon. Little Philip continues waving to the Captain and the twins as long as they remain in sight. The twins keep on watching and waving too, as though they hate to see him go.

"Come now, girls, we must finish our chores. Mother and Elsie will be coming with supper soon, and we want to show them what a good job you've been doing."

"Yes, Father. We'll do a good job. You'll see," they assure him.

There's one thing the twins love to do more than any other, and that is to please their daddy. Together they quickly sweep all the evergreen needles from off the entire deck of the ship. Then they turn their attention to the big wreath room. In no time at all, the twins have the room that the women had all left so hastily transformed from a creative mess of evergreens back into a tidy workshop again.

CHAPTER FOUR - INVITATION

The whole while, Captain Schuenemann waits on customers, selling one tree after another, sending each one off with a Christmas tree and a smile.

The winter sun is low in the horizon, shedding its hues of red and gold across the evening sky. Darkness comes early with the shorter days of winter. The sunset turns to a golden twilight. A lone figure slowly walks along the street, stopping at every streetlight, carefully reaching up with his lighter to ignite each lamp as he approaches it.

Captain Schuenemann looks up from his work just in time to notice him lighting the lamp nearest to the ship. The lamplighter sees the Captain watching and yells out to him, "Don't forget to light up your lights, Captain!"

"Good idea," he yells back. "I almost forgot." Captain Schuenemann calls to his crewmen, "Engvald, Hogie! Time to turn on the electric lights."

The two men quickly respond and soon have several strings of lights lit up across the stays and rigging, giving the ship the appearance of a well-lit city. The Captain looks up at the bright lights with a look of satisfaction as they flicker in the breeze.

Elsie and Barbara arrive, carrying a basket of food.

"Hello, Father, are you ready for supper?"

"I'm starved," he answers, rubbing his hand over his belly.

"We brought you some bratwurst, sauerkraut, and apple pie, nice and hot." Barbara greets him with a hug and a kiss. "Did the twins get here all right?" she asks, with a look of concern.

"Yes. They're in the cabin, straightening up."

"Oh, good," says Mother, with a look of relief. "Herman! Why don't you take a little break now and eat your supper while it's still hot. I'll take care of customers out here for you."

"Alright, honey, I'm coming," he says, still looking up at the lights.

"Those electric Edison lights sure are beautiful up there," says Barbara, looking up at the lights on the rigging as she climbs the gangplank.

"Yes, they are beautiful," Elsie agrees.

"I'm real happy with them, too," the Captain says, looking up at them one more time. "Business has really improved too, since we started using them. Actually, it was Hogie Hoganson's idea. He and Engvald Newhaus put up most of them. We would never have imagined such a thing as electric lights a few years ago."

"They sure make the ship noticeable from on the bridge," says Elsie. "It's like the most important thing you see when you cross the bridge, and with the lights reflecting off the river, it's just beautiful."

"I would say that we sell as many trees at night now as we do in the daytime!" the Captain boasts. "Maybe more!"

"Come on now, Herman, and eat your supper. Elsie and I have already eaten, so you and the girls can have supper together while Elsie and I mind the store."

Entering the cabin, they all look around, totally pleased to find things so nice and neat.

"Hello, children," says Barbara.

"Mommy!" The twins come hurrying over to see her.

"My, what a nice job you two have done here!" Mother compliments.

"It didn't take them long, either," Father adds.

"It sure makes it nice in here when it's all neat and clean," says Elsie.

The girls both give Mother a big hug and kiss.

"I expect you're both hungry," she says.

"I'm very hungry!" says Pearl.

"Me too," says Hazel.

"Come now, sit down here with Father and have something to eat. Elsie and I will go back out and take care of customers."

Captain Schuenemann sits down at the table. Pearl and Hazel join him.

"I met a fellow today from the old country. He and his son

stopped by for a Christmas tree. Philip Sanders. He came from Bremer Haven a few years ago, and he knows a lot of our family back there. He's really an interesting fellow to talk to."

"And his little boy was so cute," says Pearl, and Hazel nod.

"So, let me guess. You invited them to the Christmas party tomorrow," says Barbara, with a knowing look.

"Well, yes," says Herman, looking a bit sheepish.

"Herman Schuenemann! Are you going to invite the whole city? You always want to have your cake and eat it too, don't you," she says with a disapproving look.

The Captain hesitates a moment, a bit taken back by his wife's displeasure. "Well, yeah." He pauses. "What good is cake, if you don't eat it?" he says, shrugging his shoulders and bursting into laughter. Barbara starts laughing too, even though she is trying to act a bit annoyed.

"I suppose that's the way it is, when you're married to Santa Claus," she laughs. Elsie and the girls laugh too.

Barbara sets out the food. "Come now, Elsie, we mustn't keep our customers waiting."

Herman and the twins are left at the table together. "Children, let's bow our heads for a word of thanks." The twins both bow their heads as Father leads them in prayer.

"Dear God, thank you for your kindness toward us, and thank you for this food, and for all your other blessings too numerous to count. In Jesus' name we pray. Amen."

CHAPTER FIVE – CHRISTMAS PARTY

The following evening finds the Schuenemann household busy preparing for the holiday dinner party. Guests begin to arrive at their Clark Street home. The Captain's Victorian style home is attractive and kept well, yet still a rather modest place. But the Captain and his family are proud to share their home, and have decorated it with wreaths and garlands in celebration of the Christmas season.

Captain Schuenemann is in a festive mood, and greets each guest as they arrive, taking their coats and hats and showing them into the parlor.

Captain Nelson and his wife arrive. Captain Nelson is a part owner of their ship, the *Rouse Simmons*. He's an older gentleman, dressed in captain's attire. His skin is weathered and his hair is light gray, but he also has a glimmer in his eyes and a look that portrays a thousand sailing stories. His wife, Delores, is petite, with dark hair streaked with gray, and a beautiful smile. Together they make a very noble-looking couple.

The next to arrive are Mayor Carter Harrison and his wife Edith.

"Mr. Mayor, how are you tonight?" asks Captain Schuenemann, shaking his hand. "And Edith, you look lovely tonight! So glad you could come."

"We wouldn't miss it, Captain," the Mayor's wife says with a smile. "How are Barbara and the girls?" she asks.

"They're all just fine. The girls are all busy in the kitchen. Just go right in and see them. They've got a fine meal cooking for us. Just go right on in."

Another couple comes up the walk before Captain Schuenemann closes the door. "Captain Holmes, Louise. How are you on this fine evening?"

"Just wonderful," Holmes responds.

"I see you brought your lovely wife. How are you tonight, Louise?"

"Just fine. Thank you, Captain."

"And your beautiful daughter Christine. What a lovely young lady you've become. How old are you now?"

"Fifteen," she answers shyly.

"Ah, that's a wonderful age. My girls are so anxious to see you! Come on in. Give me your coats and hats."

"I suppose you not only got Christmas trees up north, but I would imagine you did some hunting up there in northern Michigan," Holmes says.

"Oh yes, we always do some hunting. It's not all work when we go up there, you know. I always carry a rifle in the wagon, so that while I'm driving the wagon in the woods I can shoot a deer, if I see one."

"Did you see any?" Holmes asks.

"Did I see any? Why they are thicker than fleas on a hound dog. I got several deer this year. As a matter of fact, that's what we're having for supper tonight. Venison roast and bear."

"Bear!" Captain Holmes snorts. "I suppose you shot a bear, too!"

"Oh yes," replies Captain Schuenemann proudly. "It was a big one. Probably around five hundred pounds."

"You've got quite the life, I tell ya," Holmes marvels.

"I'm having it made into a bearskin rug for in front of our fireplace," explains Captain Schuenemann.

"That will be nice," says Holmes.

Just then, a knock is heard on the door. It's Herr Sanders and his wife with little Philip.

"Gutten Tag, Herr Sanders."

"Gutten Tag, Captain."

"Captain, this is my lovely wife Katherine."

"A pleasure to meet you. Barbara will be so happy to meet you too.

"And Philip, how are you, young man?" the Captain asks, leaning over and smiling at the little lad. "What's that you've got there?"

"A present," he says shyly, holding a brightly wrapped

package out towards the Captain, his little face beaming.

"Oh, thank you," says Captain Schuenemann. "How thoughtful of you! Barbara and I will open it right after dinner. Come right on in and I'll take your coats and hats. Pearl and Hazel will be so happy to see you. They have been talking about little Philip all evening. They're in the dining room, getting things ready for dinner. Why don't you go in there and surprise them," the Captain says, leaning over little Philip, guiding him gently to the other room with one hand and pointing with the other.

Little Philip shyly walks into the other room. The twins let out a squeal of delight.

"Philip!" They hurry over and immediately begin to fuss over him. Little Philip smiles from ear to ear, just loving all their attention.

Captain Schuenemann introduces all of the guests to each other and pours them all a drink, keeping them all entertained with his jovial manner and interesting stories.

Barbara comes out of the kitchen and greets the guests. Beautifully dressed for the occasion, she joins the Captain in entertaining their guests. Together they make a fine-looking couple, and truly make their guests feel as though they belong to part of a big, happy family celebrating Christmas together.

All of the guests gather around the Christmas tree in the parlor and comment how lovely it looks.

The men are gathered together telling stories. Captain Holmes speaks up. "Captain Schuenemann, how are the Christmas trees selling this year?"

"It looks like this will be our best year yet," he says proudly. "It seems since we started using electric lights on the ship, more and more people are buying trees at night. I bet we sell as many in the evening as we do during the day. It looks like we'll be sold out of trees in a couple more days, so I'm hoping to get even more trees next year."

"How much land do you own up north?" asks Mr. Sanders.

"Two hundred and forty acres."

"Two hundred and forty acres! That's quite a bit of land. Is that all planted with Christmas trees?" asks Captain Holmes.

"Well, it's all cut-over land. The white pine has all been logged off about eight or ten years ago, and it's all growing back in spruce and balsam, which are perfect for Christmas trees," Captain Schuenemann explains, "so it's like having a Christmas tree plantation."

Just then, Elsie Schuenemann and Aunt Rose come out of the kitchen carrying hot platters and bowls of food. Aunt Rose is the widow of August Schuenemann, the Captain's brother, who had been lost when their ship, the *S. Thal*, had been lost with all hands twelve years earlier. "Come and get it!" the ladies announce, setting the dishes on the dining room table.

All of the guests respond and slowly begin to move into the dining room. Everything looks and smells so wonderful. The dinner table is all set with all of their best China and silverware, and the table is decorated with a centerpiece of evergreen and pinecones in a basket. Barbara joins in carrying food from the kitchen and setting it at the table. The twins are busy setting out the last pieces of silverware and napkins. By now, everyone is in a festive mood. The dining room is all decorated brightly. There are all the sights, sounds, and smells of the holidays, with everyone dressed in their best clothes. Add to all that a good dose of Schuenemann hospitality, and you can only imagine what a grand time it is to be celebrating Christmas "German style" with "Captain Christmas Tree Schuenemann" himself. There isn't a happier celebration in old Chicago this night.

The guests all find their seats around the beautifully decorated table. The shiny silverware and fine China all neatly set out over a sparkling white tablecloth appear like ornate diamonds on a fine necklace. A small sprig of an evergreen branch by each plate adds to the holiday décor.

Barbara, Aunt Rose, and the girls are all busy carrying out the last dishes of food and condiments to ready the dinner table for this finest occasion of the year. Barbara and the girls are all beaming. It is as though their greatest pleasure is derived from serving their guests.

With the sound of music flowing from the Victrola, the guests all gather around the dining room table. One by one they all take their places, till everyone is seated. Barbara is the last to join them. She turns to the phonograph, lifts the needle from the record, and the music stops. Then she quickly joins the others at the table in her place by the Captain's side.

All of the guests are complimenting, saying how wonderful everything looks and smells. Then all eyes turn toward Captain Schuenemann as he speaks up with a tone of voice fitting for the occasion.

"I would first of all like to thank all of our guests for coming to share in this wonderful Christmas celebration, and I would also like to thank Barbara, Rose, and the girls for the fine job they've done preparing this wonderful dinner. I would like to say that I helped them. But they wouldn't even let me into the kitchen!" Everyone laughs.

"We have a tradition in this house that before dinner, we all join hands and have a word of thanks." Captain Schuenemann reaches out his hands like some grand patriarch at the head of the table. They all follow his example and join hands around the table. Then, silently, they all bow their heads in prayer while Captain Schuenemann leads them in prayer.

"Dear Father in Heaven, we do thank You for all of Your blessings this past year, and for all of our family and friends gathered here at this fine meal that you have provided us. And most of all, for our Savior, Jesus Christ, whom you sent to this world to share in our joys and sorrows, and to lead us back to heaven. Amen."

Several quiet "Amens" are heard as the Captain lifts his head.

Grabbing a large knife and fork, Captain Schuenemann begins slicing the roast. "Venison and bear," he announces. "Pass your plates this way, and I'll dish you some. This is all from our trip up north," he tells them all proudly. "Barbara and Rose sure know how to cook venison, but this is the first time they've cooked bear, so you'll have to bear with me," he says jokingly.

"How much would you like?" he asks each one, placing some roast venison on their plate. "Bear?" he asks.

"Just a little piece," says Elsie, gesturing with her fingers and thumb about half an inch apart. She's trying to be polite, but at the same time she's obviously not as enthused about bear as her father is.

The Captain dishes everyone a portion of venison and bear, while Barbara and Elsie begin passing around dishes filled with delicious food, and all around the huge table everyone enjoys the meal of the year.

Conversations around the table range from sailing adventures to city politics, and from childbirth to church business, with everyone freely sharing in any of the half-dozen conversations going on at any given time. It seems that everyone is included, from the youngest to the oldest.

While they're all absorbed in the fine meal and conversation, Mayor Carter Harrison suddenly rises to his feet and rings his fork against his empty teacup. Instantly, all eyes turn to this grand old city father. Raising his glass in the air, he announces, "I would like to propose a toast to our hosts, the Schuenemann family, for their generous hospitality to us all this evening. To Barbara, Rose, and the girls, who have really done such a fine job preparing this delicious meal and decorating the house for this wonderful Christmas banquet. And I would also like to thank all of the Schuenemann family for their efforts in providing our fine city with the evergreens and donating the huge tree the city used in our Christmas celebration. And last but not least, to our host, Captain Schuenemann, for his hunting prowess that has enabled all of us to here enjoy the bounty of the northern forest!" Mayor Harrison smiles and clinks his glass as a toast with those nearest to him. Everyone around the table joins in. Even little Philip toasts his glass of milk with Pearl and Hazel.

Not one to be outdone, Captain Schuenemann rises to his feet and holds out his glass. With a broad smile on his lips and a humorous look in his eyes, the Captain announces, "I would like to take this occasion to announce the beginning of my new career in politics. It seems that evergreens are the only subject in this town that everyone seems to agree on, so tonight I would like to announce my bid for office as the next Mayor of Chicago, as a candidate of the "Christmas Tree Party!"

Everyone bursts into laughter, with Mayor Harrison nearly doubled over with laughter. Then, in a more serious tone, Captain Schuenemann announces, "A toast, to the mayor of our fine city, Carter Harrison and his lively wife Edith."

Again everyone toasts together with glasses held high. Mayor Harrison is still chuckling and smiling as he toasts with those around him. The dinner continues again, with more laughter and conversation.

"Save room for dessert," Barbara announces.

"Too late for that!" bellows Captain Holmes. "What is it?"

"Your choice of pumpkin pie or rice pudding!"

"How about a little of both? I'll just have to eat them slowly," he adds with a bit of pretended remorse.

"Let me get the coffee," Aunt Rose tells Barbara as she gets up and hurries off into the kitchen. Just as she pushes open the swinging door, the telephone rings. Aunt Rose hurries into the kitchen to the telephone hanging on the wall. She lifts the earpiece off the receiver and puts it to her ear. Leaning closer to the mouthpiece she answers.

"Hello! This is the Schuenemann's residence."

A voice at the other end says, "This is the operator. I have a long-distance call for Elsie Schuenemann."

"Yes, just a moment. Elsie! It's a long-distance call for you!"

"It must be Edward," she says, her face beaming as she hurries into the kitchen.

"Hello? Edward! Oh, it's so nice to hear from you."

Aunt Rose leaves the kitchen so Elsie can have a more private conversation. "It's Edward," she announces to the others as she enters the dining room.

The conversation immediately turns to Edward and his wealthy family, and to Elsie's budding romance.

Captain Schuenemann comments on the modern marvel of the telephone. "It's just truly amazing that we can be sitting here in Chicago having dinner, while someone on the East Coast can send a message through a wire and we're able to talk to them and hear one another's voice!"

Captain Nelson shares in the fascination with modern inventions. "I was down at the Mariners' Hall the other day and a couple of the steamship captains were talking about the new Marconi wireless. They said that they are now able to send messages somehow over great distances without any wires at all, using some kind of electric waves that can pass through the air!"

"That's amazing," Captain Schuenemann responds. "Do

you think they will be able to send messages to ships out on the ocean?"

"They already can," the Mayor chimes in. "I just read the other day about a huge passenger ship they're building over in Belfast, Ireland that will be equipped with the new wireless. The article said the ship will employ a full-time wireless operator and that the passengers will be able to conduct business transactions on both sides of the ocean while enjoying comforts that will surpass even the finest hotels in the world. The ship will be named the *Titanic,* because it's so huge."

"That's amazing," Captain Schuenemann smiles. "How many passengers will the ship be able to carry?"

"About 3,500," the mayor responds. "It's set to be launched next spring. The ship is so huge and is to be built so well, it is said that it is actually going to be unsinkable!"

"Unsinkable!" Captain Nelson and Captain Schuenemann both repeat with bated breath, and look at one another in awe.

"With that many people on board, the ship will be more like a floating city. I wonder if they'll have a full-time mayor on board," he jokes. Everyone laughs.

They all enjoy their dessert.

"More coffee, anyone?" Barbara asks.

"Yes, please," several of them nod.

Back in the kitchen, Elsie leans into the telephone, talking to Edward. She's telling him about the fine dinner they are having. "Soon we will all go into the parlor and sing carols together around the tree. I wish that you could be here, Edward. I know you would truly enjoy Christmas here with us."

On the other end of the line, Edward sits by a phone in a fancy hotel lobby, dressed to the hilt. He appears to be listening impatiently and looks around as though a bit unconcerned with the conversation.

"I miss you so much too! I wish I was with you."

"I've been so busy with my studies, I have hardly even had time to write."

"Oh, do be careful you don't overwork yourself," Elsie says, trying to give some soothing advice.

Just then a stylish young blond with a feathered hat, white gloves, and a beaded purse comes hurrying into the hotel lobby.

"Edward! Do hurry, or we'll be late for the party!"

Edward quickly puts his hand over the mouthpiece, then quickly says into the phone, "Well, I've got to go. Some friends are waiting. I'll call again soon. Good-bye!"

CLICK.

"Who was that?" the woman asks impatiently.

"Oh, I was just talking to my family back in Chicago."

"I thought you said they were all over in Europe," she says, touching him under his chin with her fingertip, looking as innocent as possible.

"Not all of them went. I still have family back home in Chicago," he answers nervously.

Elsie stands at the other end, still holding the earpiece to her ear. "Edward?" Then she slowly hangs it up onto the receiver.

Barbara comes through the door into the kitchen and sees the look on Elsie's face. "Is something wrong, Honey?" she asks Elsie.

"Oh, no! It's just that Edward is so busy with his studies, and I do miss him so!"

"I've got to get some more coffee."

"I can get it, Mother."

"All right. Just go around the table and pour them all another cup."

After enjoying dessert and visiting, Captain Schuenemann rises to his feet. "Let's all gather in the parlor," he announces. "It's time to sing a few Christmas carols."

They all casually follow him into the parlor. Aunt Rose takes her place at the pump organ and arranges her sheet music while Captain Schuenemann passes out the songbooks.

The guests all comment on how beautiful the Christmas tree looks.

"I had to fight a bear to get that tree," the captain jokes.

Together they all gather around in front of the beautifully

decorated tree. The mood is festive and yet reverent.

"Let's start out with *Oh, Tannenbaum!* We'll do it in both German and English."

Aunt Rose nods and places the sheet music in front of her, then, pumping the foot pedals of the organ, she beings to play. Her fingers move skillfully over the keys, producing a beautiful sound.

Captain Schuenemann leads them all in singing. It's obvious from his enthusiasm that the Captain loves to sing, and everyone joins in singing the words for *Oh, Tannenbaum*. The Captain's melodious tenor voice and perfect pitch make him a natural song leader. His smooth tenor voice is contrasted by the deep blasts of Captain Holmes' bellowing baritone.

The twins, looking almost angelic, join in together with their friend Christine. Little Philip stands just in front of them all and tries to join in too, while Pearl gently rests her hand on his shoulder, making him feel quite secure. At times the twins look over at one another and giggle when Captain Holmes lets out a particularly loud blast. His deep, bellowing voice and wide-open mouth remind them of a giant exploding volcano.

They sing one song after another, each one requesting their favorite, until they have sung nearly every song they know: *Silent Night, Away in a Manger, Joy to the World, It Came Upon a Midnight Clear.*

The joyous sounds of their songs drift out from the house

and out into the streets of the city, then caught by a winter breeze and carried along until met by the songs of other voices, thousands of voices, families, friends, and neighbors, all gathered around their Christmas trees singing carols. All celebrating the birth of the One who chose to leave heaven to join the human race with all of its faults and failings, and to guide them back to a place of love.

All through the city of Chicago, Christmas carolers continue singing into the night. But nowhere in the entire city is there a more joyous celebration than in the home of Captain "Christmas Tree" Schuenemann.

CHAPTER SIX – ANOTHER SEASON

It is October, the following year, 1912. Captain Schuenemann and his crew are sailing into Manistique, Michigan, a busy lumber town on the northern shore of Lake Michigan. The Captain and his crew have been transporting lumber and other cargo all summer, and now are on their final trip up Lake Michigan after making one brief stop at Beaver Island for a load of tanning bark. Then they plan to get Christmas trees for their annual shipment to Chicago.

The Captain gives orders as the crew prepares to tie up at the dock.

"Lower the mainsail," the captain shouts. "Let's tie up on the starboard side, over near them fishing boats. Bring in the jib. We'll be leaving the ship docked here until we're done unloading the cargo of bark and we have most of the trees cut and ready at the dock at Thompson."

"All right, tie her up right here," the captain orders. Deckhands jump ashore and begin tying up the ship. The captain continues, "You men prepare to unload, while I run into town and take care of some business. I want to get over to the Chicago Lumber office and get paid for that last shipment of lumber before they close for the day and maybe pick up a few supplies."

"Aye, aye, Captain," says a crewman, acknowledging.

"Lower the gangplank," the other mate responds, "the captain's going ashore!" Two deck hands instantly begin lowering the gangplank.

The moment it hits shore, the captain hurries down and is on his way into town.

Captain Schuenemann makes his way past the fishing boats and racks of nets drying along the shore. There are several sailing schooners and a couple of steamships tied along the shore nearby. The gulls fills the air with their familiar cries as they land on the rooftops of the nearby warehouses. A steam engine can also be heard in the background, and the sound of a sawmill at work nearby. There are men and boys busy piling lumber into huge stacks along the docks. They all give the Captain a friendly nod as he makes his way past. Horses and wagons move through the streets. Buggies and carriages clamber about. The Captain watches with interest as an automobile goes clattering past.

Walking up the street from the harbor, he pulls out his pocket watch. He gives it a quick glance, continuing on with a steady pace. A shopkeeper is sweeping off the steps in front of his store. A shoeshine boy polishes a customer's shoes in front of the barbershop. An angry tavern owner is throwing a drunken customer out on the street.

"And don't come back," he bellows, as he tosses the

struggling troublemaker face down onto the street. "I won't stand for any troublemakers like you in this establishment!" The bartender brushes off his clothes as he makes his way back inside.

The man on the street lies there a bit shaken, half dazed, but only for a moment, as he suddenly jumps out of the way just in time to avoid an oncoming team of horses pulling a wagon loaded with barrels.

Captain Schuenemann wastes no time, as he quickly walks through a busy intersection, past the banks and shops, to the Chicago Lumber Company office. It's a tall wooden building, giving it a commanding view of the main street.

The Captain hurries up the steps inside, through the lobby, and to the main office. As he approaches the office, a secretary looks up from her work and asks, "Can I help you? Oh, Captain Schuenemann," she says, warmly.

"Yes. Is Mr. Crowe still in?" he asks anxiously.

"Yes. He's just about ready to leave for the day. But I'll tell him you're here."

She goes to his office door, and informs him that Captain Schuenemann would like to see him. Mr. Crowe answers, "Tell him to come right in," he says expectantly, dropping his pen and rising from his chair to meet him. The two men shake hands and greet one another.

"Herman! Come on in, have a chair. How long have you

been in town?" Mr. Crowe asks.

"I just pulled into port a few minutes ago, and tied up down by the fish dock. We're unloading a cargo of hemlock bark."

"How was the weather out on the lake?" Crowe asks.

"Not bad," the Captain replies. "It did blow pretty good two days ago, but the winds were behind us, with a following sea, so we could make pretty good time. We stopped at Beaver Island on our way up the lake and took on a load of Hemlock bark for the tannery here. Captain Mannes Bonner, who lives on Beaver Island, had the cargo all ready for us to load when we got there. He's half-owner of the *Rouse Simmons*, you know," Mr. Crowe nods. He knows many of the lake captains and their ships from doing business with them.

"Have a cigar," Crowe offers, opening a box towards Captain Schuenemann.

"Thank you, Mr. Crowe," the captain replies. He pulls a cigar from the box.

"I'll get your payment for your last shipment of lumber ready. Do you have time to bring another load to Chicago before the weather turns?" Mr. Crowe asks.

"No, sir. I'm going to be getting a load of Christmas trees ready for my final run of the season," Schuenemann replies.

"Oh yes, it's that time of year already, isn't it? Well, good luck, Captain. But if you change your mind, let me know. I've got plenty of lumber that needs to be shipped."

"All right," he smiles, then asks, "Mr. Crowe, I was wondering if I could receive that payment in cash, seeing the banks are already closed today."

Mr. Crowe looks up from his paperwork and says, "I don't think it would be a problem." He quickly writes something, then tears off a piece of paper and hands it to Captain Schuenemann. "Just bring this to the cashier. He will take care of you."

"Thank you, Mr. Crowe!"

"Thank you, Captain. And good luck with those trees. How many years have you been doing that, now?"

"Over 20 years, altogether. I bought 240 acres of land just outside of Thompson. We'll begin cutting tomorrow. In a few weeks, I hope to have enough trees cut for a good load. We'll bring the *Rouse Simmons* over to Thompson and start loading them up soon."

"How many trees do you plan to sell this year?" Crowe asks.

"I could sell about 30,000, if I had them. But with any luck, I'd say maybe 20 to 25 thousand."

Mr. Crowe raises his eyebrows. "That sounds like quite an endeavor! Did you hear about my little business venture," Crowe asks.

"No, I haven't." The captain looks, wondering. "What is

it?"

"I'm in the process of buying the Chicago Lumber Company."

"The whole thing?" Captain Schuenemann sits up in amazement.

"Yeah, pretty much. Me and a few other investors have been working on it for a while now, and it looks like the deal is going to go through next month.

"That's amazing! Doesn't the Chicago Lumber Company pretty much own this whole town of Manistique?"

"Yeah! Well actually, the whole county. Who would have thought when I started out here as an office boy, sweeping floors, that someday I'd end up owning it!"

"Unbelievable!" Captain Schuenemann shakes his head. "I guess you do have a little business venture!"

"Well, we know we've got enough pine for a few more years, so that should keep us busy here for a while," Mr. Crowe says with a look of satisfaction.

"Well, I hope you have a good trip."

"Thanks again," the Captain answers. "I'm going to have Barbara and the girls come for a few days. We'll all be staying over in Thompson, at my friend Osbourn Stanley's place, so maybe we'll see you around town. If we do, I would like you to meet them."

"I would love to," Crowe replies warmly. "But hey, you better get over to the cashier's office, or he'll be closed for the day."

"Okay," the Captain smiles. "Well, good luck with your business deal. It sounds like quite a project."

The two men shake hands and Captain Schuenemann steps out of the door. He gives the secretary a nod and a smile as he walks past. She nods and smiles, but continues with her work.

The captain hurries over to the cashier's window and leans into it. The cashier turns and says, "Oh! Captain Schuenemann, how are you? Good thing you caught me. I was just going to close up the safe for the day."

The captain hands him the piece of paperwork and says, "I appreciate your patience. I just got into port."

"That's okay," the cashier responds, looking at the paper. "Six hundred dollars! That's a lot of money to be carrying around."

"Well, after I pay off the crew and buy a few supplies, it's not going to be that much."

"Yeah, that's true," says the cashier, sighing. "It ain't like the old days, when a dollar could really buy you something." He goes to the safe and gets the money together. "Here you go, Captain," the cashier tells him, and counts out the money for him.

The captain takes and puts the money in his big wallet, then into his vest pocket. A small chain is draped down from his wallet to his belt.

"Thank you," he tells the cashier.

"Have a good day, sir," he replies as the captain turns to leave. Opening the door, he walks down the front steps to the wooden sidewalk along the street. Captain Schuenemann pauses for a moment to watch as an automobile pulls up and comes to a stop right in front of him. Behind him, the captain notices the secretary turning a small sign from "open" to "closed" and locking the front door.

A young man is gets out of the automobile. The captain walks up to the automobile for a closer look, just as the young man looks up at the "closed" sign in the window and lets out a disgusted, "Darn! I suppose they're closed!"

"You just missed them. I was the last one in there."

"I just got into town," the young man explains. "I'm looking to find work in one of the logging camps, or one of their sawmills for a few months. Now I'll have to wait till they open on Monday to find out about work," he complains. "And besides that, I don't have any money left to find a place to stay."

"Where are you from?" the Captain asks.

"On the other side of Escanaba," the young man replies.

"This is a nice-looking automobile you have. It is yours?"

"No, it's my Pa's. He just bought it this summer. But he sent me up here to look for work for the winter, so he let me take the truck."

"What kind of automobile is this?" the captain asks admiringly.

"It's a Ford," the lad responded. "Pa had a carriage maker from Escanaba make the box and cab for it. It was a passenger car, but Pa thought we needed it more for hauling stuff, so he had it made into a truck, a Model T Ford truck. It can haul as much as a team of horses can, without getting tired," he tells the captain excitedly. "It can even pull a wagon!"

"Well, I'll be," says the captain, with an amused and thoughtful look on his face. "What's your name, son?" the captain asks.

"Thomas, Thomas Berger," he replies.

"Well, Thomas, my name is Captain Herman Schuenemann, of the schooner *The Rouse Simmons*," he says, reaching out his right hand.

"Pleased to meet you, sir," he says, as they shake hands.

"Son, I would like to make you an offer. I'll pay you the same wage it would cost to hire a team of horses and a teamster to drive them per day, plus room and board on my ship. I can give you work for about three to four weeks, and you will be hauling Christmas trees."

"Christmas trees," Thomas replies, in a surprised voice.

"Yes," the captain continues. "And you would be driving

some of my crew back and forth to Thompson, about five or six miles away."

Thomas thinks about it for a moment.

"That would be about $2.50 a day, plus room and board," the captain says. "Most of the men prefer to stay at the boarding house in Thompson. But if you want to save some money, you can stay on board the ship for free."

"Wow! I'll take you up on your offer, Captain. When can I start?"

"Right now," the captain replies.

"It's a deal," Thomas laughs unbelievingly.

The two shake hands again and smile.

"How about a ride down to the ship right now," the Captain asks.

"Yes sir," Thomas replies. "Jump in, while I turn the crank to get her started." Thomas gives it a crank, and the engine sputters and comes to life. They both quickly climb onto the seat of the automobile, and off they go, chugging along through town. As Thomas drives the truck through town, the Captain shouts out orders as though he is commanding a sailing ship, going to port turn to starboard. He points as though guiding a vessel down the main street of town. Both men are laughing and smiling from ear to ear as they make their way down to the fish docks and the waiting ship.

CHAPTER SEVEN – A STRANGE SHIP

The captain and young Thomas instantly become fast friends. Thomas is fascinated with the ship, and the chance to be staying there. The automobile and Thomas' eagerness fascinate the captain.

Most of the crew is busy unloading tanning bark from off the ship. The Model T pulls up alongside the ship. The captain and Thomas get out of the car while all of the men stop for a moment to watch. The captain introduces Thomas to his crew as they gather around young Thomas and the automobile.

"I would like everyone to meet Thomas Berger. He will be working with us this fall, gathering Christmas trees. I have hired Thomas and his automobile for transporting Christmas trees, but also for taking us back and forth from Thompson to the ship," the captain continues. "I decided that it's better to leave the ship docked here until we have most of the trees down by the landing, because I don't want to tie up all Mr. Chesbrough's dock space at Thompson any more than I have to while we cut the trees and haul them to the landing. There will be quite a few more ships in and out of there, yet this year for lumber," the Captain explains. "So thanks to Thomas and his truck, we'll all be able to ride in style."

The men let out an enthusiastic cheer. "Hey, alright! Yeah,

that's great!"

"Now, Thomas is going to be staying aboard the ship while he's working with us, so I want you all to show him some real ship-board hospitality."

"Yes sir, Captain! He'll want to be a permanent member of our crew," the first mate says wryly. They all laugh. Thomas grabs his bag and he and the captain climb the gangplank together.

"This is sure great weather," the captain says. "This must be our Indian summer. The temperature must be close to 60 degrees. We'll use this good weather today for unloading the ship. But enjoy it while it lasts, because it could snow tomorrow. Who knows?"

"Hey, Captain! What is that strange-looking steamer there coming into the harbor?" asks Thomas, pointing out into the lake. "It looks like it has some kind of flags on it."

The Captain and several of the men walk over to the rail and watch for a moment.

Well, I'll be…" the Captain stares wonderingly. "It looks like Captain Bundy's Gospel Ship! I heard a rumor that he was retiring."

"Gospel Ship?" asks Thomas, with a puzzled look on his face.

"Yes. It's Captain Henry Bundy. He's been sailing all around the Great Lakes as a gospel preacher. I'm not sure how long. I would guess about 35, maybe 40 years. Longer than I've been sailing, I know that. He's quite an interesting fellow, all right.

"There are a lot of stories about him along the waterfront. They say he was quite a wild character in his younger days. A lot of drinking, a lot of fighting, and a scoffer, too! The story goes, that he went to a revival meeting one time, down in Chicago, not so much to listen to the gospel, but he went there to scoff the preacher and cause trouble. He didn't know that the preacher was none other than Dwight L. Moody! Well, he ended up getting converted, and spent the rest of his life as a missionary, sailing all around the Great Lakes. He started out with a small sailing ship. Over the years, he's worked his way up to the steamer he has now. It's really quite a nice ship."

"What are those flags?" asks Thomas.

"You'll see them when he gets a little closer. He has some Bible verses on a banner," the captain tells him.

"Oh, now I can see what it says. 'Pray without ceasing,'" says Thomas.

"I remember one time," recalls the captain, "When we were docked, I think it was in Menominee, right near Captain Bundy's boat. Do any of you guys remember that?" the captain asks.

"Yes, that was Menominee," the first mate answers. "About fifteen years ago."

"Yeah, we were tied at the dock about two boats ahead of

Bundy. Tied up right between us there were a couple of young boys on a small sailboat. So Bundy sent them on an errand for him. He gave them a wooden pail and a dime. Then he sent one of the boys down to the nearest tavern. He told the lad to fetch him a pail of beer, but tell that so-and-so tavern owner to be careful not to get too much foam on top, 'Cuz it's for Captain Henry Bundy.' He evidently knew the tavern owner. So a little while later, the lad came back with an empty pail. So Captain Bundy asked him what happened. He told Bundy that the tavern owner had sent him back here with a message: "Tell that no good so-and-so Bundy that he shouldn't be spending from the people's offerings on beer, and that if he doesn't like it, to come and see me himself.

"Well, ol' Bundy, he sent the boy right back and said, "Tell the no-good so-and-so that I'm coming to pay him a visit, like I did when he was in Chicago." The lad ran off ahead with the message, with Captain Bundy not far behind with a defiant look. The lad told us that when Bundy went into the tavern, there was a terrible ruckus. The sounds of fighting and hollering and lots of breaking glass were heard. After a good while, Bundy came stumbling out the door, all red around both eyes and looking a bit disheveled, but he stood up straight, brushed off his clothes, and said, "The Lord be praised!" He walked off. The lad said he looked inside, and the tavern owner was hardly recognizable, and the bar looked like it had just been paid a visit by Carrie Nation and the Mothers of

Prohibition!"

The crew laughed together in response to the Captain's story.

Just then the old cook comes on deck, saying, "Captain, I got some potaters cooking, and I bought some fresh whitefish from the fishermen here while you were gone; it's just about ready."

"Sounds great. Count me in," the captain replies. "And cook a couple of extra pieces for our friend Thomas, here. Albert, this is Thomas Berger. Thomas, this is Albert Luxua, the most important man on this ship."

"Pleased to meet you, Thomas. I'll fix you up something to eat, too." He nods and turns to go back down into the galley.

"Listen! I hear someone shouting," says Thomas.

"Oh, that's Captain Bundy. He usually starts preaching before he gets to shore, and" (DING) the Captain is interrupted. (DING) "As I was saying, ringing the ship's bell," the captain laughs. "Listen."

A distant voice is heard shouting, "Prepare ye the way of the Lord!" in a deep, thundering voice, "Prepare ye the way of the Lord! His name shall be called Jesus, for He shall save His people from their sins. Prepare ye the way of the Lord!"

"Maybe we'll go to see him after supper," the captain smiles.

"I think I'd like that. This Captain Bundy sounds like an

interesting fellow."

"He certainly is," the captain assures him. Let's grab your bags. I'll show you to your bunk while we're waiting for supper."

"Yes, sir," Thomas responds.

The captain leads Thomas down a short set of stairs. Thomas looks around at the rugged interior of the ship. It takes a moment for his eyes to adjust to the dim lighting from two small windows and a kerosene lamp. The room is very primitive looking, with only a large table, some chairs, and some stalls along one wall where he can see some hammocks strung.

"I've seen barns that looked more inviting than this," Thomas thinks to himself.

At one end of the room is the kitchen, and there is Albert, the cook, busy working at the stove.

"Captain Nelson is part owner of the ship. He and several of the other men are staying over at the Osawinamakee Hotel until we're done offloading our cargo of bark. Then most of the men will be staying at the boarding house over in Thompson. So there are a couple of extra bunks here. I know it's nothing fancy, but until you get some money saved up, you are welcome to stay here."

"Thank you, Captain. I'm sure this will be fine. The food sure smells good. I'll be ready soon."

"I'll be up on deck if you need me."

A little later, a bell rings. "Supper's ready. Come and get it!" the cook yells. Quickly everyone lines up in the galley with a plate.

"I'm going to eat mine up on deck," the captain tells the cook.

"Me, too," comes a voice.

"I am, too," says another, and another.

"Sounds like everyone wants to eat on deck," the cook exclaims. "I can't blame ya. Well, I'll come up in a few with a pot of hot coffee and some cookies."

"Sounds good," replies the captain, as he makes his way up on deck, holding his plate full of hot food.

Finding a place to sit on one of the hatch covers, the Captain sits down outside to enjoy his meal. Young Thomas joins him, followed by the other crewmembers.

"What a beautiful evening!" the Captain says. "It don't get much better than this. A beautiful sunset on an Indian summer day, having fresh whitefish and potatoes out on the deck of a ship."

"Yes, sir, I could get used to this," Thomas replies.

"Yeah, life is good," sighs the captain. "And it has really worked out good with you looking for work and all."

Just then the cook comes out on deck with a big, blue porcelain-enameled coffee pot, full of hot coffee, and a big plate of cookies, and a pail with a bunch of cups in it hanging on his arm.

"Hey, it is really nice out tonight, isn't it," Albert says, setting them on the hatch cover. "You never know what kind of weather you're going to get this time of year. It could be snowing, or just like summer. And the nice thing about this time of year is NO BUGS!"

"Yeah," the crew all laughs.

All the while, Albert the cook is pouring cups of hot coffee.

The captain and Thomas each get a cup of coffee and a couple of cookies.

"I'm going over to see Captain Bundy. This might be his last year of ministry. They say he's retiring," the captain tells the cook.

"Yeah, he's been at it a long time."

"So, Thomas, how big a family do you come from?"

"Well, there're six of us kids, five boys and one girl. I'm the oldest," he says. "We live on a small farm, but my father is a carpenter. My younger brothers and I take care of most of the farm chores. My sister, Karen, is the youngest. She helps my mom with the house chores. So, I'm taking a year off so I can earn some money for school."

"What do you want to study for?" the captain asks.

"Photography and journalism," says Thomas.

"That sounds interesting. Do you have a camera, now?"

"Oh yes," said Thomas, "It's just an expensive hobby right

now. But I love it, and I think that it would be a great way to make a living."

"I agree," said Captain Schuenemann, sipping his coffee.

After dinner the captain announces, "Well, Thomas, I'm going to stroll over to Captain Bundy's Gospel Ship. You can come along if you like."

"Yeah, I think I will, captain. This Captain Bundy sounds like an interesting fellow."

"That was an excellent meal, Albert," the captain tells the cook.

"Yes, it was very good," adds Thomas.

"Glad you liked it," he smiles.

"We'll be back soon," reports the captain to the crew, and together they make their way down the gangplank and along the waterfront towards Bundy's Gospel Ship.

As they approach his ship, it appears that Captain Bundy has already begun his meeting. Rows of wooden folding chairs are lined up on the dock. Enough to accommodate about forty people, most seats are already filled with an assortment of men, women, and children, all listening to Bundy's preaching.

With the meeting already under way, Captain Schuenemann and Thomas quietly find some empty chairs near the front. Captain Bundy continues with his message, uninterrupted. He's an elderly man, with a thick, gray beard and a head that's bald. Not very tall, but for his age, he still has a commanding appearance. As he speaks, he often gestures with one hand. He holds an open Bible in the other.

Bundy's voice is clear and deep. His eyes are bright with expression, with perhaps a tinge of fanaticism.

"I would like to continue with a reading from the gospel of St. Mark. In these verses, the Savior admonishes us to not only be His followers, and to accept His sacrifice for our sins, but to reach out to those around us: our family and friends. The Savior even admonishes us to go out into the highways and by-ways, and into the uttermost parts of the earth, like I've done all these years with this Gospel Ship." The captain points to his ship.

"The Apostle Paul, even though he suffered persecution, traveled over land and sea to tell the world of the Savior's love for this world. He was shipwrecked twice, and arrested and taken to Rome, and still he continued to tell of the Savior's love, even till his voice was silenced."

Captain Bundy pauses and closes his Bible, holding it to his chest, looking heavenward and gesturing with is hand.

"I remember a story that helps illustrate this point," he says, raising one finger to get everyone's attention. "It was about 50 years ago," he continues, with a distant look in his eyes. It appears that he is somehow taken back in time.

"It was just before the war between the states. I was still a young man working on a tramp schooner between Buffalo and Milwaukee. The citizens of Milwaukee were in a political frenzy at the time. A group of Irish politicians from the third ward and union guards had chartered a ship to go to Chicago to support their candidate for president, Stephen Douglas, who was running against Abraham Lincoln, and to raise money for the guard to buy new rifles.

"The ship was the *Lady Elgin;* a beautiful side wheel steamer she was," Bundy continues, "one of the finest passenger ships of her time. "The *Lady Elgin* was on her return voyage after a successful time in Chicago. The passengers were all in high spirits. There was dancing aboard the ship, and a German band playing, as the ship steamed her way back towards Milwaukee. . .

"A squall came up, but the big ship made good as she continued on through the night, under the capable and able command of Captain Jack Wilson."

By now, the crowd all listens spellbound, as Captain Bundy continues.

"But out of the night came a sailing schooner, the *Augusta,* under Captain Mallot.
His ship, driven hard by the squall, perhaps her lanterns quenched by the wind, struck the *Lady Elgin* on her side, and she began to sink. Unaware that his small sailing ship had fatally damaged the *Lady Elgin*, Captain Mallot continued on to Chicago, leaving the

Lady Elgin to her fate."

Captain Schuenemann and Thomas listen intently as Bundy continues.

"The best efforts of Captain Wilson and his crew to save his ship were in vain. The *Lady Elgin* began to sink. The ship broke up as she went down. The passengers and crew grabbed whatever floating debris they could, to raft themselves to safety. All the while, Captain Wilson did his best to save and encourage others throughout the terrible night.

"It was about five o'clock in the morning before the townspeople along the shore learned of the tragedy. They hurried down to the lakeshore to assist the struggling, shipwrecked people safely to land. As the bedraggled survivors drifted within sight of land, the pounding breakers would overturn their makeshift rafts, drowning many of them within sight of their would-be rescuers. Some 300 lives were lost that night.

"But many heroic rescues were made by stout swimmers, who tied ropes around themselves, and one end held by men on shore as they plunged into the roaring surf to save as many as possible.

"Many young men from Northwestern University and the Garrett Bible Institute came to assist in the rescue work. One of them," Captain Bundy continues with a look on his face as though in vision, beholding the entire scene being played out before him,

"Edward Spencer, a ministerial student at Garrett, put forth almost super-human effort, as time after time he plunged into the cold and pounding surf to rescue another struggling human from the disaster.

"Seventeen times, he plunged into the waves. Seventeen times, he brought back another soul, until finally he collapsed, shaking and delirious on the shore. But in his delirium, he kept crying out, "Did I do my best? Did I do my best?"

"Spencer never became a minister," Bundy continued. "He had so ever-exerted himself in rescuing others, he never fully recovered, and was forced to abandon his studies for the ministry. But oh, what an example he left for you and me to follow!

"In this dark and dying world, with war, and disaster, and pestilence on every hand," Bundy exclaims vehemently, "Each one of us will soon pass from the scene. And in the brief time that we are given here, I want each one of us here to ask ourselves two questions.

"The first is: Who will you choose this day? Whom you will serve? Satan once showed Christ in a moment of time all the kingdoms of the world, and the glory of them, and said 'I will give them all to you, if you will just bow to me.'"

"Satan offers the best that this world has to give. Is that the goal for your life? A short glimmer of glamour, power, or fame, only to end in the corruption and in the grave, or will you choose the One who said, 'I am the resurrection and the life,' and offers us hope beyond the grave? Will you choose the One whose kingdom will last forever; the One who said, "Father, forgive them, for they know not what they do," as He died at the hands of those he came to save?

The crowd listens breathlessly.

"The choice is yours: the king of heaven, or the prince of this world. Choose you this day whom you will serve." Bundy pauses to give his audience time to reflect.

"The second question I would like you to ask yourself, like that of the young Edward Spencer, lying delirious on the shore, is: 'Did I do my best? Did I do my best?'

"Perhaps you have chosen the Savior and His everlasting kingdom, but are you allowing those around you to perish without so much as a word of hope? If you have already chosen to follow the Savior, I would like you to ask yourselves each day the question Edward Spencer kept asking, 'Did I do my best?'"

Then Bundy slowly asks one more time, "Did I do my best?"

Young Thomas looks over at Captain Schuenemann. He appears a bit shaken and deep in thought.

Captain Bundy closes the service with a word of prayer. Though the meeting is short, Bundy's words are attended by a power that seems to linger in the air after he is through preaching.

The soft notes of organ music come from the Gospel Ship, as Bundy's daughter plays a hymn on the ship's organ.

Thomas and Captain Schuenemann rise from their seats, as the crowd begins to disperse. Many of them go forward to pray with Captain Bundy.

"I'm going to talk to Reverend Bundy for a few minutes," Captain Schuenemann tells Thomas. "I'll meet you back at the ship."

"Okay, Captain," Thomas replies, "I'll see you later," and makes his way toward the fish dock.

Captain Bundy is talking to a crowd of people at the front, but he excuses himself and turns to greet the captain.

"Captain Schuenemann!" he says cheerily, as he holds out his hand. "Good to see you."

"I was surprised to see you, Captain Bundy. I heard that you were retiring!"

"Well, old steamboat captains never really retire, they just lose their steam!" he laughs.

"Well, I have to admit that I was quite moved my your message tonight."

"Well, the Lord be praised," Bundy said softly. "Sometimes the Lord can even use an old fool like me. You heard right, though, I'm going to have to give it up," Bundy says. "The ship, that is. I'll still preach now and then. But I'm on my way back down to Chicago. I already sold the ship, so this is my last voyage; I've been at it now a long time, my wife passed away last year, and my health just ain't what it should be anymore, so I'm selling the ship."

"How long have you been at it?" Captain Schuenemann asks.

"Over forty years," Bundy replies. "I started out back in 1868. I just had my old sailing schooner, then worked my way up through several ships, till I was blessed with this fine steam ship."

"I see fewer and fewer sailing schooners on the lakes," Bundy adds, "And even the small steamships are getting to be a thing of the past. The railroads and the big steamship companies are pretty much taking over."

"Yeah! We're a dying breed," Captain Schuenemann adds. "But I'll be damned if they will make a tow barge captain out of me, if you'll excuse the language, Reverend." Bundy shows no emotion, but appears lost in thought for a moment.

"A dying breed," he repeats with a distant look in his eyes. "That's for sure, like the passenger pigeons. When I was a boy, there were so many that the flocks would darken the sky for days, as they passed, but now there is only one left, and it is in a cage at the zoo in Cincinnati. The last of its kind on earth," he says emphatically. "I preached tirelessly that the slaughter should stop. Now they're all gone, and there won't ever be any more," Bundy exclaimed, shaking his finger. "The Lord will come someday, and destroy them that destroy the earth," he says vehemently.

Captain Schuenemann, realizing that the conversation has gotten off track onto one of Bundy's pet subjects, quickly brings him back around. "Well, I'd like to thank you again for that message; I feel I was somehow touched by the message tonight," Captain Schuenemann says. "I'm sure I'll carry your words in my heart and mind a long time. And I would like to say that even though you have a few rough edges, your ministry has been a blessing to me, and many others around the lakes all these years.

"I guess you showed us all one thing: that accepting Christ isn't the end of faith, but the beginning, and that you didn't wait for some church group to send you as a missionary. You just went. In that respect, you taught us all a lesson."

"Well, Lord be praised," Bundy responds. "I'm going to miss traveling the lakes too, Captain. God bless you!"

The two captains shake hands again, and Captain Schuenemann slowly walks back to the ship. He contemplates the words of Captain Bundy's message. The words, "Did I do my best?" seem to echo in his mind.

The warm evening makes a pleasant walk back to the ship. It is already starting to get dark. As Captain Schuenemann arrives at the ship, he hears singing, and music playing. Some of the men on the ship have broken out their instruments. One man is playing a small accordion, another has a ukulele, another has a mandolin, and another with a fiddle, joined occasionally by the first mate on the harmonica. They're singing together an old familiar tune, "What Do You Do With a Drunken Sailor?" The entire crew sings along, and even young Thomas joins in on the chorus. What great fun for a beautiful Indian summer evening.

"What do you do with a drunken sailor?

What do you do with a drunken sailor…"

Captain Schuenemann laughs and applauds as he finds a seat on the ship rail. "Sounds good, gentlemen. Hey Albert, how about that tune you made up about Captain Bundy's Gospel Ship?"

"Yeah, let's hear it!" they all ask.

"Alright," Albert replies, and begins to strum on his ukulele and sing. "Captain Bundy's Gospel Ship." The other instruments join in to accompany him. The rest of the crew joins in on the chorus, "Sail away. Sail away."

CAPTAIN BUNDY'S GOSPEL SHIP

Captain Bundy's Gospel Ship
Is sailing in the bay
I hear that bell ringing
I hear that organ play
I hear the captain shouting
O'er the crashing of the waves
We've got to save some sinners
Before we sail away

CHORUS

Sail Away, Sail Away
We've got to save some sinners
Before we sail away
The Captain was a sailing man
Of many stormy seas
Drink and swear and cuss and fight
He'd do just what he pleased
They say he was a scoffer
Just as proud as he could be
The revival that he went to scoff
He wound up on his knees
Pray without ceasing
I heard the Captain say
We've got to save some sinners
Before we sail away.

CHORUS

There's hell to be shunned
And a heaven to be gained
We've got to save some sinners
Before we sail away.

CHORUS

The Gospel Ship is leaving port
The ten's all packed away
The captain's words have all been preached
His prayers have all been prayed
Superior Shores are calling me
I heard the Captain say
We've got to save some sinners
Up there in Grand Marais

CHORUS

The song ends and Thomas and the captain both laugh and applaud.

"Well, Thomas, what do you think of our crew here?"

"They sure are a jolly bunch," says Thomas.

"Yeah, they are. But I'm going to turn in now. Tomorrow is going to be a big day for us, harvesting trees and all. I'd like us all to be ready to go sometime just after sun-up."

"I'm with you on that, captain," the cook replies. "I'll have breakfast ready by six bells, and have a lunch ready for you by the time you're ready to leave."

"Albert, you're the most important man on this ship!"

All the men laugh and begin to make their way down below.

"Tomorrow night I'll be staying over in Thompson, at my friend Osbourn Stanley's place. My wife Barbara and my three daughters are going to arrive Wednesday, on the train. They'll be staying there, too. And all of the woodsmen will be staying at the boarding house in Thompson. So, after tomorrow night, you can stay in my cabin," the Captain offered Thomas.

"Oh, you don't have to do that, sir."

"Well, you might as well. I'm not going to be staying there."

"Yes, sir," Thomas replies.

"Well, good night, men."

"Good night, captain," they all reply.

The Legend of the Christmas Ship

CHAPTER EIGHT – HARVESTING TREES

The next morning, Thomas awakens to the sound of pots and pans, the smell of bacon cooking on the griddle, and the cook scurrying about in the galley, preparing to feed the crew.

The smells and sounds slowly roust the men, and they all begin preparing themselves for the day. Soon the cook rings the dinner bell, and they all gather around the table. The cook, Albert, brings out a pile of plates and the men all start passing things around the big table. "Flapjacks, bacon and eggs, stewed prunes, and hot coffee," the cook announces. Everyone digs in, and the pile of pancakes soon disappears. Likewise, the bacon and eggs follow. Then the cook brings another huge plate of pancakes.

"Don't worry about trying to eat all these now," the cook says. "I'm going to wrap them up with some jam for your lunch."

Captain Schuenemann comes and joins in. "How did you sleep, Thomas?" the captain asks as he digs into his stack of pancakes.

"I was out like a light," says Thomas, "I don't remember anything."

"That's good," smiles Captain Schuenemann, "'Cause we're going to have a long day today, ain't that right?"

"Ooooh, yes," reply some of the men.

"Hey, captain, I got that wagon you asked me about yesterday," the mate tells him. "I traded the fisherman one of them new ropes that we brought back with us from Chicago. He said we could use the wagon till we're ready to leave."

"Excellent," Captain Schuenemann replies. "Things are really working out good for us, so far." The captain is anxious to start the day. When he finishes his breakfast he announces, "Well, it's daylight, boys, let's get sailing. Thomas and I will go get the wagon, while you men get all our gear ready and set it all on the dock. We'll be back in a few minutes."

"Aye, aye, Captain," the men respond, and they all spring into action.

The captain and Thomas hurry down the gangplank to the Model T, and Thomas cranks the motor over. "Hop in," he tells the captain.

Captain Schuenemann looks like a kid on Christmas morning. He's still very excited about riding in the automobile.

"I'll grab a piece of rope," the captain says, running back to the ship.

"Okay," says Thomas, "But we might not need it."

"Why is that?" the captain asks, as he grabs some rope and hurries down the gangplank. He throws the rope in back of the truck and climbs in.

"Well, my dad had a hitch made, so that a wagon hooks

right on."

"Great," says the captain. "Let's go." The Model T goes chugging off.

Soon they're back at the dock, pulling the wagon behind. The truck stops, and the men all start loading stuff on: tools, axes, and saws.

"Captain Nelson and some of the others will stay behind to finish unloading the bark," Captain Schuenemann explains. "The rest of you climb aboard."

Then the men climb on and Thomas drives off, the Model T chugging along, pulling the wagonload of workmen down the main street and through the town.

Captain Schuenemann and Thomas talk together as they jostle along the main road to Thompson.

"Last year at this time, the mill in Thompson still had quite a few ships in the harbor, loading lumber. That's why I'm keeping the *Rouse Simmons* in Manistique till we're ready to load the trees. Mr. Chesbrough, the owner of the mill at Thompson, said that in a couple of weeks, he'll have a lot more room for the *Rouse Simmons*," the captain explains as he looks back at the wagon.

"So, your father bought this automobile last spring, you say?" the captain asks, still showing a great wonderment for it.

"Yes," says Thomas as he drives along, "It was late one evening, and the family was just getting ready to go to bed there on the farm, when we heard this automobile driving up our road to the house. Then came to a stop right in our yard. Well, the dogs were barking, and my dad went out to see who had come driving up. By then all us kids were awake, too, so we got dressed real quick, so we could go out and see who it was that had come with the automobile.

"We had only seen a few automobiles before, but never up close like this, and right in our yard, besides. Well, it was a man named Charlie Behrend. He was the meat cutter at the IXL Store in Hermansville, but now he sold Ford automobiles," Thomas continues. "So he asked my father if he wanted to go for a ride. He said he would, so Charlie took us all for a ride in the new automobile. After we rode it for a while, he asked my father if he wanted to learn how to drive it. So right then and there, he traded places with my dad and explained to him how to drive. He told him that it was like driving a team of horses. When you want to turn this way, instead of pulling on the left rein, you turn the wheel like this." Thomas turns the wheel to the left, to show the captain. "And when you want to go right, instead of pulling on the right rein, you turn the steering wheel this way," and Thomas turns slightly to the right. "And that's how you do it. So by the end of the evening Charlie had sold my father the Model T, and that's how we got it."

"What an amazing machine," the captain marvels.

"This here is the throttle lever on the steering column. When you push it up further, it makes it go faster!" Thomas demonstrates, as the Model T Picks up speed.

But as they do, they hit a bump in the road, and the passengers and tools in back nearly come bouncing out. The men in back yell, "Hey, slow this buggy down!"

The captain and Thomas both laugh together as they go careening down the bumpy road, like there's not a care in the world. Soon they arrive in Thompson, at the home of Captain Schuenemann's friend, Osbourn Stanley.

He sees them pull up in his yard, and comes out grinning. "Captain Schuenemann, where in God's creation did you get that?"

Schuenemann can't hold back his smile, and says, "It's the modern age, isn't it?"

"Yeah, but who would have thought?" Osbourn replies.

"Osbourn, this is Thomas Berger. Thomas, this is Miles Osbourn Stanley."

"Pleased to meet you," they both say.

The other men greet him also.

"But he usually goes by Osbourn. And he's our Christmas tree guide. Ain't that right, Osbourn?"

"Well, I guess so," he raises his eyebrows and scratches the back of his head.

"Let me grab this bag of apples and my tools, and I'll take

you to a good spot where the trees are. The captain here has 240 acres of Christmas tree land. It was all cut over, and the spruce and balsam are all coming up like weeds."

"Okay. Put that stuff back there, and come on and sit up front here, with me and Thomas," the captain says.

"Boy, oh boy, I didn't think I'd be riding in an automobile today," Osbourn replies excitedly.

"Well, you won't believe this thing. And look at us, pulling that wagon. We were going so fast on the way over here that the men back there just about bounced out," the captain laughs with an amused look on his face.

Thomas eases the Model T ahead. The men in the wagon pretend they are driving a team of horses. "Giddy-up!" they shout, as the automobile moves forward, the whole bunch of them grinning like a bunch of schoolboys on a holiday picnic.

"This way, about a mile," Osbourn points out, "There's some places that are just thick with them."

The Model T slowly works it way along a narrow two-rut road, weaving its way through a forest of giant pine stumps. The morning sun glistens on the heavy dewdrops resting on the branches of hundreds of young spruce and balsam trees. Soon they arrive at the spot. Thomas stops the Model T and they all get out and grab their tools.

"Okay, boys, let's have at her!" the captain says.

They all shoulder their axes and saws and disappear into the trees.

CHAPTER NINE - WINDS OF FORTUNE

"Well, gentlemen, just spread out here and start cutting, then we'll take and set them along the road," the captain orders. "We'll all meet back here at high noon. Thomas, here, will blow the horn on his automobile, like this," the captain signals to Thomas to blow the horn. He squeezes the rubber ball on the end. "Honk, honk."

"I bet you didn't think you'd be using this automobile for a dinner horn," the captain laughs.

"No, but it should work great."

"Okay, let's shove off," the captain orders, and all the men spread out to gather trees.

"Try and keep a count on how many trees you cut," the captain orders, as they all go their separate ways.

"Okay," they all holler back.

The men all work feverishly till noon. Then they hear the horn blow, and gather back at the Model T. Albert, the cook, has the lunch spread out on the back of the wagon.

"Well, I've got rolled-up flapjacks with jam and butter, cheese, smoked chubs, some nuts and raisins, and a keg of water to wash it down," the cook says.

"Albert, you could make any meal you serve into a picnic,"

the captain jests.

"Hey, how many trees did we cut so far?"

Each one gives the captain a number, as they line up for their dinner. Some say fifteen, some twenty. The captain writes their answers in a small notebook. "Well," the captain exclaims, "We got a pretty good start. That's 123 trees cut the first morning.

"Ya done good, Osbourn," the captain says. "You found us a good spot."

"This whole area here is like that," Osbourn replies. "It was all logged off about six or eight years ago, and these small spruce and balsam are coming up like weeds."

"Well, we'll thin them out," the captain jokes, as he grabs a rolled-up pancake and takes a bite.

"After lunch, Thomas and I will start hauling them back down to the dock with our 'iron horse'," the captain teases.

"Don't forget, I brought a bag of apples, too," Osbourn reminds the men. He goes over and takes the bag out of the back of the truck and places them with the rest of the food.

After lunch, all the men help load the truck and the wagon with trees, and then go back to cutting. Thomas and Captain Schuenemann take a load of trees back down the bumpy road, talking as they go.

"Who's that one older guy that never talks at all?" asks Thomas.

"Oh, that's Engvald Newhouse. He talks a little, but it's very unusual to get him to really say very much. He's just a shy old bachelor from Sweden. I guess nobody really knows why he doesn't talk. He's worked for me for years now, and he's become a trusted part of my crew. Albert kind of looks after him."

"He seem as though he's somehow sad all of the time," Thomas adds.

"Yeah, I think Albert knows why he's like that more than anyone. But he never talks about it, so no one really knows. But it was Engvald's idea to put lights on the ship when we're at the dock there in Chicago. And it sure has helped me sell more trees!

"Well, you know, Thomas, every year that goes by, I bring more trees to Chicago, and every year I sell more. Selling trees has become the best part of my business. As far as our other cargoes, well, that's our bread and butter, but the Christmas trees! That's our gravy! Ah, there's something about them I just love. For one thing, it's my own cargo, for another thing, my own customers; no middlemen," the captain muses. "Another thing is the people. I like dealing with the people. But, there's a lot of risk in this business. For one thing, if the trees are harvested too early, the needles fall off. But then again, if the trees arrive too late, there's no time to sell them. And suddenly, trees that are worth a dollar or two each are worth nothing. So all the time and money invested in them can go up in smoke."

Thomas nods as he listens.

"And, there's also the danger," the captain pauses. "The weather in November can be pretty nasty. About twelve years ago, my brother, August, and I were in business together. He and his whole crew were lost when the *S. Thal* went down in a storm. I would have been with him, but I stayed home that year. My wife, Barbara, was about to give birth to our twins, Pearl and Hazel. Otherwise, I would have been with him." His voice cracks a bit.

"I'm sorry to hear that, sir."

"Yeah. So, there are a lot of risks. But still, it's the best part of my life," the captain says, wiping a tear from his eye. "It's become a tradition in Chicago to buy a Schuenemann Christmas tree.

"Hey, what about fuel?" the captain asks, changing the subject.

"Oh, yeah," says Thomas. "We should probably get some gasoline tonight after we're done working. I saw a place on the corner in Manistique that had gasoline. Sometimes it's hard to find gasoline, so if I think I'm going to run low, and I can't find a place that sells it, I can usually find some kerosene. But, I don't like using it straight, it seems to run a lot better if there's some gasoline in the tank already to mix with it," Thomas explains.

"Let's unload the trees right over by the end of the break wall," the captain says, pointing towards the dock. "There's a lot more room there."

"All right," Thomas replies. "I'll pull up as close as I can."

"So how did you learn to drive so well," the captain asks.

"Well, my father showed me. It really didn't take too long. Pa showed me how, and I guess the rest is just practice." He shrugs. "When we're done unloading these trees, I'll show you how."

"Show me how to drive it?" the captain asks.

"Yeah, on our way back to get more trees," Thomas replies.

"Hey, it would be a good place to learn. There's no one else around, and we could take turns driving then," said Thomas in a logical tone of voice.

"Really," the captain says, in a tone of disbelief. "This is really exciting! It's a modern marvel. Me! Learning to drive an automobile? What next!"

Quickly, the captain and Thomas unload the trees, and Thomas gets ready to start the truck.

"Okay, captain, just sit here in the driver's seat."

"Who would have thought the day would come when I would be learning to drive a horseless carriage? Next thing you know, it will be one of them flying machines!"

"Orville and Wilbur, look out! Here comes Captain Schuenemann," Thomas says, laughing.

"Okay, captain, there's two levers here by the steering

wheel. This one is your throttle, for your fuel, and this lever advances the spark. So, move that a little, but it doesn't need much, because the engine is already warmed up. So, just make sure it's turned on here, then I'll crank it over."

Thomas turns the crank, and the engine sputters to life. "There we go!" Thomas jumps up on the seat next to the captain. "Okay, now remember what I told you. It's like steering your horses. If you want to go left, instead of pulling on the left rein, you turn the wheel this way, to the left. And, when you want to go right, instead of pulling on the right rein, you turn the wheel to the right. That's the way Charlie Behrend showed my dad how to drive when he bought it."

"All right, I got that," the captain answers. "What about my feet?"

"Okay, this pedal on the left is the high and low gear. You push that when you want to go forward. Half way is neutral, for when you want to stop. Push it half way in and push the brake on the right with the other foot. The middle pedal is for reverse, when you want to go backwards. You got that, now?"

"Yeah, the one on the left is for forward, the one in the middle is reverse, and the one on the right's the brake."

"Yeah, for when you want to stop," Thomas adds. "Okay, give the throttle lever a little push, about one-fourth the way, then push the forward pedal all the way down. That's it, captain! Okay, let's go," Thomas encourages.

"All right," the captain smiles, with both hands locked on the wheel, and a determined look on his face, "Here we go!"

The truck lurches ahead. "Whoa!" the captain shouts, with his eyes as wide as saucers.

Thomas laughs, and yells, "Yippee! Ride 'em, cowboy!"

"To port! To starboard!" the captain yells, as he turns the wheel from left to right.

"All right, now, let the pedal out all the way into high gear. Keep it between the buoys, captain," Thomas cautions, laughing.

The captain and Thomas go swerving back and forth down the road with the wagon bouncing along behind. Together, they spend the rest of the day driving back and forth to the dock, each time with a fresh load of trees. By evening, the size of the pile of trees is quite impressive.

At evening, the captain honks the horn and shouts, "Let's call it a day. Climb aboard, men. This train is leaving for Thompson."

"We got a pretty good start on it today, and I learned to drive an automobile besides. Well, Thomas, how am I doing?"

"You're doing great, captain. A little more practice, and you'll be ready to get your driver's license."

"Driver's license?" the captain asks.

"Yeah, you've got to have a license to drive one of these

things."

"I didn't know that," he says.

"Well, it makes sense. You wouldn't want just anybody driving one of these things," he says sarcastically, looking around. The men all laugh.

Soon they pull up in front of the boarding house and the woodsmen all get out and grab their bags. Thomas drives to Osbourn's house.

"Drop me and Osbourn off at his place. We'll leave the wagon there, too. Then I'll give you some money for gasoline, so you can feed this thing."

"Aye, aye, captain," replies Thomas, and off they go, wagon and all.

When they reach Osbourn Stanley's place, the captain and Osbourn get out and grab the tools. "Pull up over here," Osbourn points. "I'll unhook the wagon. Hey, that's a pretty fancy hitch you got."

"Yeah, my dad had the blacksmith make it out of a horseshoe," Thomas says.

"Well, we'll see you tomorrow morning, Osbourn," says the crew, as they climb in the back of the truck.

"We'll see you in the morning, Osbourn," tells him. Then they drive off towards Manistique.

CHAPTER TEN - FIGHT

The Model T bounces along the road towards Manistique. The sun is getting low in the sky, and reflects in warm yellow colors from the huge sand dunes, as they follow the coast of Lake Michigan back to Manistique. The deep blue waters of the lake blend with the blue of the sky, and the horizon of water stretches out as far as the eye can see.

As they approach Manistique, the captain asks himself a question out loud, "I wonder what they're going to do here, when the pine is all gone?"

"What's that, captain?" Thomas asks.

"I wonder what these saw mill towns, like Thompson and Manistique, are going to do when the pine is all gone," the captain says, a little louder. "In, let's say another ten or so years, when all the pine has been cut. The loggers, the saw mills, the ships, all depend on the pine."

"I don't know," Thomas answers.

"Hey, what are all them shacks over there on our left?" Thomas asks.

"That's Indian Town," the captain answers. "A lot of the Indian families live there. The world is changing so fast around them, they're not sure if they want to live in the old world or the new. So, many of them just live in huts here in the winter, and they live in other places in the summer. Some live out on High Island in the summer. Others, out by Indian Lake, and other places."

"I guess I kind of know how they feel. It's kind of like captains of the sailing ships. We want to hold on to the old ways, because that's been our way of life for so long, but soon the sailing ships will be gone, too."

Thomas nods silently, taking all of the captain's words.

"When it gets a little cooler, I have some of the my Indian friends here make Christmas wreaths to bring to Chicago. They gather a lot of greens and are very good at working with their hands. They also make beautiful moccasins and baskets. I always bring some of them back to Chicago with me as well. The extra money helps them make it through the winter."

The little truck rolls along into town. Horses with wagons and buggies travel up and down the street.

Thomas says, "There's a place to get some fuel," and turns to pull in. "There's the pump," Thomas points out.

"This must be new," says the captain. "It wasn't here last year," he says as they pull up along side the pump.

"The glass tank up there holds twenty gallons," Thomas announces, and he begins pumping a lever back and forth. "See, it fills up this glass container at the top, there, and the marker shows how many gallons of fuel. So, you just fill the glass to the right amount, and then put this hose right into the tank, and let it drain right into the tank!"

"Well, I'll be," says the captain, as he looks at the pump. "That's a pretty fancy outfit," he nods.

After fueling up the truck, they start the truck and roll on through town down to the dock, pulling up along side the ship. They all begin unloading, and Albert, the cook, says, "I left a big pot of boiled dinner on the wood stove before we left, so it won't take long and I'll have some supper ready. I probably just have to get the fire going again, and it should just have to warm up a little."

"Now you can see why Albert is the most important man on this ship!" the captain comments.

"I sure can; that's amazing," Thomas exclaims.

The men all climb aboard the ship, and busy themselves with their various chores, while Thomas helps the cook prepare for dinner.

"I don't know how you do it, Albert; cook for such a big crew, and still you worked all day cutting trees."

"Well, I don't expect to go every day," he explains, "But when the weather is nice, I like to go along. The way I got it figured, good food is one of the few pleasures in this world that God gave us to enjoy, so I try and make it my priority to make meal time one of the best parts of the day."

"Well, you do that!" Thomas replies.

"Thanks," says Albert with a twinkle in his eye.

Soon the dinner bell rings, and the crew gather around the table. Each one dishes up a hot plate of boiled dinner.

"This is good bread," Thomas comments. "Did you make this, too?" Thomas asks Albert.

"No," he answers, "the captain's daughter made that, and gave it to us just when we were ready to sail from Chicago. She's really a sweet gal. Is Elsie coming up on the train tomorrow with Barbara and the twins?" he asks the captain.

"I think so. She's twenty now, and you know when kids get that age, they've got a mind of their own. But Barbara and I wanted her to come. So, I'll know for sure tomorrow."

"Well, I didn't get a chance to pay you men last night, so I would like to take care of that right after supper."

"Okay, captain," they all agree. After supper, the captain pays each of the crew.

"Thomas, I'm going to give you a little advance, so you have some money in your pockets," and the captain hands him some money.

"Thank you, captain."

"You're quite welcome. You've already shown us what you're worth. I appreciate your help."

"Thank you, captain."

"My pleasure. Well, I'm going to my quarters. I have some paperwork to catch up on. I'll see you men in the morning. Have a good night."

"Okay. Good night, captain," they reply. "Good night, all."

Thomas sits and listens as Charles Nelson and the mate, Steve Neuson, talk about some of their sailing adventures. Philip Larson is working in the galley with Albert, the cook.

The two deck hands, Hogie and Andrew, leave the table and make their way up to the deck. As they do, Hogie turns and silently signals to Thomas to follow him. So Thomas quietly excuses himself from the table and follows them up on deck.

Hogie Hoganson is well built, in his early thirties, with dark hair and blue eyes. His well-trimmed beard and mustache only seem to accentuate his friendly smile.

"Hey, Thomas, Andrew and I were thinking about going into town for a bit. And we both have never ridden an automobile till today, and we'd love to take a ride."

"Yeah. Sure," said Thomas, sounding very interested.

"Well, I'll buy you a couple of beers, and maybe we could shoot a game of billiards."

"Well, I've never played billiards," Thomas says cautiously.

"That's okay, Andrew and I can show you!"

"Okay," says Thomas, "Let me grab my jacket."

The young men walk down the gangplank together.

"This should be fun," Hogie says. "You know, that wagon ride this morning was pretty wild. A horse would never have pulled us along that fast."

"Yeah, it's an amazing machine," Thomas says. "I guess Henry Ford is selling them by the thousands."

Thomas adjusts the throttle and the spark, and walks around front and turns the crank.

"I'm not going to bother lighting the headlamps, yet. Maybe we will, later."

"How do they work?" Andrew asks.

"They work off of acetylene gas," Thomas explains. "See, this here is an acetylene generator. I just put some carbide rocks in here, and then some water in this top part. The water drips down on the carbide, and it produces acetylene gas. The gas then goes through these tubes to the headlamps, so then I just have to flick this striker against the flint to light them."

"Wow, that is really handy!" Andrew exclaims.

"Carbide lamps are what all the miners are using now on their hard hats, and they're a lot brighter than a kerosene lamp or candles," Thomas adds.

"That's really interesting," says Hogie. "Henry Ford is sure using a lot of new ideas in his automobiles."

They all climb into the front seat together.

"A couple of years ago, in Chicago, there was never any automobiles. Now we see them quite often!"

"Do you think they'll replace the horse and buggy?" Hogie asks.

"It sure seems like they just might, someday, the way Ford is manufacturing them. I heard that they were making a new automobile every few minutes."

"That's impossible!" Hogie scoffs. "Nobody could build one that fast."

"No, it's true," Thomas exclaims, as he steers the model T towards town. "They say he has big factories, where they make all the parts, and then all they have an assembly plant with an assembly line, where each man adds the same part all day as the assembly line moves the frame of the automobile past them, so they all get really good at adding their parts, so they can do it in seconds. And with a whole line of men adding their part, it comes together really fast."

"So they just add one part, all day long?" Hogie asks.

"Yup, that's the way they do it," says Thomas.

"It's hard to believe," says Andrew.

"Yeah, it ain't like the carriage makers, who only make one carriage at a time. No wonder Ford can sell these automobiles for the price of a good carriage, and that's not counting the price of the horse to go with it," Thomas adds.

"Well, that's why so many people are getting automobiles," Hogie acknowledges.

"Hey, where are we going, Hogie?"

"Let's go to Ekburg's Tavern. I'll show you. Andrew and I was there a couple of times before, when we were in port here. They had some really good beer."

"Yeah, and we watched a fight, too," Andrew adds.

"Yeah, a couple of lumberjacks must have been drinking whiskey, and they got a little crazy."

"Well, let's stick together, and just have some fun," Hogie advises.

The Model T rattles its way into town.

"It's right there, on the other side of the street," Hogie points.

Thomas does a U-turn, and pulls up right in front.

"Wow, you sure can turn this thing!" Hogie said, with a surprised look on his face. "I don't think you could have done that with a horse and buggy."

Thomas parks the truck and shuts off the engine.

"Yeah, makes you feel kind of important, riding around town in an automobile," Andrew says with a bit of pride.

"Everybody here probably thinks we're some kind of businessmen," Hogie adds.

"C'mon, Thomas, I'll buy us a pitcher of beer."

"Okay, I'm coming."

The saloon looks rather busy as all three walk in together and find a place at the bar. Hogie orders a pitcher of beer and three glasses. The three belly up to the bar and stand together. Hogie fills their glasses with beer.

"I worked up a thirst today, cutting those trees."

"Yeah, it was a good day. How 'bout you, Andrew?"

"Yeah, I had a good day. I like cutting trees a lot better than handling lumber."

"I'll take Christmas trees over lumber, any day," Hogie agrees.

The men all sip their beer as they talk together.

"So, how long have you guys been working on the ship?"

"This is my fourth year now, and Andrew, he just signed on this spring. Andrew is thinking about learning to be a mechanic, and working on automobiles."

"Yeah, I was working at a bicycle shop, before. I like mechanical stuff. I hope to save enough money to start my own repair shop, for bicycles and automobiles."

"That's a good idea," Thomas replies. "With all these new machines nowadays, you would have plenty of work."

"I'm learning a lot about ships from Captain Nelson," Hogie says. "He's the real master of the vessel. Captain

Schuenemann is lucky to have him with us as a partner. He's been a sea captain all his life, and has sailed all the oceans of the world. He and Captain Schuenemann are both part owners of the ship. Captain Schuenemann runs the Christmas tree business and makes sure things are running smoothly, and everyone is paid. But don't get me wrong, Captain Schuenemann is a great man, and a captain in his own right. But when it comes to sailing the ship, Captain Nelson really knows his stuff. I think he's going to retire in a couple more years, and Captain Schuenemann wants to learn all the old tricks that he can from him, while he's still around."

"Eventually I want to get on one of the new lake freighters," Hogie says, as he sips his beer. "That's where the future of the shipping is on the lakes. Maybe work my way up to captain, or a first mate."

The three men talk together, and soon the pitcher of beer is gone.

"The bar in this place is something," Hogie points out. "See behind the bar there, the woodwork and mirrors are really something to see, aren't they? They were moved from the Brunswick Bowling Alley in Chicago, about a year ago. I guess they had one heck of a time, transporting them up here, and installing them was even more of a chore."

"Wow, this place is really something to see," Thomas marvels. "Should we order another pitcher of beer?"

Just then, Thomas feels a big hand on his shoulder. "Hey! I would like to buy you boys a drink!" comes a booming voice. They all turn to see a barrel-chested mountain of a man, with a captain's hat and a broad grin on his face. "So, what are you boys doing in town here, with that fancy automobile?" he bellows.

"We're with the crew of the *Rouse Simmons*," Hogie speaks up.

"Well, pleased to meet you." He sticks out his big hand. "I'm Captain Dan Seavey."

"I'm Hogie Hoganson."

"I'm Thomas Berger."

"I'm Andrew Morris."

They all shake his big hand.

"Bartender, bring me and my friends a round of whiskey."

"We were just drinking beer tonight," Thomas mentions politely.

"Nobody refuses to drink with Dan Seavey," he growls.

"Yes sir," they all respond timidly.

The bartender pours them all a shot of whiskey. Seavey places his money on the bar.

"Here's to your health," he says, as he hands them all a glass, then gestures for them to toast their glasses together. Seavey quickly drinks his in one gulp. Thomas, Andrew, and Hogie sip theirs, obviously not used to drinking whiskey.

"So, you boys are from the *Rouse Simmons*, eh?"

"Well, Andrew and I are," Hogie chokes out, trying to clear his throat after sipping the whiskey. "Thomas, here, was hired to haul Christmas trees with his automobile."

"Christmas trees?" Seavey roars. "Isn't it a little early for that?"

"No, sir," Hogie answers. "Captain Schuenemann brings thousands of trees to Chicago every year, and sells them for as much as $1 or even $2 apiece."

"Two dollars!" Seavey bellows. "They're worth their weight in gold!"

"Yeah, so the Captain hired Thomas, here, to haul trees down to the dock in Thompson, and to transport us back and forth to the ship. We'll be keeping the ship docked here in Manistique until we're ready to load the trees, because Mr. Chesbrough, owner of the mill in Thompson, said he has a lot of ships loading lumber at his dock right now. So Captain Schuenemann is going to wait till most of the trees are cut before he ties up at Chesbrough's dock. Then we can load them up all at once."

"That makes sense," Seavey replies. "So, how many trees does Captain Schuenemann plan to carry?"

"Oh, I'm not sure exactly," says Hogie. "But I think he said he would like to have twenty-five thousand."

"Twenty-five thousand," Seavey choked. "That would be

worth over thirty thousand dollars! How would he carry that many?"

"Well, he fills the cargo hold, and then just piles them up out on the deck."

"A deck load," Seavey responds knowingly. "I suppose they don't weigh a heck of a lot, so you could carry quite a load," he says, pondering the idea. "So Thomas, here, brings you back and forth here to the ship until you're ready to load, right?"

"That's right," Hogie acknowledges, "and we'll load the ship the second week of November, so we can make it to Chicago in plenty of time to sell them for Christmas."

"That's interesting," Seavey says thoughtfully. "Well, it was nice meeting you boys. Hey! Do you see that big lumberjack over there, in the corner, with the green shirt and suspenders?"

"Yeah," they answer.

"Well, before the night is over, I'm going to kick his ass," he says, glaring at him. "You just wait and see. But right now, I see an old friend of mine down at the other end of the bar. I'm going to buy him a drink. I'll see you boys later." Seavey struts off down to the other end of the bar.

"Whew!" Hogie gives a sigh of relief. "I'd hate to get in a fight with that guy."

"Me, too," the others agree.

Thomas turns toward the bar. "I'll get our beer."

"Yeah, we need something to wash down that whiskey."

Thomas signals the bartender, and the bartender comes over and fills the pitcher. Thomas reaches in his pocket and pulls out a dime, and hands it to the bartender. Then Thomas reaches for the full pitcher, but just as his hand gets close to it, another hand quickly reaches out and grabs it before he does.

It's a tall, cocky-looking young man, with shoulder-length hair and a beard, standing at the bar.

"Hey, that's my beer," Thomas protests.

"I take what I want!" the bully says in a challenging tone, looking at Thomas defiantly to see if he'll do anything about it. The two men stare silently at one another for a moment.

"No, you don't," a voice comes from behind. The bully quickly turns to see who spoke. It was Hogie. The two men square off and look at each other in a defiant stare down, like two gunfighters in the old west ready to draw. Then, like a flash, they both explode into action, fists and elbows flying in every direction. The crowd draws back in amazement.

Hogie and the bully have at it, and though Hogie is smaller than the bully, he looks more like a prizefighter warming up on a punching bag with the bully's head bouncing back and forth. In an instant, the bully is falling on the floor, with Hogie all over him, with fists flying.

Out of nowhere, the bartender and another man grab hold

of Hogie and throw him out the door. "Not in my place!" the bartender is yelling. A group of patrons pick the bully off the floor, with his nose bleeding. They shove him out the door. Instantly, all the customers in the bar all spill out into the street to watch, and the fight resumes.

The bully is shoved right toward Hogie and the fight continues. But by now, Hogie's pumped up with adrenaline, and the bully doesn't stand a chance. Within seconds, he's falling to the ground again.

But suddenly, appearing like a ghost, another man springs out of nowhere and takes a swing, and Hogie finds himself duking it out with someone even bigger than the first bully.

It happens so quickly that Hogie hardly realizes he's fighting someone else! The fight continues with renewed zeal, his new opponent towering over him, even larger than his last opponent. But Hogie, with almost super-human effort, totally defies all the advances of this giant, landing one punch after another so rapidly that this new assailant is driven back.

In the midst of the battle, Hogie realizes he is fighting none other than Dan Seavey, and through his punches, he yells, "Why am I fighting with you?"

"I just wanted to try you out," Seavey snorts back. Hogie realizes that if he lets an experienced fighter like Seavey get the upper hand, he'd pound him to bits. Hogie lets him have it with every bit of force imaginable, not letting up for a second.

Someone in the crowd marvels, "That guy's been eating dynamite!"

Then, to the amazement of everyone in the crowd, Seavey begins to fall back. His legs look like rubber, and then, like a mighty white pine, Dan Seavey slowly topples onto the street, with Hogie still pursuing with an endless volley of punches.

With his opponent momentarily unconscious, Hogie leans over and appears almost puzzled what to do next. But before he can stand up, a punch came from in back of him, catching him by surprise. Hogie spins to meet his opponent. It's the first bully he'd subdued. As with most bullies, the only fight they want is with someone he is sure he can beat. Sucker punching Hogie from behind, the bully makes his move, thinking he's got enough of the advantage.

Though momentarily dazed, Hogie jumps back and turns to see what hit him. When he sees the coward who jumped him from behind, his sense of injustice turns to anger, and where before he had been fueled by adrenalin, he is now fueled with the fires of rage. Hogie comes back on him with a fury of indignation, driving back his attacker with a look of anger and flying fists. But his rebound is short-lived, when all of a sudden Hogie realizes he's now fighting two men. Seavey has regained his feet, and is back after him, both bullies seizing the opportunity to pay back their tormentor and to regain some of their lost pride.

Now they pound Hogie from both directions while Andrew and Thomas watch with horror at the sudden turn of events. They feel helpless, as the two bullies gang up on their friend.

Hogie gallantly fights back, and does surprisingly well, but an unexpected blow sends Hogie reeling off balance and falling to the ground, hitting his head on the front bumper of his Model T.

The first bully seizes the opportunity, and starts kicking him, knowing he at last has the upper hand. But in an instant, Hogie crawls under the Model T to protect himself. The two bullies look a bit puzzled as to what to do next, while Hogie climbs farther under the Model T.

Just then, the sound of galloping hoof beats comes up the street, and a policeman on a horse yells out, "Hey, what's going on here!"

Instantly the two bullies disappear into the crowd, as the policeman circles with his horse, trying to determine what the disturbance is all about. Meanwhile, Hogie lies motionless under the Model T.

The policeman, assuming that whatever or whoever was causing the disturbance is now over, shouts, "Okay everybody, let's move along there," and the patrons from the tavern quickly make their way back inside. With the crowd dispersing, the policeman turns his horse and continues on down the dimly lit street.

Andrew and Thomas find themselves standing alone on the street, almost paralyzed in unbelief. Then, realizing their friend is still under the truck, they hurry over to help him.

"Hogie, are you all right?" they ask. For a moment, there's no answer, then slowly, the words, "Yeah, I think so." He groans.

Thomas and Andrew climb under the truck and help pull him out.

"Can you move?" Andrew asks, wiping the blood from Hogie's nose and mouth.

"Yeah, I'll be all right," Hogie says as he dizzily sits up. "Let's get out of here before those guys come back," Hogie moans.

"Yeah, let's get you out of here," they agree. Helping Hogie to his feet, they place him on the seat of the truck.

Andrew holds onto him, while Thomas hurries around to the front of the truck and gives it a crank. The engine rattles to a start. Quickly he jumps in and drives off, leaving the tavern far behind.

"I didn't have time to light the headlights," Thomas complains, as he drives into the dark. "I guess I can see okay."

"That's alrihgt. Let's get out of here," Andrew says.

"I just wanted to get out of there before those guys came back outside. Are you all right now, Hogie?"

"Yeah. I got an awful bump on my head from when I hit it

on the bumper, and my ribs hurt when I breathe, but I think it would have been a lot worse if I hadn't crawled under the truck," Hogie moans.

"That's for sure. You only gave them a few seconds to both pound on you like that."

"Hey, we better go back and get that pitcher," Hogie says slowly, trying to sound funny.

"We'll just take one away from that bully next time," Andrew assures him. "That guy sure as heck won't ever want to mess with you again."

"Yeah, you whipped the snot out of both of them guys, Hogie. You had them both on the ropes, till they double-teamed you. Thomas and I were just about ready to jump in and help you, but when you jumped under the truck, it was all over so quick. We just froze."

"It was best you didn't. Those guys are used to fighting, and you probably would have got hurt," Hogie tells them. Thomas hastily drives on into the darkness toward the docks. With the light of the street lamps ending at the edge of town, Thomas strains to see ahead.

Then all of a sudden, BUMP, BANG, CRASH!

"Oh no!" Thomas cuts the wheel to the right and comes to a sudden stop. "I hit something." Thomas gets out and looks around. "It looks like I just hit a pile of fish boxes. I didn't see them in the dark."

"We'll pick them up in the morning," Andrew says.

"All right," says Thomas, climbing back in behind the wheel. "We've got to get back to the ship."

Pulling up near the ship, Thomas turns off the engine.

"Just help me to my bunk," Hogie asks, "But don't tell Captain Schuenemann. I'll be all right in the morning."

They both help Hogie onto the ship and down to his bunk. Then quietly they all climb into their bunks. The only sound they hear is the occasional snoring of some of the other men on the ship.

CHAPTER ELEVEN - RECOVERING

The next morning, Albert is up early, cooking breakfast, and soon the crew gathers for breakfast. "Hot coffee, biscuits and gravy, and some sweet rolls," the cook announces.

The captain comes in and sits down at the table. "How are you boys this morning?" he asks Thomas and Andrew.

"Fine," they answer quietly, looking straight ahead, sipping their coffee.

"How'd your trip into town go last night?" the captain asks, as he dishes himself a plate of food.

"All right," they answer quietly.

The captain eats his breakfast. "Good job on the biscuits and gravy, Albert."

"Thank you, captain," the cook responds. "It's my Aunt Bev's secret recipe."

"Hey, where's Hogie this morning?" the captain asks, looking around.

"He's still in his bunk," Andrew replies sheepishly.

"You better get him up. We got work to do today!"

"Well, he's not feeling too good this morning," Thomas responds quietly.

"What did he do, get drunk last night? I suppose he's hung

over," the captain growls angrily.

"Well, no, but he got in a fight," Thomas answers.

"A fight? Is he all right?"

"Well, not exactly," Andrew says. "He's got some kind of banged up."

"Banged up," the captain exclaims, rising from his chair. "Why didn't you tell me!" and he hurries off towards Hogie's bunk.

"Hogie, are you all right?" the captain asks. There's a moment of silence.

Slowly, Hogie responds, "Yeah, I'm all right," and turns his head toward the captain. His face is black and blue. One eye is almost swollen shut. There are a couple of red bumps on his head, and dried blood around his nose.

"Oh my God! Hogie, you're a mess!"

"Oh, it's not that bad, captain."

"Andrew! Thomas! Come here and give me a hand. We'll put him in my cabin."

"C'mon, Hogie," the captain coaxes, "You're going in my cabin."

The two young men help him up, and they half-carry him to the captain's cabin and help him onto his bunk.

"Where you hurting?" the captain asks.

"Oh, just the bumps on my face and head, and my ribs right here on this side. It hurts when I breathe," he gasps.

"Probably a bruised or broken rib. Well, it could be a lot worse. Do you still have your teeth?"

"Yeah, I still got 'em," he says, opening his mouth wide so the captain can see.

"Well, I'm going to run over to the fish house and get some ice for those bruises. You two get yourselves ready for work."

"Aye, captain." Andrew and Thomas nod and hurry off. Captain Schuenemann helps Hogie to his cabin. Then he hurries down the gangplank with a pail to get some ice. Soon he returns to his cabin with the ice.

"Here you go, Hogie. Hold some of this ice on your bruises. It will help the swelling go down. I just want you to lay low today, and hopefully, you'll feel better tomorrow. Barbara and the girls are supposed to arrive in Thompson by train this afternoon, and we'll all be staying at Osbourn's place. I promised my bunk to Thomas, so you two can work that out. But I'd like you to stay here today and rest up."

"Thanks a lot, captain. I'm sure I'll be okay. Just a few bumps and bruises."

"I think you'll be okay. I've got to get going now." The captain hesitates a moment. "So, Hogie, how are things going with you?"

"They're okay, captain."

The captain continues again, a bit awkwardly. "Ah, I mean

with you and the Lord?"

"Well," Hogie pauses. "It could be better. I guess I used to be a pretty good Christian when I was younger, reading the Bible almost every day, and praying. I had asked Christ into my life and really meant it, was even a deacon in the church. But when my wife and I split up, things just started to unravel. I felt out of place in the church, and slowly quit praying or reading the Word." He pauses. "But, I would like to get back into it."

"I went and listened to Bundy's sermon the other night," says the captain, "and it kind of made me think, 'what am I doing to help save others?'"

"Yeah, I was there and heard it, too. I've been thinking the same thing," Hogie says thoughtfully.

"Well, before I go, I'd like to have a word of prayer for you. Would that be all right?"

"Yes," Hogie nods. The men both bow their heads.

"Dear Lord Jesus, watch over my friend Hogie here, and help him to recover his health. But most of all, Lord help him to follow you closer, so that he may be ready to meet you when you come in your kingdom. In Jesus' name we pray. Amen."

"Amen," Hogie adds.

"Hopefully, I'll see you tomorrow."

"Okay, captain. I think you probably will."

As the captain turns and walks out the door, Hogie says,

"Hey, captain." The captain backs up a bit and turns his head. "Thanks, hey."

The captain nods, closes the door, and hurries off down the gangplank for another day's work.

CHAPTER TWELVE - SEAVEY

Thomas and the rest of the crew are waiting in the Model T.

Captain Schuenemann climbs in and off they go, chugging along through town.

"So, what happened last night?" the captain asks.

Thomas speaks up. "Oh, we went to a couple of taverns and bought a couple of pitchers of beer. We were just talking a bit. I went up to the bar and bought another pitcher of beer when out of the blue, this big bully comes along and takes our pitcher of beer. He says, 'I take what I want.' Well, Hogie didn't go along with that. So he gave the guy a real spanking. But then, in jumps this other guy even bigger than the first, just to try him out. Well, Hogie whopped him, too. But then, the first guy jumped him from behind, and that's when things really got nasty," Thomas explains.

"They both knocked him down, and the first guy started kicking him. I think Hogie's head hit the bumper on the truck when he fell, too. But if he hadn't crawled under the truck real quick, I'm sure he'd really be hurting a lot worse," Andrew agrees. "The funny thing is, the second guy he got in a fight with was the captain of the *James Hall*, and had just bought us all a drink a little while earlier, and we talked to him a while."

"What was his name?" the captain asks.

"Dan Seavey," Thomas replies.

"Dan Seavey!" the captain repeats excitedly, sitting up straight. "Did you say Dan Seavey?"

"Do you know him?" Thomas asks.

"Yeah, I know him. Everyone knows Dan Seavey. He used to own a couple of taverns in Milwaukee, not far from the waterfront. Then he went up to the gold fields in Alaska, and came back broke. I heard he had gotten a schooner called the *Wanderer*, and was carrying whatever cargo he could find; fruit from Lower Michigan, and whatever else he can get into. Most of the time, he's doing something illegal. Whatever he can make money at. That's Dan Seavey. And oh yes, fight. He loves to fight. Hogie's lucky he's only got off with just a few bumps and bruises.

"Yes, I know Dan Seavey. He's known all around the lakes as a fighter and that he loves to fight. There's one story where Seavey heard of a real tough fighter by the name of Mitch Love. Seavey went looking for him, and found him over in Frankfort. They decided to have a fight out on the ice, and take bets on who would win. I guess they battled it out for about two hours and finally Seavey was the winner.

"I heard he has a place now, out on the Garden Peninsula. Osbourn could probably tell us more about that. He knows a lot more about the area around here."

"I think Hogie knew he was fighting for his life, 'cuz he

was like a punching madman when he finally knocked Seavey down," says Thomas.

"What," the captain gasped. "He knocked Seavey down?"

"Yeah. But that's when the trouble started. That's when the first bully came back and jumped him from behind."

"Not many can say they knocked down ol' Dan Seavey," the captain marvels.

"So Hogie ended up fighting two at once," Thomas continues. "Then, he was knocked down. I think that's when he hit his head on my front bumper when he went down. Then the first bully started kicking him. That's when Hogie climbed under the truck, and that pretty well ended it. Just about that time a policeman came along riding a horse and everyone just kind of disappeared," Thomas explains.

"I don't think the policeman even saw Hogie under there, so when the policeman left we loaded Hogie in the truck and headed back to the ship."

"So, why didn't you tell me last night?" the captain asks.

"Hogie told us not to tell you."

"Well, I still say he got off easy, especially fighting two men at once." The captain laughs and shakes his head.

Thomas continues driving the six and a half miles to Thompson along the bumpy road.

"Yeah, there are a lot of stories about Dan Seavey," the

captain muses. "If anything is missing on the waterfront, everyone blames Seavey. One of his favorite tricks it to pull up to the docks at night and load up any cargoes that he can find. I heard he even took a team of oxen, once. Another time, he showed up back in Chicago with a load of gloves, shoes, and leather goods he salvaged from a stranded steamer, the *G. M. Nickles*, off Big Summer Island. When the crew had gotten off, he went aboard and salvaged all her cargo before they returned.

"It seems there was some false buoys near the reef." The captain frowns. "Another time, he showed up down there with a boatload of caviar and other high-class goods for sale, cheap."

Thomas listens intently. "Why didn't they catch him?" Thomas asks.

"Well, he's so darned slippery. Not too long ago, they did get him arrested for piracy of the *Nellie Johnson*. I can't remember if it was out of Grand Haven or Frankfort. He was having a card game with Red McCormick and his crew. He ended up drinking ol' Red and his whole crew flat on their backs. While they were out, he left them lying on the dock, weighed down with an old anchor chain, and took off for Chicago with his ship and a full load of cedar posts. When Captain McCormick finally came to, he reported his ship missing, but he was such a mess, no one believed him. Finally, he convinced them, and the revenue cutter *Tuscarora* was sent looking for Seavey, and finally caught up with him."

"What did they do with him?" asks Thomas.

"They brought him in to stand trial for piracy back in Chicago, where he got some slick lawyer. So when he went in before the judge, he told him Captain McCormick sold him the ship for a gambling debt. Well, ol' Red and his crew had been too drunk to remember for sure, so Seavey got off."

"Did he get to keep the ship," Thomas asks.

"Well, no. Gambling is illegal. Besides, he didn't have a bill of sale, so the ship was returned, too. But I don't think Seavey really got in any trouble for it.

"I'm sure there's a lot more stories than what I've heard," Captain Schuenemann continues. "I heard that sometimes his cargo is painted ladies. He takes them from one town to the next, when their shine wears off, if you know what I mean.

"I live in Chicago, and I spend a lot of time up here too, so I hear stories about him at both ends of the lake. The latest one I heard is that some of the underworld gangs that operate in Chicago were a little unhappy with Seavey, because he wouldn't deal with them, and sold his black market goods direct. Not being able to get their cut, they sent a boatload of thugs up here after him, and I heard they worked him over pretty good, telling him that he needed to walk the line and deal through them. Well, on their way back, they were overtaken by Seavey's schooner, and he had somewhere gotten a cannon."

"A cannon?" Andrew and Thomas exclaimed.

"Yeah. Blew their boat right out of the water. I guess they'll think twice about trying to make HIM knuckle under!"

"Wow! This guy is like some kind of modern-day pirate," Thomas exclaims.

"That's what everyone calls him since his heist of the *Nellie Johnson*. I don't think he'll ever live that name down. He does have a good side, though, so they say. He contributes a lot of money to some of the orphanages, and has helped others who are down and out. But that still doesn't make stealing right." The captain scowls.

The little truck makes its way into Thompson.

"We'll go over and get the wagon, then pick the woodsmen up at the boarding house. Osbourn won't be coming today; he'll be working at the sawmill. And with Hogie laid up, we will be a little short-handed. But I'm sure they'll have more than enough trees for us to haul. Just pull up by the wagon. I'll hitch it up."

So Thomas and the captain hitch up the wagon and stop at the boarding house, and pick up the woodsmen for another day's work.

CHAPTER THIRTEEN – DRIVER'S LICENSE

"It's a lot cooler today," Thomas points out.

"That's okay," replies the captain. "The cooler the better. It helps keep the trees fresh, and the needles stay on better."

The little truck rolls on down the bumpy road, back into the woods. The men are all anxious to get started, and they all spread out to find a fresh supply of trees. Thomas and Captain Schuenemann begin their routine of loading the wagon and hauling them down to the dock.

After a couple of trips, Thomas has the Captain drive again.

"Your turn to drive, captain. You're getting pretty good at the wheel. You should get your driver's license. I've got a letter to mail to my folks. Maybe, after the next load, we could run over to the post office. We could get you a driver's license at the same time. Then you can drive anywhere you want to by yourself."

"Good idea! I'll be a captain by land or by sea," he laughs.

So, after unloading another batch of trees, Thomas and the captain drive the truck back into Thompson, down the main street, and over to the post office. Stopping in front of the small, white wooden building, they get out of the truck and go inside. The postmaster is busy sorting mail, and looks up from his work.

"Oh, Captain Schuenemann! How are you?"

"Well, I can't complain."

"Are you here for a while, getting trees?"

"Yeah. I just pulled in two days ago. But I'm keeping the ship over in Manistique, till I'm ready to load up. Mr. Chesbrough didn't want his dock space tied up that long. Guess he still has quite a few ships coming and going, before the weather gets bad."

"Yeah, he's been shipping a lot of lumber. What can I do for you, captain?"

"Well, my friend Thomas, here, would like to mail a letter, and I would like to get a driver's license."

"A driver's license!" the postmaster exclaims. "I have never issued a driver's license before. But they sent me the forms. Here, let me take care of your friend first, and I'll find you the forms."

Thomas hands him his letter. "That'll be three cents, please." Thomas reaches in his pocket and hands him three cents.

"Okay, captain. I'm reading the form here and it says that you must have received proper instruction in the use of an automobile."

"I've hired Thomas, here, to haul trees for me. He showed me how to drive his Model T."

The postmaster looks up from his form at Thomas and asks, "Can he drive pretty good?"

"Oh, yes," Thomas assures him.

The Postmaster says, "Okay then, that will be two dollars," as he stamps the form. "You just have to sign your name right here, and carry that in your wallet, and you'll be all set."

"That wasn't as tough as it was getting my captain's license." The captain laughs and signs his name on the license. Then he pulls two dollars out and hands them to the Postmaster.

"Okay. Thanks a lot, Don."

"All right, gentlemen, have a good day." He turns again to sorting the mail.

The captain and Thomas walk out to the truck. "Well, that was easy. Hey, Mr. Licensed Captain, do you want to drive?"

"Why, sure!" the captain says excitedly. "Won't Barbara and the girls be surprised to find out I can drive an automobile, and that I have my driver's license!"

A light snow begins to fall as they step out of the post office. Thomas cranks the engine to a start. "You drive, captain."

The two drive off together through the snowflakes. Then an idea comes to Captain Schuenemann. "You know, I was thinking." He pauses. "How much did you say this thing cost?"

"I think it was $675," Thomas answers.

"You know, I think after this year's Christmas tree sales, I just might go out and buy my own automobile. Wouldn't that be something! I can see it now," Captain Schuenemann says, "Imagine what it would be like with me driving my own automobile through downtown Chicago, with Barbara and the girls riding along with me. It almost seems like a dream. A dream? Heck, I AM going to get an automobile, Thomas! My mind is made up!" the captain says, with a determined look on his face, and excitement in his eye. "Ha! I can see it now!"

The captain breaks out into a song, ad-libbing to the tune of *Jingle Bells*: "Dashing through the snow, in a shiny automobile, over the hills we go…" The captain turns the wheel from side to side, to the time of the song. "...Laughing all the way. Ho, Ho Ho." Then he laughs. "But, we won't have any horses to put the bells on bob-tails to ring! Oh well, I'll have to figure something out."

The two of them talk together and laugh as they bounce along on the seat of the automobile. The rest of the day flies by, while the two of them haul one load of trees after another, back and forth down the bumpy road to the boat landing.

By afternoon the light snow begins to fall more heavily, and by late afternoon the ground is covered with snow.

"It looks like winter might come early," Thomas comments.

"Well, you never can tell," answers the captain. "This time of year, it comes and goes. Just look at it this way: it will help keep them trees fresh."

"Well, it's about time to bring the woodsmen back to the boarding house. Osbourn and I will be meeting the girls at the railroad station this evening. I'm sure looking forward to seeing them," the captain sighed.

Thomas and the captain arrive at the spot where the men are cutting trees. Thomas blows the horn to signal them that it's time to go. The men all gather at the truck, load their gear into the wagon, and climb aboard. Thomas engages the clutch on the truck. The Model T lurches ahead a bit, but then stops with the tires spinning helplessly.

"Darn!" Thomas curses. "That little bit of snow, and we can hardly move! Some of the men will have to push to get us moving."

The captain jumps out and gives some instructions. Several of the men jump out and get ready to push.

"When it gets moving, jump on," he yells.

Together they push, easily getting the truck rolling again.

"Hop on!" Thomas yells. The truck moves ahead, gaining speed. The men who are pushing all dive on or climb on as hastily as they can, so they're not left behind. Soon they arrive at the boarding house, and the woodsmen all climb off and unload their gear.

Thomas drops Captain Schuenemann and the wagon off at Osbourn Stanley's place. "I'll see you in the morning," the captain says.

"Yes sir, bright and early, captain!"

Thomas and the rest of the crew drive back to the ship at Manistique.

CHAPTER FOURTEEN - VISITORS

Captain Schuenemann watches as Thomas and the crew drive off into the snow, then climbs the steps onto the wooden porch. Osbourn's wife, Florabell, meets the captain at the door. "Come in, Captain Schuenemann," she says with a warm smile. "It's cold out there!"

Florabell is a beautiful young woman in her mid-twenties, very curious but at the same time giving the impression she was a bit of a tomboy when she was younger. She gives the captain a big hug. "You must be frozen, working outside all day, captain!"

"Well, even though it's been snowing all afternoon, it really wasn't too bad. It seems to be cooling off more, now. But it's nice and warm in here," the captain says, taking off his coat and hat. "And, m-m-m, what's that smell, Florabell?"

"Oh, I've got bread baking in the kitchen, so come on in and have a cup of hot coffee and sit by the wood stove. Osbourn should be home from the mill in a little while."

"How have you been, Florabell?"

"Oh, just fine. I've been busy getting things ready for your visit. I can't believe another year has gone by already. It just seems like yesterday since you were here. Oh, I just can't wait to see the twins," Florabell says excitedly. "They are just the sweetest children!"

"Yes," the captain beams. "Those two are the joy of my life. But they can be trouble, too, because what one doesn't think of, the other will." He grins.

"Is Elsie coming too?"

"Yes, I think so," the captain answers. "Barbara wanted her to come along and help this year. She has a mind of her own lately, but I think she's coming."

"Well, by the time you and Osbourn get back from the train, I should have supper ready. Here comes Osbourn, now."

He comes in and hangs up his hat. "Hey, captain! It's a little snowy out there. It's cooling off some, too. A little early for snow, don't you say, captain?"

"Yeah, well, it'll probably melt in a couple of days."

"How did you do today?" Osbourn asks.

"Well, not as good as yesterday," the captain sighs. "We were short a couple guys, of course you weren't there, and one of my crew, Hogie Hoganson, wasn't there, he had gotten into a fight down at the tavern last night and was pretty sore this morning. I hope he's back on his feet tomorrow. He got in a fight with Dan Seavey."

"Dan Seavey!" Osbourn spouted.

"Yeah, and another guy, too," the captain adds.

"No wonder he's hurting," Osbourn comments.

"Isn't Seavey living around here somewhere?" the captain asks.

"Yeah, he got himself some land on the Garden Peninsula down at Govley's Harbor and built a sawmill. Married some young girl, Annie Bradley, from right over here at Little Harbor. I guess her parents were just sick about it, but what could they do?" He shrugs. "I heard the residents of Garden got tired of his antics real quick. He's been causing so much trouble around there that the village board passed an ordinance that says he can't dock his ship at Garden anymore."

"The boys said he's got another ship now. What's he sailing now," asks captain Schuenemann. "Does he still have the *Wanderer*?"

"No, he's just got a pretty nice two-master, the *James Hall*. It has a gasoline engine, too."

"A gasoline engine?" The captain raises his eyebrows. "Then he doesn't need to use a tug."

"Yeah. So when anything is missing around the docks, Seavey is usually given the blame," Osbourn says, with a disgusted look.

"How did your man get in a fight with him?" Osbourn asks.

"It was Hogie Hoganson. I guess he got in a tussle with some other bully over a pitcher of beer, and after he whipped that fellow, Seavey jumped in and wanted to try him out. Thomas said he knocked ol' Seavey for a loop, too. But while fighting Seavey, the other guy came up from behind and sucker-punched him a couple times. Knocked him down, and gave him a few kicks. But, I guess he's all right now, and hopefully he'll be back to work tomorrow." Osbourn just shakes his head.

"Well, it's about time to go and pick up the girls from the railroad station," the captain says, looking at his pocket watch.

"I'll go out and get the carriage hooked up," says Osbourn.

"All right. I'll give you a hand," the captain says, taking the last drink of his coffee.

The two men make their way out to the barn and hitch up the carriage.

"It sure has been nice having Thomas around with that automobile," the captain comments. "He taught me how to drive it already, and I even got my driver's license."

Osbourn looks up, surprised. "Your driver's license?"

"Yeah. Thomas showed me how to drive it, then we went to the post office and got my driver's license."

"Well, I'll be darned," Osbourn replies in disbelief. "I didn't know you even needed one."

Soon they are on their way to the railroad station. The snow on the ground forms a blanket of pure white. The sky clears, just as the evening sun begins to set, casting its colors of red and orange across the sky.

"It will probably get colder tonight, if the sky clears," says Osbourn.

"Yeah, it probably will," answers the captain.

The clip-clop of the horses' hooves made a steady sound as they track through the snow to the Thompson railroad station. The smoke from the giant sawdust burner at the sawmill lingers in the air, giving it the familiar odor of a sawmill town.

When they reach the station, the train is already stopping at the station. The black smoke from the steam engine's stack rises above the train like a flag blowing in the breeze.

The steam whistle sounds, and the conductor steps off the train and checks his watch. Soon the passengers are unloading. Captain Schuenemann climbs the steps up onto the wooden train dock. Barbara and Elsie step off the train, carrying two large carpetbags. The twins, Pearl and Hazel, are just ahead of them. Just then, they catch sight of Captain Schuenemann.

"Daddy!" the twins yell, as they run toward him with their arms outstretched.

With his big smile on his rosy cheeks, he bends down and picks them up, one in each arm. They both put their arm around his neck and hug him tightly, and each one kisses him on the cheek.

"How are you, my little dollies?" he says through his beaming smile. "Did you take good care of your mother?"

"Oh, yes, and we have been on the train all day," they tell him.

"Oh, Herman, it's so good to see you!"

Letting go of the twins, he leans over to give Barbara a big hug and a kiss.

"How was your trip," the Captain asks.

"Oh, it seemed to take forever. Next year, I think I'd like to sail up here on your ship," she says.

"Elsie! I'm so glad you decided to come."

She reaches out and gives her father a hug and a kiss. "It's so good to see you, Daddy!"

"C'mon, now, let's get your bags loaded onto the carriage. Osbourn is waiting for us. Florabell is expecting us too, and has a wonderful dinner planned for us."

They all greet Osbourn as if he were part of the family. The captain and Osbourn load the luggage onto the carriage. On the way back to the house, the sky is now almost totally clear. The last rays of the red and gold sunset color the sky. The happy group talks together as the carriage rolls along over the blanket of fresh snow to the little farmhouse on the edge of town. Osbourn pulls on the reins as he approaches the house.

"Whoa, boy," he tells the horse.

The children jump down and grab a handful of snow, and throw it at each other.

"Come along now, children. I don't want you getting all wet." The captain helps Barbara and Elsie down from the carriage and hauls the suitcases into the house.

The twins are met by Sandy the dog. Sandy is eagerly greeting all of the visitors with a wagging tail and friendly look.

"Oh look, here's Sandy, Mama," the twins reach their arms around the dog's neck and fuss over her. The dog is a beautiful golden-yellow lab, with smooth fur, and very friendly. Elsie bends over and pets her, too. Running both hands along the sides of the dog's head, she looks into her face and says, "Oh, you are a pretty dog. How are you?"

She's answered with a lick.

The twins run in to see Florabell.

"Florabell," the girls yell excitedly.

"Oh, you little darlings," she says, giving them a hug. "And I won't stand for any more of this Florabell. I just want you to call me Flora."

Osbourn drives off to park the carriage and put the horse in the barn.

"Come on in, everyone. Take your coats off and get ready for supper. It should be ready soon. Come to the table. Oh Elsie, I'm so glad you decided to come too. Barbara, so nice to see you," she says, giving them both a big hug.

"I was surprised to see snow when we got off the train. But

this IS Northern Michigan," Barbara exclaims.

"Yes, winter comes early here," Flora answers. "Elsie, could you finish setting the table for me? Barbara, please come and mash the potatoes? Then everything will be ready. It is so good to have everybody here again. I just love this time of year!"

Osbourn comes in from the barn, and they all gather together around the table.

"Everything smells so delicious. What are we having?"

"Chicken dinner, with mashed potatoes and gravy, acorn squash with maple syrup, and cooked carrots," Flora announces.

"And everything right from the farm?" Hazel asks.

"That's right. Everything right from the farm," Flora answers.

"Oh, I love to come to the farm," Hazel replies. "Everything is so good."

"Let's all come to the table now," Flora announces.

Everyone gathers at the table. They all pass the food around and enjoy the meal together, catching up on old news. But during dinner, Captain Schuenemann notices Elsie is rather quiet, but he doesn't say anything about it.

As everyone finishes eating, Flora announces, "Carrot cake for dessert." She brings over a plate full of sliced cake.

"Oh, I love your carrot cake!" the twins chime together.

"Coffee? Who wants coffee?" Flora asks.

"Yes, please," says Barbara. "And milk for the girls."

"Oh, yes, Flora," they answer.

"Coffee, Elsie?" Flora asks.

"No, thank you," she says quietly.

"You didn't eat much tonight, honey. Are you feeling all right?"

"Yes," she nods, but as she does, Flora notices Elsie wipe a tear from the corner of her eye.

"Could I be excused?" Elsie asks quietly. "I do need to get a breath of fresh air." She slides her chair from the table and goes over to take her coat from the rack. Quietly she slips out the door.

As Elsie closes the door the captain looks over at Barbara and asks, "What's the matter with Elsie?"

"Yes, she doesn't seem to be herself," says Flora with a look of concern.

Barbara tries to explain. "She's a bit heartbroken," she whispers in a quiet voice.

Captain Schuenemann asks, "Why is that?" with a concerned look on his face.

"Well, Edward Harkness, the young man who's been her sweetheart, has been away to college for some time now. He just sent Elsie a letter telling her he intends to marry a girl he met from Vermont. She's been heart broken all week. I was hoping the trip up here would help take her mind off of him."

"Oh, that's too bad," Flora sympathizes.

"It takes time to get over that kind of thing," she says. They all agree.

"Well, that was an excellent dinner, Flora!" the captain compliments.

"Yes, Flora. And we love your carrot cake," the curly-haired twins both say.

Meanwhile, Elsie walks down to the lakeshore and strolls along the snow-covered beach. She needs a little time to herself. The stars are out now and the air is crisp and cool. It seems to have gone from fall to winter in just one day.

Elsie scuffs her feet through the sand along the Lake Michigan shore. The gentle lapping of the waves has a soothing effect, helping her to forget her loneliness and the one she had placed her hopes on. Even with her family and friends close by, the future looks so empty to her now. Never has she felt so alone. Elsie stops for a while. Heartbroken, she stands looking out over the lakeshore. In the distance she can see the lights of Manistique reflecting on the dark waters of Lake Michigan.

In her sorrow, she turns to the one who she has always felt she could share her joys and sorrows with, and in her anguish, she prays to God for comfort and hope. She asks, "Will this sorrow ever end? Will I live my life alone? Oh God, I know that you are always there for me, but will I ever love again?" Nothing but the graceful lapping of the waters on the shore seems to answer her prayer. The stars twinkling in the night sky and the sound of the water are the only response. In the vast silence of the night sky, she feels as though her prayer is lost somewhere in that endless expanse. Can God even hear my prayer, she wonders. Tears well up in her eyes. It seems as though God Himself has forgotten her.

"Why would he care about me?" she wonders. "Why would he be concerned about me?"

Suddenly, a bright flash lightens up the sky. A falling star, with a brightness she has never before seen, streaks out of the sky, so bright it even lights up her tear-filled eyes. Elsie gasps in amazement. Never has she seen such a celestial display, so close it seems she can almost touch it. Forgetting her sorrow, she hastily makes a wish. "I wish that soon I will meet my true love." Somehow, in that brief moment, her heart is changes from sorrow to joy; from hopelessness to faith. A sign that the one who rules the vast universe cared for her and was even now answering her heartfelt prayer.

Little does she know that on the other side of the bay, a lonely young man is out on the deck of a ship, and that he, too, sees that same falling star, and he, too, makes that same wish.

DREAM ON A WINTER'S NIGHT

Dream on winter's night
When there's nothing left
Inside you to believe in

A falling star cross the winter sky
So bright it even lightens up your tear filled eyes
Sparks a hope inside
That someone else is wishing on
That star tonight

So you make a wish on a falling star
Make a wish. May your dreams go far
That you'll find the one, the one that
You've been waiting for on that cold
And lonely starlight winter night

Dream On a Winter's night when there's
Nothing left inside you to believe in
You pray a prayer that you'll find someone
The one you know will be the one who really cares.

Dare to Dream the kind of dream
They say just don't happen no more
The kind of dream that's only meant
For you and me, but for you and me
Our dream's come true
To love you and to be loved by you

Dream on winter's night
When there's nothing left
Inside you to believe in

A falling star cross the winter sky

So bright it even lightens up your tear filled eyes
Sparks a hope inside
That someone else is wishing on
That star tonight.

That someone else is wishing on
that star tonight.

Elsie walks along the shore back to the house. The burden she has been carrying seems to have lifted, and the world around her looks more beautiful again. She returns to the house and goes inside to join the others.

By now, the dishes have all been washed and put away, and everyone is gathered together in the living room. Osbourn has his fiddle out, and is playing a few familiar tunes, like *Turkey in the Straw, She'll be Riding Six White Horses, and Oh my Darling Clementine.* Elsie quietly joins them, with a new and peaceful look on her face.

Now it's the twins' turn to entertain. The two girls sing songs for their little audience, and keep them amused for hours with their antics.

Then Captain Schuenemann and Osbourn take turns swapping stories of ships and sea captains, of lumberjacks and Indians, well into the night.

Finally, they all decide it's bedtime, and Flora helps them all get settled in for the night. After a full day, sleep comes easily for the household. A sense of peace seems to linger in the air, as they all go to sleep for the night.

CHAPTER FIFTEEN - STUCK

The next morning, the crew of the *Rouse Simmons* is up and moving, after Albert fills them with a hot meal. They're ready for another day. Thomas leads the crew down the gangplank to the Model T. Hogie, feeling recovered enough to work, joins the crew. They all climb aboard and Thomas cranks up the engine and off they go. Soon they are bouncing along the road toward Thompson.

"How are you feeling today, Hogie?" Thomas asks.

"Not too bad," Hogie responds. "My ribs are still sore, but at least they're not broken," he says as he smiles with his black eye. Thomas laughs as he looks at him.

Soon they arrive at Osbourn's. The captain is already outside and as Thomas pulls up, he begins hooking up the wagon.

"I see you're back in the saddle," the captain yells to Hogie, over the sound of the Model T.

"Yeah," he says, lowering his head sheepishly.

"You still have a pretty good shiner there," the captain teases.

"Yeah, but you should have seen the other guys," Hogie retorts.

They all laugh together as the captain climbs onto the truck and off they go to the boarding house to pick up the woodsmen.

At the boarding house, the woodsmen are all waiting and climb into the wagon. They all give Hogie a joking remark about his black eye or about taking the day off. Hogie just smiles and takes it all in stride.

"You think you could have found someone a little tougher than Dan Seavey to pick on," one of them says in a sarcastic tone.

"Oh, he saved him for a second," Andrew spouts in Hogie's defense.

Hogie just grins and shakes his head.

The truck pulls ahead with the wagonload of men behind. They continue laughing and teasing Hogie, actually quite proud that one of their group had given the legendary Dan Seavey a whooping.

The morning sun is out now, but the air remains cool. The snow makes it much more difficult to pull the wagon, and now as Thomas tries to drive ahead with the Model T, the wheels slip and slide every time Thomas tries to pull with the wagon. Again Thomas engages the clutch on the Model T, but the tires just spin helplessly.

"Darn! This little bit of snow sure makes pulling this wagon a lot harder," Thomas complains. Trying again to pull the wagon, Thomas again engages the clutch. Again the tires spin in the slippery snow. "That darn snow is like trying to catch a greased pig at a county fair," Thomas complains.

Captain Schuenemann watches intently, studying the situation.

"Darn!" yells Thomas in a note of disgust. "I don't think I can pull this wagon in this snow!"

The woodsmen in the wagon look on bewildered for a moment. One of them yells out, "Get a horse!" adding to Thomas' frustration and embarrassment.

Thomas tries pulling the wagon one more time. *Whirrrrrrr...* The Model T spins helplessly.

"I guess it's no use," Thomas says in a defeated tone. "Maybe we need to get a horse after all."

"Wait a minute," the captain orders. "I've got an idea." Taking some rope out of the back of the truck and jumping down from the Model T, he wraps the rope through the spokes of the wheel, around the tire. Then he repeats the process on the other wheel. "Okay, pull ahead a little," the captain orders. Completing his task of putting rope on the back wheels, he secures the ropes tightly.

Thomas climbs down and watches intently, wondering at the captain's positive attitude and quick thinking. The captain makes quick work of the task as hand. "Okay, let's try that."

Thomas jumps back in the driver's seat and engages the engine. The truck easily moves ahead. "Wow, that's a big improvement!"

The two men jump in the truck and away they go. "Wow, that rope works great, captain. That was really a good idea," says Thomas, with his face beaming as he steers the truck down the road.

"I just thought about those big metal clogs I've seen on those big steam tractors," the captain explained with a look of satisfaction. "I bet a piece of chain would work even better, 'cuz the rope will get kind of slippery, and it will wear out real fast, too," he adds. "When we get back into town, we'll stop at the livery, and I'll buy a couple of pieces of small chain, then we'll fasten them on with some leather shoelaces."

"That sounds like a great idea," says Thomas. "You're not only a captain, you're an inventor, too!"

"Just call me Thomas Edison Schuenemann," he laughs. Then they both laugh as the Model T easily pulls the loaded wagon along.

The little truck chugs along now over the blanket of fresh white snow. In every direction as far as the eye can see, a whole forest of snow-covered spruce and balsam trees seem to be popping up among the giant stumps of the once great white pine forest. The captain smiled. He points all around.

"Look at all the young trees coming up," he marvels. "There are a lot of Christmas trees out there!"

Thomas just smiles and looks around as he steers down the road.

Arriving at the place where they will be harvesting trees that day. Thomas stops the truck and the woodsmen all unload their stuff and get ready for another day of harvesting trees.

"Could you give us a hand loading these here trees before you go?" the captain asks. "Thomas and I need a head start this morning to make up for our delay."

Instantly, the men all grab trees. In nothing flat, the truck and wagon are both quickly loaded.

"Thank you, gentlemen," he tells them. Then they both climb into the truck and head for the dock. Thomas and the Captain unload the trees then drive into town to the store.

"Boushour's Livery will probably have some chain. Pull up over there," the captain points. "Before you shut off the engine, let's take these ropes off the wheels. Then we can use them to get an idea how long our chain should be."

"Yeah, good idea," says Thomas.

The captain cuts the rope, and unwinds it from the wheel. "Okay, back up a little." Soon the captain has the ropes in his hand and together they go into the livery store.

The captain greets the man inside.

"George, how are you doing?"

"Herman! Good to see you. I was wondering who that was

with the automobile. I've seen you go through town with it. How do you like it?" he asks.

"Oh, it's great. It actually belongs to Thomas, here. We've been pulling a wagon with it, but with this fresh snow, the back wheels keep slipping. So, we need a couple of short pieces of chain and some leather laces to wrap them around the tires to keep them from spinning. The chain should be about this long." The captain holds up a piece of rope.

"All right, I'll fix you right up," George tells them. Soon he returns with the two pieces of chain and the leather laces. "That will be $1.50," he tells him, placing the chains on the counter.

Captain Schuenemann pays for the chains. "Thanks, George."

"Okay, captain. Hey, do you think the day will come when those automobiles will ever replace the horse and buggy?"

"I think it's already happening," the captain answers. "I think that it will soon be like the steam ship and the sailing ship. The sailing ship is becoming a thing of the past." The captain looks him in the eye. "It's just a matter of time," he adds with a prophetic tone of voice.

George nods his head and for a moment contemplates the future of his livery business.

"Have a good day, captain."

"You, too," the captain says, as he and Thomas step out the

door.

"Well, let's get these chains on, so we can haul our next load."

"Okay, captain," Thomas replies.

Quickly the two of them work together. Soon they have the chains installed and they're on their way back for another load of trees. After loading the trees, Thomas tries out the new chains.

"Wow, no comparison!" He smiles. "This is going to work a lot better now!

So off to the dock they go, with another load of trees. The day passes quickly while the two men haul one load of trees after another. The number of trees at the dock steadily increases with each trip.

I think we've got that problem solved," Captain Schuenemann says confidently.

"I think so too," Thomas agrees. "That was one thing my pa didn't like about the automobile. He said it would get stuck too easy. I wonder what he'll say about it now!"

"Hey, let's get one more load, and then we'll have to call it quits for today. But before we go back and pick up the men, I want to stop at the house for a moment and show Barbara and the girls the automobile. Maybe I could take them for a little ride?"

"Great idea, captain. I know you were anxious to show them that you know how to drive."

"Don't say anything about my learning to drive the automobile until they're all aboard, then I'll jump in the driver's seat at the last minute," the captain says with a sly grin. "That way I'll really surprise them."

"All right," Thomas agrees, going along with the captain's little plan.

So off they go for another load, and in a short time they are on their way back with another load of trees to unload at the dock.

"There," the captain says, taking off his wet gloves, "That's one more load. Let's head over to the house now, and show Barbara and the girls the automobile." The captain seems so excited he can hardly stop smiling as they pull up alongside the house. "I'll be right back," he says, with a mischievous look on his face.

Captain Schuenemann goes into the house to get Barbara and the girls. Thomas sits at the wheel and leans back, thinking to himself about how much he enjoys working for Captain Schuenemann. The captain seems more like a friend than a boss and how often he makes him laugh. Thomas also thinks about the members of his crew, how they feel about the captain, and their loyalty to him. As he thinks about these things, he realizes how fortunate he is, to have the opportunity to work for Captain Schuenemann.

The captain hurries out the door, anxiously leading his wife and daughters. They all gather around, admiring the Model T.

"Thomas, I would like you to meet my family," the captain says proudly.

Thomas steps down from behind the wheel and politely stands facing them as they approach.

"This, of course, is my beautiful wife, Barbara. Barbara, this is Thomas Berger, who, I might add, has been a great help to me." She smiles and nods.

"Nice to meet you, Thomas."

"Pleased to meet you, Ma'am," Thomas answers softly.

"And this is my daughter, Elsie," the captain says, placing his arm around her shoulder and giving her a little hug.

"Pleased to meet you," Thomas says, looking into her deep blue eyes.

"Pleased to meet you," Elsie answers. For a moment, they are lost in one another's gaze.

"She's beautiful," Thomas thinks to himself.

Then the captain's voice draws his attention again. "And these are my two little twins, Pearl and Hazel," the captain announces, wrapping his arms around them and giving them both a little squeeze. Their curly hair, rosy cheeks, and innocent but mischievous smiles make them an instant hit. It is easy to see why the captain beams every time he talks about them.

"Nice to meet you," they both say together.

"Nice to meet you," Thomas smiles.

"Is that your automobile?" Pearl asks.

"Can we go for a ride?" Hazel adds.

"Yes," answers Thomas, to both at once. "Well, actually, it's my father's," he tells them. "But I'm using it to haul trees for your father."

"I'll unhitch the wagon. Maybe we could go for a little ride," the captain suggests.

"Good idea," Thomas replies.

"Barbara and I will ride in front. Elsie, you and the twins can ride in back. It's a Ford Model T truck," the captain explains. "You girls can sit up here in back, on the rail. But hold on tight!" he warns them.

Thomas goes around to the front of the truck and gives the engine crank a turn. The captain helps Barbara and the girls into the truck. Then at the last moment, Captain Schuenemann climbs into the driver's seat, while Thomas jumps in back alongside Elsie, and off they go, clamoring out of the yard and up the street.

"Hang on!" the captain yells.

"Herman Schuenemann! You never told me you knew how to drive an automobile! Aren't you supposed to have a driver's license?" she asks.

"I've already got one," he says with a twinkle in his eye.

After a short spin around Thompson, the captain returns to

the yard. Enthusiastically, he gets out and explains some of the features of the automobile to Barbara and the girls.

But all the while, Thomas and Elsie are rather quiet. They both are a little shy, but at the same time both want to speak. There's a mutual attraction that is hard to explain, but they both know something is happening inside them.

The captain, ever observant even though his attention is absorbed in the automobile, for a brief moment glances over and notices the two of them, looking over at one another.

Never one to miss an opportunity, he immediately blurts out, "Oh, and Thomas, would you like to join us for supper tonight?"

"Oh, thank you, sir. I would like that very much," he answers, half smiling, sensing the captain's opportune invitation.

"We'd better go back and pick the men up now, so you'll have time to get ready," the captain says, gesturing for them to get back in the truck.

"Goodbye, Thomas. We'll see you later," Barbara and the girls chime in together.

"Good-bye! It's been a pleasure meeting you. I guess I'll see you at dinner tonight!"

"We'll be looking forward to having you," Barbara answers. The girls all nod and smile.

Thomas and the captain hitch up the wagon, and off they

go, back up the Little Harbor Road to pick up the workmen. After dropping the woodsmen off at the boarding house, they stop to leave the wagon at Osbourn's.

"Hurry back, now, Thomas! Oh, and here's some money for gasoline. We have to remember to feed that thing!"

"Yes, sir," Thomas replies, smiling. He takes the money, and off he goes with the crew back towards Manistique.

When they arrive at the ship, the men begin to unload.

"I won't be eating supper on board the ship tonight," Thomas tells Albert, the cook. "Captain Schuenemann invited me to eat with them over at Osbourn's place, so I'm just going to get cleaned up a little and then I have to get right back over there."

"All right, I've got a pail of warm water on the stove you can use," Albert tells him. "I left it on the stove before we left here this morning, so it's probably still warm."

"You're always thinking ahead, Albert," Thomas answers.

"We'll have you looking dapper in no time," Albert teases. "I don't know if you noticed or not, but the Captain's daughter, Elsie, is not a bad looker. Maybe a little romance could come of this," Albert says loudly.

The crew all laughs.

"Yeah, I noticed," blushes Thomas.

Then Thomas notices Engvald, the old Swede who never talks, step forward and for a moment look as though he's going to say something. Thomas pauses expectantly, but Engvald quietly turns and walks away, leaving Thomas wondering what he would have said.

"Well, quit daydreaming there and get yourself ready. Time's a-wastin'," Albert says, throwing him a towel. "Here's the wash tub. Have at 'er."

Thomas gives himself a quick sponge bath, and quickly dries off, then takes his shaving cream and lathers up his brush. He grabs his strait razor and gently shaves his face. All the while, he feels as though he's in some sort of dream.

Quickly dressing in the best clothes he had brought with him, he hurries up on deck. "See you later," he says to the others.

"Have a good time," they tell him.

He rushes of down the gangplank and out to the Model T. Grabbing the handle, he gives the engine a crank. In a moment, he's rolling through town. When he reaches the edge of town, he stops suddenly.

"Oh, shoot! I forgot to get gasoline." Turning the truck around, he drives back into town to the place that sells the fuel, only to find that no one is around and the pump is padlocked. Thomas hurries to the door of the shop and pounds on the door. As he knocks, he notices a sign in the window of the door that reads: "Will be back tomorrow."

"Oh, great," he says to himself in a disgusted tone of voice.

Thomas runs back to the truck, opens the fuel tank, and checks the dipstick. It's almost empty," he mutters. "I'll run out for sure." Jumping back in the truck, Thomas races back through town to the dock. Stopping near the ship, he runs up the gangplank.

"I forgot to get gasoline on the way home," Thomas announces desperately, "And the place that sells it is closed till tomorrow. Do we have any gasoline here?"

"No, we don't use gasoline for anything on this ship," Hogie tells him.

"What am I going to do? I'll never make it to Thompson on the fuel I've got in the tank!"

"We have a couple gallons of kerosene for the lanterns. Will that work?" Hogie asks.

"Yeah, it will have to," Thomas answers. "And oh, I should light the headlamps," Thomas says, looking as anxious as a schoolboy that's about to wet his pants.

"How about if I get the kerosene and pour it in the truck for you, while you get the carbide and water for your lights," Hogie says assuredly.

"That would be great," answers Thomas, turning again and hurrying down the gangplank.

While Thomas gets the acetylene generator charged with some carbide and water, Hogie hurries down the gangplank carrying the can of kerosene. Opening the fuel tank, he pours it in.

"How does this thing run on kerosene?" Hogie asks.

"Oh, not bad. There's a little gasoline left in the tank, too, so I should be all right."

"Well, as soon as you light your headlamps, you should be ready to go," says Hogie as he empties the kerosene can into the tank. Thomas lights the acetylene lamps.

"Thanks a lot, Hogie!"

"That's okay. You get going now, and have a good time."

"Oh, I will," says Thomas. He turns the crank and the Model T rumbles to a start. Thomas jump in behind the wheel. "See you later," he says, as the truck lurches forward.

Hurrying back through town and across the bridge, Thomas slows the truck to a crawl on the bridge, so as not to scare the horses pulling a wagon. Back through the dark he hurries along the lake shore the six and a half miles to Thompson. Finally he pulls into Osbourn's yard. There to greet him is Sandy, the dog, with her usual tail wagging and a couple of friendly barks. She is always happy and looking for some attention.

Captain Schuenemann meets Thomas at the door. "Come on in, Thomas, we're all waiting for you. Dinner's ready!"

"Sorry I'm late. I forgot to stop and get fuel on the way back to the ship, so I had to use some kerosene from the ship, because the place where we got the gasoline was closed," Thomas explains.

"That's all right. Just hang your coat up and come into the dining room."

"The food sure smells good. I just realized how hungry I am."

Thomas sits down at the table.

"Thomas, this is Florabell Stanley."

"Pleased to meet you, Ma'am."

"Pleased to meet you, Thomas. Glad you could join us. Dinner is ready. I'll start serving," Flora announces.

"We're having fresh lake trout, baked with Florabell's secret recipe," Captain Schuenemann boasts. Everyone seems so happy to see him, Thomas feels right at home. The twins are always a source of amusement, with their glowing smiles and their funny comments. Then there is Osbourn, with his interesting stories of people and places he knew from the area.

Florabell and Barbara make a wonderful team. It is obvious they enjoy one another's company. And of course, Captain Schuenemann, who always seems to bring out the best in everyone, is everyone's best friend and at the same time commands their respect.

Then there's Elsie, with her beautiful blue eyes and golden hair, her gentle and friendly manner, makes him feel so at ease in her presence that he feels as though he has known her all his life.

Although this is really the first time he has been away from the farm for any length of time, Thomas feels just as though he belongs here.

"So Thomas, you said that you were saving money to go to college. Have you decided what you want to study?" Elsie asks.

"Yes, I have always been interested in photography, and writing, and hope to pursue a career in one of those fields, and the way I see it, they both go hand in hand."

"That sounds interesting. With so much happening in he world today, you would certainly have a lot to write about."

"I find that there are so many interesting people and places, that I just think that it would be a great way to make a living. As a matter of fact, I have a camera and have been taking quite a few photos already, but there's a lot to learn about photography."

"Yes, that sounds exciting. I have always been interested in photography, too," Elsie joins in. "I think it's amazing how much smaller the cameras are today than just a few years ago," she says.

"Does anyone want more fish?" Florabell asks everybody. "Let's eat it up."

"I'll take another piece," Captain Schuenemann responds. "Thomas and I were unloading trees at the dock, when the *Dorothy S.* came in with a fresh load of fish. Bill Sellman was telling us what a good catch he had, so I decided to buy some for supper."

"This sure is a busy harbor here," Captain Schuenemann

comments. "That's why Mr. Chesbrough wants us to keep the ship tied up at Manistique till we are ready to load. There's been quite a few ships in here to get those piles of lumber shipped before the weather gets too bad."

During supper Thomas and Elsie converse freely. At times it seems the two of them are completely absorbed in each other's company.

Captain Schuenemann notices and quietly gestures to Barbara in a way that would be unnoticed by the others. She in turn returns a knowing glance of satisfaction that the two are so at ease in one another's company.

After supper, the ladies gather in the kitchen to do the dishes, while the men do other chores. Thomas volunteers to go out to the pump and fill some pails of water and carry them into the house. Captain Schuenemann splits some wood and brings it in, filling the wood box next to the stove. Osbourn goes out to the barn to tend to the animals.

After chores, they all gather in the dining room. Captain Schuenemann brings in a large piece of sailcloth and covers the table. Then he carries in a large pile of greens. "This is what we do for entertainment in the evenings. Everyone gathers around, and we make wreaths and garlands to sell back in Chicago."

Everyone sits down at the table, and starts working. Thomas and Elsie sit together.

"I'll show you how to make a wreath," she says. "First, you make a wire loop, like this," she demonstrates. Thomas mimics her every action.

"Then we wrap some princess pine around the wire, like this." Elsie demonstrates.

Thomas marvels at how quickly her fingers form a wreath. Within minutes, she has a beautiful wreath.

"That's amazing," he tells her.

"Okay, now you try," Elsie says, handing him a piece of wire.

"How many of these do you make?" Thomas asks.

"As many as we can," Captain Schuenemann interjects, and they laugh.

"I want this to be my best season ever," the captain continues, "And when this season's over, we're going to buy an automobile."

"An automobile," Barbara exclaims. "Herman Schuenemann, what will you think of next?"

The captain laughs and answers, "My mind is pretty much made up. I don't see any reason why we shouldn't have an automobile. The way Henry Ford is mass-producing them, it seems that a lot more people will be buying automobiles than horses and buggies, and thanks to Thomas here, I know how to drive one." He gives Thomas an approving nod.

"And besides that, you girls wouldn't have to feed horses or shovel the manure."

They all laugh. "Oh Daddy," the twins answer with a disapproving look. Really they enjoy his attention even when he's teasing them.

The evening flies by, and the Christmas wreaths stack up. They all enjoy one another's company, with the captain and Barbara telling stories of Chicago, and the grand and busy happenings around the city.

Thomas' evening visits become a regular part of the day, until nearly every evening is spent together with them.

CHAPTER SIXTEEN – ANOTHER SURPRISE

The following day starts pretty much the same as any other. The captain and Thomas drop the woodsmen off to cut trees while they carry as many loads of trees down to the dock as they can. After a short lunch break, the captain and Thomas continue their ritual of hauling trees. After a full day of hauling trees, the sun is getting lower in the sky and the captain voices his satisfaction with the day's efforts.

"This will be the fifteenth load of trees today. That makes it our best day so far. When we're finished unloading these, we'll go back and pick up the men in the woods and call it a day!"

"Yeah, I'm whipped, captain. But it does feel good to get so much done today. No problems and no breakdowns!"

Soon they're on their way back, both very tired but both feeling good about the day's production. The captain dozes a bit as the little truck bounces along.

Thomas blurts out, "There's a deer!"

The deer has been standing near the side of the road, and bolts quickly across the road, right in front of the truck.

"That was a buck!" Captain Schuenemann exclaims.

Thomas brings the truck to a sudden halt, reaches behind the seat, and pulls out a rifle. Cocking the lever to place a shell in the chamber, he leaps out of the truck.

"He's running through those small spruce trees!" Captain Schuenemann reports, pointing in the direction.

Thomas leans out over the hood, rests his elbow on the Model T, and takes aim. The white tail of the deer flashes with each leap. As the deer reaches the edge of a small clearing, it stops briefly and turns to look back.

That's the moment Thomas is waiting for. Thomas squeezes the trigger. BLAM! Fire shoots from the end of the barrel and sends the bullet flying.

"Good shot!" Captain Schuenemann shouts.

The bullet has met its mark, dropping the deer on the spot. "That's the way we do it up here in the U. P. (meaning Upper Peninsula)," says Thomas coolly, lowering the rifle.

"You sure surprised me. I've been so busy with these trees I forgot that we had my rifle along with us."

The two men hurry out to the place where the deer is lying. Captain Schuenemann grabs the deer's antlers and holds the deer's head upright.

"It's a nice eight-point," he announces.

"Wow, it's a beautiful deer," Thomas marvels. "Really a nice rack on it."

"That was a nice clean shot, Thomas. I don't think he felt a thing."

"Do you have a knife?"

"Yeah, I've got a pocket knife right here. It should be good and sharp."

So the two men work together to dress out the deer, and are soon dragging it out to the road.

"It's a good-sized deer," Captain Schuenemann comments. "Let's load it onto the truck. Florabell is sure going to be surprised when she sees this. She loves to cook venison. You get up on the back of the truck, and I'll lift the horns up to you. Then, you pull on the horns while I lift on the legs."

"Okay," says Thomas, grabbing the antlers from the captain.

"Okay, pull!" the captain grunts. "Ho boy, I bet he's over two hundred pounds!"

Thomas finishes pulling the deer onto the truck.

"Hey! When we go and pick up the other guys from the woods, don't say anything about it. Let's surprise them, and see what they say," the captain says mischievously.

"Let's go pick them up now. It's about quitting time anyway."

So they both climb into the truck, and off they go, prouder than a couple of peacocks.

A little later, they pull up at the spot they were to meet the woodsmen, and honk the horn. Hogie and Albert are the first ones to come walking out of the woods. Thomas and the captain look over at one another with a slight grin. Neither of them said a word about the deer.

Hogie and Albert put their tools in the wagon. The rest of the woodsmen are gathering around the truck.

"Hey! What the heck have you guys been doing? Going hunting all day, while we're working?"

"Yeah, what's with this?" Albert asks.

"Hey! Thomas and the captain got a nice buck in the back of the truck," they holler to the others. Quickly the men all gather around the truck.

"Wow, that's a nice buck!" "How did you get him," came a barrage of questions.

"We ran over him with the truck," the captain laughs. "No, really, the deer ran across the road in front of us, and the next thing I know, Thomas jumps out and pulls a rifle out from behind the seat, and BLAM! That was it. Just one shot."

"Oh wow." They all take an admiring look, each taking the antlers in their hands.

"Don't worry, you guys, I'll send half the venison over to the ship, and leave half at Osbourn's place. You guys at the boarding house will just have to come for supper on the ship one evening, if you want to have a taste. How does that sound, Albert?"

"Sounds good. The more the merrier," Albert says, in a jovial tone.

"Sounds good to us," the others add.

"Well, let's get going, gentlemen," the captain prods, "And remember, we won't be working tomorrow 'cause it's Sunday, so get rested up for another hard week. In a few more days we'll be bringing the ship over here to Thompson, and we'll start loading her with trees."

They all climb into the wagon and the truck and are off for Thompson. After dropping the woodsmen off, they head back over to Osbourn's place, and pull into the yard. Thomas and the others get out to unhitch the wagon. Captain Schuenemann hurries inside. "I'll tell Osbourn and the girls to come out and see the deer you got," the captain announces anxiously. "They'll all be surprised."

A few minutes later, they all come out of the house and gather around the truck.

"What a beautiful deer," the ladies compliment. Osbourn walks over and grabs the horns, straightening the head up, so everyone gets a better look.

"Let's get a photograph," Thomas suggests, getting out his camera. "Elsie, could you take the picture?" Thomas sets his camera on the tripod and gets it all ready. "Let's get the captain and I, one on each side of the deer. Just hold it steady, and look through here. When we're ready, just push down on this lever. All right, we're ready."

Thomas holds the rifle while he and the captain pose. Barbara and the others watch.

"Okay, smile," Elsie tells them, and then clicks the shutter.

"All right, good job," says Thomas.

"Now, let's go out back and hang the deer up, back by the shed. I've got a spot where I hang mine," Osbourn instructs.

So they go out back and hang up the deer. Sandy, the dog, follows close behind, sniffing everything with her big nose while the guys hang the deer up on Osbourn's buck pole.

"Come on back over for supper, when you drop the crew off," Captain Schuenemann tells Thomas, "And don't forget to stop and get gasoline."

"I won't forget," says Thomas, sheepishly.

"Okay, we'll see you later, Thomas," he says, and off they drive to Manistique.

On the way back to the ship, Thomas stops to get gasoline. "I'm not going to forget again this time," he tells the others, stopping for fuel.

Soon they're back at the ship, and Thomas quickly gets ready. The crew all razz him about cozying up to the captain's daughter, but Thomas takes it all in stride. Then, just to add a little spice to the conversation, Thomas adds, "I think I'm going to ask her if she would like to go on a picnic tomorrow. As long as Barbara and the captain approve, of course!"

This gets more of a rise out of the crew. "Next thing you know, you'll be getting married," Hogie and Andrew tease. The rest of the crew joins in poking fun at him. "Hey Thomas, watch out for the ball and chain!"

"Yeah, you'll be taking orders from the captain's daughter instead of from the captain," they joke.

Suddenly, out of nowhere, Engvald appears, and to everyone's astonishment, Engvald is standing in front of Thomas, and actually giving his advice. Everyone is so shocked to hear him talking, that they are all instantly silent, straining their ears to hear what this silent, private shipmate has to say. For a moment, his eyes grow bright with a light the others have never seen before. Then he speaks.

"Ton't vait til yer too olt to look for a vife," Engvald advises in his thick Scandinavian brogue.

Thomas looks up, startled to hear Engvald speak at all, much less give his advice. "How come you never got married, Engvald?" Thomas asks.

"Oh, it vas vone of dose tings dat I vish dat I hat tone tifferent," he sighs. "Ven I vas young, I vas in love vonce," he says. The distant look in his eyes makes it appear that somehow he was transported back in time. The others are so quiet now you could hear a pin drop, and they all listen as he continues, "I vas living in ta olt country, back in Shveeden. I vas in love vit a putiful, younk schoolteacher der. Ve vere very much in love. Vone time ve vent on a valk together. It vas in ta autumn time, and ta mettow vas chust so creen. Ve valked together tru da fielts, laughing and talking together," he continues. "Ta autumn flowers vere int ploom, ant she picked some of tem, ant she took ta flowers ant put dem in her colten blond hair. Ta sun on her shone chust like ta colt of heaven. Den I put my arms arount her and helt her close to me ant ve kissed. She vas so putiful dere in tat vite tress, I chust never vanted to stop kissing her and holting her in my arms.

"Tat vas ven I shoot have asked for her to marrvy me. Put ta vords chust tidn't come out, Den time vent py. I chust never hat ta right chance to ask her again. Ten somevone else asked her first," he says sadly. "So ton't vait too lonk, 'cuz now I'm chust too darn olt. I vill alvays remember her tat summer evening, put now, she's chust a memory," he sighs. Tears run now from the corner of his eyes as he finishes his story.

JUST A MEMORY

She was walking in the autumn sun at evening
Golden sunlight touched the flowers in her hair

Shadows dancing on the white dress
She was wearing, she was wearing, she was caring for me.

She was walking in the autumn sun at evening
Golden sunlight touched the flowers in her hair

A warm smile on her loving face
She was wearing, she was wearing, she was caring for me

She was walking in the autumn sun at evening
Golden sunlight touched the flowers in her hair

A sweet kiss on her soft lips
She was sharing, she was sharing, she was caring for me

She was walking in the autumn sun at evening
Golden sunlight touched the flowers in her hair

There was music in the sweet words
She was sharing, she was sharing, she was caring for me

But now she's Just a Memory

Thomas and the crew are so moved by the lesson, that for a moment they all stand speechless, and perhaps for the first time they understand the burden carried by this silent and mysterious man.

Reaching out and placing his hand on Engvald's shoulder, Thomas breaks the silence. "I'll keep that in mind, Engvald. Thank you for the advice."

Engvald nods and turns to go up on deck, but at the same time appears to be relieved of some great burden, as though his words of warning, if held back, would be lived out again in others, and in that by speaking out this one time, he is somehow redeeming himself from the guilt and remorse he felt for not speaking up at an earlier time in his life.

As Thomas finishes cleaning up and hurries back to Thompson, he thinks about Engvald's words. "Well, I'm not ready to ask her to marry me," Thomas jokes aloud, "But I do want to ask her to go for a picnic with me," he says, laughing out loud to himself. "I'll make sure and ask her that much anyway," he says with great resolve.

CHAPTER SEVENTEEN - ADVICE

Arriving at Osbourn's, Thomas is greeted by Sandy's cautious, but friendly barks. Giving her a quick pat on the head, he says, "Good dog, Sandy," and enters the house, and joins the others at the table.

While dinner is being served, Thomas thinks about what he's going to say, but somehow, just can't think of the right words. He hesitates as he passes a dish of potatoes around, then Engvald's words seem to ring in his ears. "I chust never hat ta chance to hask her again."

"Elsie, I was wondering, if it's all right with your parents, if tomorrow afternoon you would like to take a ride with me and maybe you could show me the Big Spring," Thomas asks. "Maybe have a little picnic or something, too."

"Oh, that sounds like a great idea," Elsie replies. "You have never been to the spring, have you, Thomas? Oh, it's beautiful," Elsie describes. "I've been there quite a few times, but each time I visit there, I find it more beautiful. It's very deep, and the water is crystal clear, so that you can see all the way to the bottom of the spring. It's beautiful, it really is. There is a raft that is pulled across by a rope, so you can look right down in the spring. The water is a deep blue-green, and oh, you can see all of the moss-covered logs and fish, just like looking through a piece of glass!" The enthusiasm in her voice and the light in her eyes makes Thomas all the more anxious to go.

"I've heard so much about it, I would really like to see it."

"Oh, can we go, too?" Pearl and Hazel chime in.

Thomas looks a little embarrassed and tries to let them know that he wants to be alone with Elsie without making it too obvious. "Well, I was just thinking it would be nice if Elsie and I just went together," he says, feeling a little put on the spot.

"That sounds like it's okay to me," Captain Schuenemann answers, looking over at Barbara to get her approval.

She nods an approving yes, and adds, "Florabell and I will pack you two a picnic lunch."

"A picnic! Could we go too?" the twins plead.

"Now girls," Barbara frowns, "They don't need a crowd. Elsie and Thomas want to take the automobile and go by themselves."

That night, after supper, the table is covered again with the sailcloth, and then piled high with evergreens. Thomas joins Elsie in making wreaths. Again, Thomas marvels at Elsie's agile and skilled hands.

"I've been doing this since I was just a little girl," Elsie says, looking over at Pearl and Hazel kneeling together on the floor playing a game of jacks, bouncing a red rubber ball and picking up jacks while chattering together about the picnic. The evening once again flies by, and all too soon it's time for Thomas to get ready to travel back to the ship.

Thomas says good night to everyone and slips on his coat and hat.

But this time, Elsie slips out of the door to say goodbye. For the first time, they are actually alone together, both of them thinking that this is all far too good to be true. There seems to be a magnetic attraction between the two.

"That was nice of you to ask me about going to the spring tomorrow."

"Well, it sure sounds like a beautiful place. I think it would be nice to get a couple of photographs of the place. You would look nice in some of them, too!"

As he looks at Elsie, he can picture her in his photographs. Even now, in the dim light, she looks so beautiful to him. Never has he wanted to kiss a girl's lips like he wants to right now. Never has he wished he could hold someone so close as right now. "Should I kiss her," he wonders. "Would it be too forward of me?"

Then Engvald's words seem to echo in his ears, "Ton't vait too lonk," so, as he says good night, he leans forward and holds her gently in his arms, and puts his lips close to hers, their lips finally meet as though they were meant to be together, both of them lost in the moment, both of them feeling as though, for a moment, everything in the world is right. Two people in a great, big world, perhaps guided together as though by an unseen hand.

All too soon, the kiss is over, but both of them know in their hearts that there will be more.

"I'll see you tomorrow, around noon," Thomas says softly.

"I'll be waiting," Elsie whispers.

"Look, the stars are out." Thomas points into the night sky.

"Oh, how beautiful," Elsie sighs. "I have never seen them look so bright! That's why I love coming up here each year. It is so beautiful here."

"Oh, I just remembered I've got to light these lamps, so I can see," Thomas tells Elsie.

"There's no moon out tonight, so you better take it slow," Elsie cautions him.

"Yeah, I will," he says, then works at lighting the lamps.

"Well, good night," says Elsie, as she walks to the house.

Thomas gives the Model T a crank, and the engine coughs to a start. Elsie stands with her hand on the doorknob, and waves as Thomas climbs in and starts backing down the drive. They give one another one last wave.

Elsie steps into the house, and Thomas chugs off into the night. Never has his heart seemed so light, never has the night seemed so pleasant to him as tonight. The drive back to Manistique seems to be as though it were a dream.

Back along the lakeshore, he drives toward Manistique, then through the town and down to the ship. Thomas parks the Model T alongside the *Rouse Simmons* and shuts off the engine. The carbide lamps are still burning as he walks up the gangplank. All is silent aboard the ship, so Thomas walks slowly across the deck. Stopping along the rail of the ship, he stands looking out over the water. The silent stars now seem brighter than ever. "I have never seen the Milky Way like this," Thomas says to himself out loud. "I wonder if anyone else feels this way, when they're in love. I feel like I could just reach out and touch the stars tonight," he tells himself. "I don't feel like going down to my bunk just yet. I just want to stay here, out under the stars."

So Thomas walks back down the dock and walks along the shore to the harbor break wall. He finds himself strolling down the break wall towards the lighthouse at the end, its bright beacon flashing through the night. In his heart, he asks the stars to witness the way that he feels tonight.

"How many stars are shining in the night? There's never been a star that shines quite so bright."

How Many Stars
The night Thomas falls in love with Elsie

How many stars are shining in the night
There's never been a star

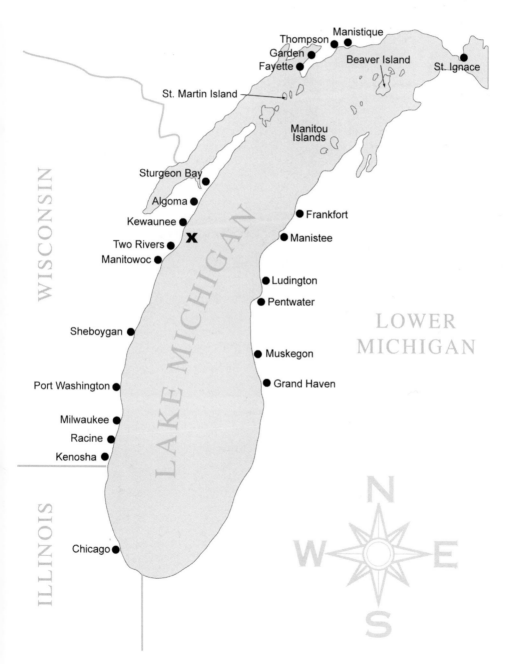

UPPER MICHIGAN

Manistique
Thompson
Garden
Fayette
Beaver Island
St. Ignace
St. Martin Island
Manitou Islands

WISCONSIN

Sturgeon Bay
Algoma
Kewaunee
Frankfort
X
Two Rivers
Manistee
Manitowoc
Ludington
Pentwater
LOWER MICHIGAN
Sheboygan
Muskegon
Port Washington
Grand Haven
LAKE MICHIGAN
Milwaukee
Racine
Kenosha

ILLINOIS

Chicago

N
W · E
S

Left: The Rouse Simmons at the dock in Chicago with Christmas trees on deck.

Below: Captain Schuenamann and two of his friends abaoard the Christmas Tree Ship at Chicago. Captain Jack Colberg is on his right and Captain Vanaman is on his left.

Right: The city of Chicago preparing for the holidays with a wagon of Christmas trees.

Above: Captain Herman Schuenemann, part owner of the Rouse Simmons.

Above: William S. Crowe, through the ranks, rose from office boy to become General Manager and part owner of the Chicago Lumber Co. and Weston Lumber Co. in the newly formed Consolidated Lumber Company.

Above: A good photo of the Rouse Simmons under full sail.

Above: Inside the Chicago Lumber office in Manistique.

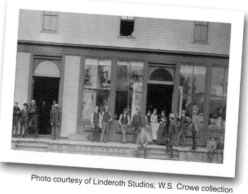

Above: Front steps of the Chicago Lumber Co. in Manistique where Thomas meets Schuenemann.

Above: The Christmas Ship loading tanning bark at Iron Bay on Beaver Island.

Left: Mannes Bonner on his boat. Captain Bonner used this boat to ferry passengers to his hotel on Beaver Island.

Above: A small fishing boat offering to sell a catch of suckers to the crew of a docked ship at Manistique.

Left: Another great photograph of the Rouse Simmons taking on a cargo of tanning bark at Beaver Island.

Left: Captain Bundy's Glad Tidings Gospel Ship.

Below and Left: Captain Bundy's Glad Tidings Gospel Ship.

Above: Captain Henry Bundy.

Above: Sailing ships docked at Manistique Harbor.

Left: Glad Tidings Gospel Ship at the dock at Manistique.

Left: A photo of the Rouse Simmons, better known as the Christmas ship.

Below: The Hart Line Steamer provided package frieght and passenger service to Manistique.

Above: Model T truck on the main street of Manistique, Michigan. The tall darker building was Ekburgs Tavern in the story, now the Harbor Bar, where the fight scene takes place.

Left: Sailing ships in the harbor at Manistique.

Above: A photo of Dan Geavy's ship "The Wanderer."

Above: Captain Dan Geavy getting his photo taken wearing his new set of clothes purchased for his trial for the piracy of the Nellie Johnson..

Below/Right: Several photos of the James Hall, one of Dan Geavey's ships. The James Hall was equipt with a gasoline engine. The ship caught fire on Thunder Bay in 1914 near Alpena and burned to the waterline.

Above: Elsie Schuenemann at the wheel of a schooner with Christmas trees.

Above: Model T truck with a boat in back.

Right: An early picture of the Kichitikipi Big Springs raft.

Below: Giving everyone a ride in the Model T Ford truck at Thompson.

Above: Wolcott's Photography Studio in downtown Manistique where pictures are developed in the story.

Above: The Boarding House at Thompson where the men from the Rouse Simmons stayed while harvesting trees and loading the ship.

Below: A good photo of the Rouse Simmons at a dock at Sheboygan, Wisconsin.

Right: The sawmill at Thompson.

Above: The Rouse Simmons.

Below: A birds eye view of Thompson, the sawmill can be seen in the background. Notice the stumps in the foreground.

Below: The mill pond at Thompson.

Above: Florabel Stanley posing with her rifle and trophy buck. The Schuenemann's sometimes stayed with them while harvesting trees.

Above: Loading lumber onto a schooner by the dock in Thompson.

Below: A sailing schooner similar to the Rouse Simmons loading lumber at Thompson.

Above: White Pine Days. Lumberjacks with a team of horses pulling a load of logs.

Above: Mill Pond at Thompson Harbor.

Below: Indian women selling baskets.

Above: The Sawmill in Thompson, Michigan.

Above: Millworker at Thompson. Miles Osbourn Stanley is in middle of photo.

Below: Horse and buggy in front of house at Thompson.

Above: Fish tug at Thompson Harbor. Cedar posts are piled on the dock ready to be shipped.

Left: The Christmas Ship with snow covered trees on deck.

Below: Kewanee life savers practicing breeches buoy drill.

Above: Railroad Car Ferry Ann Arbor No. 5 with sailing ship entering the harbor.

Below: The Kewanee lifesaving crew ready for action.

Above: Ann Arbor No. 5 next to the Kewanee Lifesaving Station.

Photo courtesy of Rogers St.
Fishing Village Museum

Left: Capt. Gogge, lifesaving Captain of the Two Rivers Lifesaving station led his men in a daring search for the troubled schooner.

Photo courtesy of Superior View

Above: The Two Rivers Lifesaving Station had recently been issued a powered surf boat, like the one pictured above, capable of speeds up to 10 MPH.

Photo courtesy of Rogers St. Fishing Village Museum

Above: Two Rivers Lifesavers in oar powered surf boat.

Photo courtesy of Rogers St. Fishing Village Museum

Above: The Two Rivers Lifesaving crew attempted to rescue the crew of the doomed Rouse Simmons.

Below: The Kewaunee Lifesaving crew notified the Two Rivers Station of a ship in distress..

Photo courtesy of Roger Street Fishing Village Museum

Above: The Two River Lifesaving Station with surf boats in foreground.

Photo courtesy of Kewaunee Historical Society

Above: underwater rail of the Rouse Simmons. The ship was found in 1971 by Kent Belrichard.

Above: Christmas trees still in the hold of the Rouse Simmons. The ship lies in 165' of water off of Two Rivers, Wisconsin.

Above: Kewaunee Lifesaving Crew in front of station pulling a beach cart.

Above: Steering wheel and steering gear from the Rouse Simmons, found by divers 1.5 miles upwind of the wreck. Read more in Rochell Pennington's book, The Historic Christmas Tree Ship.

Above: underwater photo of anchor chain winders on the Rouse Simmons.

Above: More Christmas trees in the cargo hold.

Photo courtesy of Bowling Green State University

Above: Revenue Cutter Mackinac searched the islands of Northern Lake Michigan

Below: The Revenue Cutter Tuscarara, built in 1902, searched the lake for survivors or signs of wreckage.

Photo courtesy of Bowling Green State University

Photo courtesy of Algoma Historical Society

Above: The Two Rivers Lifesaving Station with crew in the foreground.

Below: Kewaunee Lifesaving crew practicing thier boat righting drill.

Photo courtesy of Algoma Historical Society

Photo courtesy of Chicago Historical Society

Above: A later photo of Captain Schuenemann's daughters Pearl and Hazel. The Captain's wife, Barbara, and her three daughters continued to sell Christmas Trees in Chicago for 21 more years untill Barbara's death in 1933.

Below: The Author, Carl Behrend, best known as the singer/songwriter of Great Lakes ballads. More about Carl at the end of the book.

Photo courtesy of the Author's Collection

Above: The author, Carl Behrend.

That shines quite so bright.

I needed love and you were there
You showed me that you really care
How can I show
The love I have for you.

How many stars are shining in the night
There's never been a star
That shines quite so bright.

I caught a glimpse of you last night
I never saw a star so bright as the love
You have for me

How many stars are shining in the night
There's never been a star
That shines quite so bright.

I looked up in the big night sky
I never thought I'd feel so high
As the night I saw
The love you have for me

How many stars are shining in the night
There's never been a star
That shines quite so bright.

I never will forget that night
That in my arms I held you tight
And saw your love
That awesome love for me

How many stars are shining in the night
There's never been a star
That shines quite so bright.

Each time I look up at the stars
I remember just the way you are
and your love you have for me

How many stars are shining in the night
There's never been a star
That shines quite so bright.

Your love is like the brightest star
Now I know just what you are,
You're the star of my life you'll always be

You're the star of my life
You'll always be.

Finally satisfied with the expressions of his heart, Thomas makes his way back towards the ship. The cool evening air reminds him that although he feels like touching the stars, he isn't in heaven yet. The chill of the night brings him back to reality and hastens his steps back to the ship, wishing in a way that the night would never end, and yet, desiring to get back to the warmth of his bunk.

Shivering a bit, Thomas climbs up the gangplank and makes his way down below to his bunk. Quietly he climbs under the blankets, and drifts off to sleep, his heart still full from the night's events.

CHAPTER EIGHTEEN - SERMON

The next morning is a busy day at Osbourn's place. Barbara and the girls are getting ready to go to church. Captain Schuenemann and Osbourn are sitting at the table, talking over cups of hot coffee and home made sweet rolls. Florabell is working in the kitchen. There's a clanging sound as she puts another piece of wood in the wood stove and places the metal lid back on the stovetop. It's nice and warm around the kitchen stove, so Pearl and Hazel are busy getting dressed for church near the stove's warmth.

"It looks like it's going to be a pretty nice day," Osbourn tells the Captain. "I've got to run over to the mill for a while, so I'll see you later."

"Have a good day," he tells them all as he gets his coat and hat on and opens the door.

"Good bye, Uncle Osbourn," the twins say together.

He turns and smiles. "Good bye," he tells them.

The Captain pulls out his pocket watch and gives it a quick look. "We better get going if we want to make it to the church on time."

"I'll help the twins get ready," Elsie says, getting up from the table. "Mother should just about be ready. Oh, here she comes."

"I'm ready," Barbara announces. "Just get the girls' coats on, and we'll be ready."

Off they go, walking down the road together. It's a clear, sunny morning, and the birds are singing.

"It looks like it's going to be a good day for a picnic," says Barbara.

"It sure does," agrees the captain, glancing over at Elsie. The look on her face is so different from when she had arrived. "Yes, it does look like a good day," she adds quietly.

"I still want to go with Elsie and Thomas," says Pearl.

"No, you're going to stay with us, honey," says mother firmly.

"It's always nice to attend church when we're here in Thompson," Elsie says. "Everyone here seems like old friends."

"Well, they are," says the captain. "We've been bringing you here since you were a child."

"Yes, it's nice having all these friends here, and at home in Chicago, too."

Singing can be heard coming from the church as they approach.

"It sounds like the church service has already started," the captain says, tilting his head and straining to hear what's going on inside.

"I've got a good excuse for being late, though, because I'll be walking in with four women." He smiles with a mischievous look.

"Daddy," Elsie says, pretending to scowl at him but not able to hold back a smile.

The singing gets louder as Captain Schuenemann holds the door for Barbara and the girls. Together they all walk down the aisle to the sound of the hymn, *How Great Thou Art,* joining in singing as they find their places together.

Several families nod in recognition and smile to welcome them as they make their way to their seats.

Not long after being seated, the music stops and Reverend Gustafson invites the congregation to kneel together for opening prayer. Just as they all bow their heads, Pearl drops a small red ball, and it goes rolling out into the aisle, right towards the front of the church, with curly-haired Pearl following close behind. Reverend Gustafson pauses momentarily and waits for Pearl to retrieve her ball. Ducking back into the church pew, she resumes her closed-eyed kneeling position, as if she were a perfect angel.

Barbara looks over at Herman with a half-embarrassed, half-disapproving look. They all close their eyes as Reverend Gustafson leads them in prayer.

After the regular opening ceremonies, he ascends to the pulpit and reverently opens the Bible. "I would like for you to turn in your Bibles to the Gospel of Mark, chapter 13, verses one through five. He reads the verses. Then, looking out at the congregation, he begins to speak.

"Last night, when I had gone to bed, I did so feeling as though I was fully prepared to give you the sermon I had prepared all through the week, but as I slept last night, I became aware of a divine presence guiding me, and although I was asleep, it seemed as though I was totally conscious. My thoughts were directed to passages of scripture, and in my mind a clearer understanding of God and His love was revealed to me in His word. So when I awoke, I immediately wrote down what had been revealed to me in the night. The theme of my sermon is *From Eden Lost to Eden Restored.*

"Perhaps you have at times asked the question: If there is a God who is all-powerful, all-knowing, and all-loving, why does he allow suffering and war and death as in our scripture reading this morning? Jesus is informed of some worshipers whose blood was spilled by Herod's soldiers while in the very act of offering sacrifice to God. Those who informed Jesus evidently were quite certain that God had allowed this to happen as some great punishment for their sins.

"But Jesus, reading their misconceived ideas, cites another example of some recent tragedy, the collapse of the Tower of Siloam and the persons on whom the tower fell. Were they worse sinners than any others? Jesus tells us, "No." But with all the uncertainties of this life, it is best to be repentant of our sins, lest we meet our life's end unprepared. Quite often, these and other tragedies are referred to as acts of God, as if it is God's will that this one died, or that a certain tragedy took place. I would like to suggest that in doing so, we are really giving God a bad name."

Reverend Gustafson pauses for a moment, looking out at the congregation.

"We all are still quite shaken by the loss of the *Titanic* earlier this year. Was this an act of God," he asks.

"The only way we can even faintly grasp the answer to such deep questions is from the Holy Scriptures. So turn with me to the Book of Genesis, Chapter two, verses 15 through 17. We find God places Man, His new creation, in the Garden of Eden, and instructs him that he may eat fruit from all the trees in the garden, except for the Tree of Knowledge of Good and Evil. God clearly instructs that it is not to be eaten from, lest they surely die. And prior to this, God had given our first parents free access to the Tree of Life.

"So herein lies the answer to our question of God's will, that ultimately it was God's will that Man should not die, but live forever. So in the light of the scriptures, it is not God's will that anyone should die, but that he had made Man to live forever.

"God was the One Who had made everything for their

enjoyment and had formed Eve from a part of Adam's own body, and what had Satan done for them, that they should believe him? Nothing. That's how powerful lies can be," Reverend Gustafson tells the congregation.

Captain Schuenemann looks over at Barbara, then turns back and listens more intently, his ear bent to hear every word spoken by the minister.

After describing the fall of man and the loss of eternal life, Reverend Gustafson goes on to explain that it was not God's plan that man should die, but that it was the work of an enemy. Then Reverend Gustafson leads the congregation to several scriptures that reveal the origin of evil and how Lucifer, Son of the Morning, would eventually, through jealousy of God, lead a revolt that not only resulted in a war in heaven, but he would lead the inhabitants of this earth to join in his rebellion, and how Christ, though the Son of God, would suffer the most cruel and humiliating death at the hands of the ones He came to save, foreshadowed first by the sacrifice of the lamb, then later, after His death, by the ordnance of the Lord's Supper. All the while Reverend Gustafson leads the congregation to God's final solution to the problem of sin and suffering in the great battle between good and evil.

Captain Schuenemann listens with rapt attention to how Christ is to return again and the dead in Christ would rise again to forever be with the Lord.

Reverend Gustafson concludes his sermon with a few more scripture readings. "In Nahum 1:9, the Bible says affliction shall not rise up a second time. The reason for that is that this earth will be the dwelling place of God and Christ, as John tells us in Revelation Chapter 21 and 22. The holy city the new Jerusalem comes down from God out of heaven and you and I will forever remember the Savior's love and what he has done to redeem us. And that is what will keep sin and disobedience from occurring a second time. That is what will forever end all doubt about God's love.

"And so you see suffering war and death are not a part of God's plan and the war will soon be over. Christ Himself has suffered terribly, more so than any man. But someday soon, the suffering will be over. Tell me whose side you will be on when the war is over and God wipes every tear from our eyes.

"Turn in your Bibles to Revelation 22, verses 12 through 14." They all read aloud together. "What a beautiful story of salvation God has revealed to us in His word! Let us conclude this service with a word of prayer together." Reverend Gustafson says.

"Dear God, it has been good to be here today in this house of worship, and we truly do worship You as our Lord and our Savior, and we cannot thank you enough or praise You enough for the beautiful thing you have done for us in redeeming us through the blood of Your Son, and reaching out to save us in this great conflict between good and evil. And thank you for your written word that has revealed to us this beautiful plan you have for us from Eden lost to Eden restored. Amen."

After church, Captain Schuenemann and his family slowly walk down the aisle and to the door, where Reverend Gustafson stands greeting the congregation as they slowly exit the building. Captain Schuenemann stops to shake his hand.

"That was a great sermon, I must say. I think that I understood things clearer today than I ever have before."

"So have I," Reverend Gustafson answers. "So have I." He nods. Their eyes meet for a moment of mutual understanding. Then the line moves on.

Next Barbara thanks him and says she too was touched by the message today.

"I hope that you can carry it with you in your heart," Reverend Gustafson replies. "We all need a Savior, and we truly have a friend in God."

"Thank you, Reverend," Barbara says as she enters the sunshine.

Many friends greet the Schuenemanns as they make their way down the steps. It's a beautiful morning, and the Schuenemanns share their last greetings as they walk back to the Stanley's home. The twins are running ahead as usual. Elsie runs to catch them, showing she has some girlish energy, too.

Catching up to them, they walk together towards the house, while Herman and Barbara join hands and follow behind.

"What a beautiful day," the Captain exclaims. "All of our snow is just about melted."

"Well, it's going to be a great day for a picnic."

"I'll say," the captain responds. "I don't know what it is," he says with a mystified look on his face, "If the preachers are getting better, or if what they are saying is just starting to make more sense to me. I think I've been blaming God all this time for the death of my brother, August, and his crew, but it's not really God's will that they died. It's a result of this battle between good and evil, and the uncertainties of this life. God has placed Himself at the very heart of this battle, and he too has suffered terribly. You know, I feel as though some great weight has been lifted form me, and that I can now bear the loss of my brother, August, and not blame God."

Barbara reaches out and places her arm in his. They walk together arm in arm in the sunshine, with Elsie and the twins up ahead.

"Elsie sure looks happy, too," Barbara comments.

"I think she is quite fond of Thomas," the captain adds.

"Oh, yes. A wonderful young man, and he's been a real godsend to me. The use of his truck has made him invaluable too."

"I hope that Thomas and Elsie have a nice time together

today," says Barbara.

"Oh, I'm sure they will," the captain smiles reassuringly. "Just think of us when we were that age!"

"That's what I'm afraid of," Barbara laughs. The two of them look at each other and smile, then walk arm in arm together, basking in the warm sunshine.

When they reach the house, Thomas is waiting there near the house, sitting on the running board of the truck and petting Sandy. The dog enjoys every second of attention.

"It looks like it's going to be a beautiful day," says Thomas, greeting them. His eyes meet Elsie's, and a warm smile comes across their faces.

"I was wondering if you were coming."

"The preacher got a little long-winded," said Elsie.

"Oh, but it was a great sermon," the captain adds. "I was just telling Barbara that either I'm getting wiser, or the preachers are getting better."

The twins greet Thomas with a hundred questions about everything from his automobile to his level of affection for Elsie. Thomas just laughs and tries his best to answer all their questions.

Barbara and Elsie excuse themselves. "I'll make sure everything is ready," Barbara says, hurrying into the house.

"Come now, and get changed," she tells the twins.

"Okay, Mama," they answer, but they obey rather

reluctantly. They both seem to enjoy Thomas' attention.

Barbara is insistent, and they finally come with her into the house, leaving the captain and Thomas waiting outside.

The captain speaks up. "Well, tomorrow morning we'll be bringing the *Rouse Simmons* here from Manistique, and we'll start loading the ship. Then I'll be sailing in a few days."

"That will be great," says Thomas. "I have really enjoyed working for you, captain."

"Yeah, well, the feeling is mutual. You've been a great help here, and I hope that if you're not too busy next year that you will come back and help us again."

"Thank you, captain. I'll keep that in mind."

"Well, the church service today was really interesting. Reverend Gustafson in his sermons can really make the Bible interesting and understandable. I didn't realize it but, in a way, I guess we all blame God for tragedies in this world. I think I was blaming God for my brother's death and the loss of his ship, but he cleared that up for me. I have a little better understanding of why some events are allowed to take place in this world, and that suffering and death aren't God's will at all, but the work of the enemy in this battle between good and evil."

Thomas looks on with great interest, while Captain Schuenemann relates what he has just learned. Summing it all up he explains, "And Christ also suffered in this war between good and evil. But he will soon return, not as a suffering human, but as King of Kings to settle the score once and for all and his kingdom will be an everlasting kingdom. And we will remember his great sacrifice he made by coming to this earth to win this battle."

"Wow, that's pretty deep," says Thomas. "I guess I never really understood all that. It makes more sense when you look at the bigger picture," says the captain. "Rather than just looking at small segments. It's like a big puzzle. We spend all our time working on the pieces, and rarely take time to look at the whole picture."

"That's right," muses the captain. "Well, that's what he spoke about this morning, and so in a way I made my peace with God today. So for me, it's a beautiful day in more ways than one. I have seen this day that Jesus Christ is not only a Savior from sin, but from suffering and death also, and someday the war will be over. Then there will be peace like we have never known.. Now that makes the bigger picture that much better." The captain sits quietly, contemplating what he's just said.

Soon Elsie comes out, carrying a picnic basket and looking lovelier than Thomas has ever seen her before.

"Sorry to keep you waiting," Elsie says shyly, but with a look of pleased excitement.

CHAPTER NINETEEN – THE BIG SPRING

Thomas can hardly believe his good fortune. Elsie places the basket in the back of the truck and climbs into the seat. She looks so fine sitting there in a white cotton dress with a slight splash of color, sitting so straight and tall with a smile that Mona Lisa would die for.

"Are you ready?" she asks with a warm smile.

Thomas snaps out of his dazed look. "I'll start the truck," he says, turning to the front of the Model T. He turns the crank, and the truck sputters to a start. He jumps up into the driver's seat and they take off together.

As the little truck sputters through Thompson, they see an occasional horse-drawn carriage. But theirs is the only automobile on the road. The sun is now shining and it's a picture-perfect day.

"Wow, what a perfect day," Thomas says excitedly. "It's hard to believe we had a snowstorm the other day. Today seems almost summer."

"Did you bring your camera?" Elsie asks.

"Oh yes," Thomas assures her. "I can't go anywhere without it, especially an occasion like this." He glances over at Elsie from the steering wheel.

Elsie can't conceal her delight. "This is so exciting, riding together in your automobile. And you're just going to love Big Spring. You're not going to believe it!"

"I can't wait," says Thomas. "I've heard so much about it. It must really be something."

"Oh, it's a true wonder of nature. I would say it's one of the best that I've ever seen," she assures him.

"I think that you are a wonder of nature," Thomas gives a quick glance and smiles, then he quickly turns back to watching the road, making a special effort to concentrate on his driving. He's a bit surprised at the boldness of his own comment yet happy he made it at the same time.

Caught up in the moment, Elsie presses closer to Thomas' side, resting her head on his shoulder. The two jostle on down the road together. Thomas is feeling prouder than a peacock strutting his tail feathers, and Elsie feeling as though, perhaps for a moment, the whole world seems right.

The little truck bounces its way down the two-rut road and disappears into the countryside.

"Thomas, look out!" Elsie shrieks. Thomas instantly swerves to avoid hitting a deer. He slams on the brakes, bouncing to a stop just short of a group of birch trees.

"Wow, that was close," says Thomas, with a sigh of relief. "Are you all right?" he asks, suddenly realizing that Elsie is hanging on to his right arm with both of her arms around his.

"Yeah, I'm all right." Then she too realizes that she's clinging to Thomas. They both stop and look at one another and their eyes meet for a moment. Time stands still, with both of their faces just inches apart, both remembering their first kiss the night before. Their lips are just naturally drawn together as if by some unseen force, and once again their lips meet. They kiss long and warm.

Out of the corner of his eye, Thomas notices a carriage coming around the bend, and they both look up with a start, realizing that they are still halfway off the road, in the automobile.

They both sit up quickly and try to look as proper as time will allow. Thomas pulls the Model T back onto the road and he begins to drive. They both look straight ahead with sheepish looks on their faces. Thomas gives a slight wave as they pass the carriage. The staunch-looking carriage driver and his wife stare in disbelief with a "What's this world coming to" kind of look. After they pass, both Thomas and Elsie burst into laughter.

Elsie lets out a squeal, covering her face with her right hand, but not letting go of Thomas' arm. Their laughter continues all the way to the Big Spring.

They aren't sure what it is, but the whole incident has put them both in a giddy mood, adding to the joy of spending time together.

Arriving at the spring, Thomas parks the truck. Elsie is

obviously anxious to show Thomas the spring.

"You aren't going to believe your own eyes," she tells him, "So don't forget your camera."

"Don't worry. I'm looking forward to getting some great pictures. I'm going to bring the tripod to hold the camera steady." Thomas reaches into the truck and rests the tripod and camera on his shoulder.

Together they hurry down the path to the spring. The spring is the size of a large pond or small lake, surrounded by cedars. Even the lumber barons, when cutting over the forest, didn't have the heart to completely strip the spring of trees, and even though the large stands of white pine are now gone for miles around, the area around the spring appears as a small oasis of cedar in a desert of pine stumps.

"See, there's the raft, over there. We can go out across the spring and look down into the water."

Thomas looks down at the water along the edge of the path. "Wow, that water really is clear, isn't it?"

"It's beautiful," Elsie says. "I've never seen anything like it. I can see right down to the bottom, just like looking through the air, but under water. It gets even better," says Elsie, "when you look from the raft. You'll be able to see all the fish swimming around way down in the water, and the springs bubbling way down deep."

"This is just unreal," Thomas goes on. "I have never seen anything like it."

The two of them walk along through the thick cedar forest surrounding the spring. The path leads on to a raft made of large logs and planks with some makeshift hand rails made of poles.

"I told you it was a beautiful place," Elsie smiled with a pleased look on her face.

"Yeah, but I couldn't even imagine that it was this beautiful."

"Let's go out on the raft," she says. They carefully make their way onto the raft, as they continue to look down into the clear, cool water.

"Holy whaa! Look at all the minnows! There are thousands of them, all in a huge school. And look at those trees down there," Thomas points out. "They look haunting, with that little bit of moss covering them. They must be ancient!"

"Come on, let's go across," Elsie urges him on. "See? This rope is stretched across the spring, so that we can pull ourselves across on the raft."

"Elsie, could I get your photograph?"

"Well, of course. How would you like it?" she answers, standing on the raft facing him.

"I'd like you to be leaning on the railing, looking down into the water. I just wish that somehow I could get an image of what you are looking at in the same shot. Maybe I'll learn how to do that when I go to photography school.

"How's this?" Elsie asks.

"Great! Now, turn this way just a bit more."

Ca-click goes the shutter. "Oh, wonderful," says Thomas. "You look just great through the camera lens. I think it will be just a great shot! Now, let's get one of us together."

"How will we do that?" asks Elsie. "There's no one here to take our picture."

"Oh, you'll see. Just stand right there, and I'll stand beside you."

"Then who will take the picture?" Elsie asks in a puzzled voice.

"You'll see," says Thomas, setting the camera onto the tripod. Thomas takes a piece of string from his pocket and threads it through the shutter lever. "Rigging the string up in this way, I'm able to stand in front of the camera with you. I just have to pull the string," he says, backing up next to her on the raft.

"All right, are you ready?" Thomas and Elsie lean with their heads together and smile.

Click, Click!

"I got it!

"Thomas, this is so exciting," Elsie squeals. "I am so glad we met!"

"Oh, and I am too! I never thought I'd be out on a picnic with a beautiful woman to model for photos, and help me besides."

"Is that all?" asks Elsie.

"No, better than that," Thomas draws close. "I'm crazy about you!"

Embracing one another, they kiss long and tender. This time there is no one around, and so there is no reason to stop. For a moment, it is as though time stands still and the world revolves around one boy and one girl.

After a good while, they draw apart.

"I thought I would be in the woods with a bunch of lumberjacks, cutting timber. Instead, I am here on this raft with you."

"Oh, that's right. We're on a raft," Elsie says, as though waking from a dream.

"Yes, and perhaps we should cross the spring," Thomas answers, as though reminding her that they're back to reality.

"What a great idea," Elsie answers back as they both give each other a smile.

Grabbing hold of the rope, they both give a long, steady pull. The raft responds, slowly gliding out across the spring. The two of them are looking down into the water.

"They say that the spring never freezes," Elsie recounts. "There's an old legend about an Indian princess who was about to become the bride of a young chief. But they say she was carried off by a rival chief while her husband-to-be was out hunting. She ran from the rival chief to the edge of the spring, leaped in, and slowly sank. Legend has it that the girl was changed by the magic waters of Ki-Chi-Ti-Kipi into a graceful white fawn. That is why no Indian since then has killed a white deer. Whoever would kill a white deer would be sure to meet with some great misfortune."

"That's really interesting. Where did you learn that?"

"Osbourn told me, and he said that he had heard it from Chief Osawinamakee himself. They consider this place sacred. The Indians call the spring the mirror of heaven."

"I can see why," Thomas answers. "This is amazing. I can see all the way down to the bottom. How deep is it down there?"

"The spring is over forty feet deep in the middle, and stays about forty-five degrees all year 'round, so it never freezes. This is one of my family's favorite places to go. Father tries to bring us here at least once each year."

"Your father is quite a guy. I have really enjoyed working for him. He's the best boss I've ever had. He has a way of bringing out the best in people. It's as though shipping Christmas trees is all of our endeavor."

"That's my dad," says Elsie, smiling proudly. "He has us all involved, too. It really is a family business. I can't imagine this time of year without harvesting evergreens."

"Oh, look down there!" Elsie points. "We're right over one of the springs."

"Oh, I see it now. Wow, look at that sand bubbling away down there. It's hard to believe it's really that deep. I've never seen anything so clear!"

Looking into the depths, they are both caught up in the scenes deep below them, and for a moment even their youthful passions are forgotten as they reverently behold this awesome gem of nature. The bubbling sand looks like some ancient volcano continually bubbling out molten lava. The spring continually bubbles out thousands of gallons of cold, clear water, making this giant spring a wonder to behold!

Elsie is obviously proud to be showing this beautiful place to Thomas. They spend hours slowly pulling the water-logged raft across the beautiful spring, savoring every moment they spend together, laughing and talking, then occasionally interrupted by a few sessions of passionate kissing. Unaware and unconscious of time, the two young lovers slowly pull the raft back to the landing.

"I'm so happy you showed me the springs, Elsie. I never knew such a beautiful place existed. I have really enjoyed this."

"Oh, I have too! And as many times as I have been here, I never get tired of it. Especially today, showing it to you."

The two kiss and embrace again.

"Are you getting hungry?" Elsie asks, looking into his eyes.

"Yeah. Where are we going to have the picnic?"

"You'll see," says Elsie, with a mischievous look in her eyes. "We can build a fire along the shore of Indian Lake. That way we can stay nice and warm while we eat. I know a good spot."

"You sure know your way around here, Elsie."

"Yeah, well, my family has been coming here for years. In a way, this is like home for me here. C'mon, let's go."

CHAPTER TWENTY – INDIAN LAKE

Together they hurry off. When they reach the Model T, Elsie climbs in. Thomas walks around to the front to start it.

"Elsie, could you advance the spark for me?"

"Sure," she says, slipping over to the driver's side of the seat.

"Just move that lever up a little."

"This one?"

"Yeah," says Thomas. "Hey, how would you like to learn how to drive this thing?"

"Oh Thomas, I don't think women drive automobiles!"

"Yeah, well, they do now! You're going to learn right now. Here we go!"

"Oh really!" Elsie sits up straight at the wheel with a determined look.

Climbing up beside her on the seat, Thomas shows her how to steer.

"All you do is turn the wheel like this when you want to go this way, and turn the wheel that way when you want to go right."

Elsie nods, but looks rather skeptical.

"I'll help you steer for a while," Thomas reassures her. "Now give it a little throttle." He shows her.

"Now push the left pedal down and it will move forward. The middle one is for reverse, and the right one is the brake, for when you need to stop quickly. Okay, are you ready?"

She nods nervously.

"Push the pedal down all the way!"

Elsie pushes down, and the Model T drives ahead.

"Oh, this is so exciting," says Elsie, holding the wheel tightly. Thomas holds the wheel with his left hand, helping Elsie steer. The truck pulls slowly forward.

"Yer doing good," Thomas encourages her. "See? It's not that hard, is it?"

"No. This is really easy," says Elsie, gaining more confidence every moment. "I never thought it would be this easy!"

"You're doing great," says Thomas, taking his hand off the wheel. "You're in charge now. All right, now let the pedal out all the way."

"All right," she says, letting it out. "Oh!" she screams as they move faster.

"That's high gear, for when you want to go faster."

They bounce along together.

"Thomas, this is wonderful! I can't believe I'm doing this."

"You're doing good. Now, I want you to practice stopping, so push the left pedal in half-way and then push on the right pedal to stop."

Elsie obeys with a determined look on her face then she does what Thomas tells her.

"Good job!" The Model T comes to a stop. "Okay, let's start over now, so that you can get used to it."

Elsie nods with both hands firmly on the wheel. I remember," she says. "I push the pedal all the way down to get going, then let it out all the way to go faster, half-way down and push the right one to stop."

"You catch on fast. All right, let's go!"

Elsie pushes the pedal all the way down, and the Model T slowly moves ahead.

"Okay, let it out all the way, and away we go!"

The two roll through the countryside, laughing and talking as they go in the warm sunshine, without a care in the world. After a while they arrive at Indian Lake.

"Here's the place by the lake," says Elsie, as the automobile bounces along.

"Do you remember how to stop," asks Thomas.

"Yes, I think so," says Elsie. "Push this pedal down half-way, and push on the brake pedal. I'll stop over by the lake."

"That's right. You're doing great," Thomas says, praising her driving.

Elsie slows the Model T to a stop.

"All right now, move the throttle lever like this, and turn

this to stop the engine."

Elsie quickly obeys.

"Fantastic," Thomas applauds.

Elsie sits back and laughs. "This is so exciting! Won't Father be surprised to hear that I drove the automobile!"

They both smile at one another.

Thomas looks around at the sandy beach along the calm waters of the lake shore, with the sun and trees reflecting on the surface.

"This is a beautiful spot here, Elsie."

"Let's go look at the lake," says Elsie, grabbing the picnic basket.

So they both hop down from the Model T. Elsie leads Thomas down to the lake.

"Wow, this is a pretty big lake," says Thomas. "It must be five or six miles across to the other side, and it looks like about half of the lake is covered with logs. Look at that!" The two stand on the shoreline gazing out over the water together for a moment.

"They say the lumber companies here keep a year's supply of logs cut ahead of time," explains Elsie.

"Wow, that's incredible! I bet we could walk right across the lake on top of the logs," Thomas marvels. "That's a lot of logs!"

"Let's build our fire right here on the shore," says Thomas.

"I'll get some birch bark," offers Elsie.

"All right. I'll find some wood."

Working together, they soon have a nice, blazing fire.

Sitting on a large log near the fire, Elsie unpacks the basket.

"Just look at all of this food! This is the most wonderful day I have ever had in my whole life," says Thomas. Elsie spreads out the food and the two of them casually eat their lunch. The sun reflecting on the calm waters of the lake, the warm glow of the fire, the fine meal laid out before them, and most of all the charm of each other's company gives them both a feeling of "I can't believe this is true!"

Together they laugh and talk while they enjoy their picnic dinner. Thomas throws another piece of wood on the fire, as Elsie offers him a fresh piece of apple pie.

"Apple pie," says Thomas.

"Yes, Flora and I made it yesterday." Elsie takes a piece of pie over to Thomas. She leans over and holds it up to his mouth. He takes a bite.

"Mmmmm, that's delicious!"

But before Elsie can feed him another bite, Thomas reaches out and wraps his arms around her and the two embrace and kiss for a good long while. Elsie holds on to Thomas, still balancing the piece of pie in her other hand.

Finally Elsie looks Thomas in the eyes and asks, "Are you

ready for more?"

"I never thought you'd ask!" Thomas leans forward and kisses her again. Elsie leans back and continues balancing the pie once more in her hand. After passionately kissing, their lips finally part.

Elsie says, "I meant, more pie!"

Holding the piece of pie between them, they both laugh and Thomas takes another bite of pie.

"I was just testing to see which one was sweeter. I think it's the pie," he says, teasing her.

"All right, I have more pie here," she says, playing along with him. "More pie and no more of me." She smiles tauntingly.

Thomas grabs her again, and the two embrace and kiss, this time even longer and more passionately.

The evening sun reflecting on the water silhouettes the two lovers as they embrace together there on the lakeshore. All too soon the day has passed.

"I wish this day could last forever," Elsie says, looking into Thomas' eyes.

"So do I," says Thomas, "But we better get going soon, or the captain will have me walk the plank for bringing you back too late."

"Yes, I suppose we should go," agrees Elsie.

"I want you to drive on the way back," says Thomas.

"Oh, really?"

"Yes. I think with a little more practice, you'll be a pretty good driver."

"I would love to," she says.

The two lovers take one last look out over the lake.

"I'll put the basket in the truck," says Thomas.

"I'm going back down to the lake to make sure the fire is out all the way. I'll be right back," says Elsie.

She walks back down to the lake and scoops more sand onto the fire, making sure it's completely out. Then she turns and walks back up to the truck.

Thomas stands near the truck, waiting for her with his camera. He stands watching as she walks up to the truck. The red and golden rays of the evening sun reflect from her golden hair. Shadows dance on her white dress as she walks back towards him. The colors of the sunset give her an almost surreal appearance. Thomas watches, spellbound, as if he were watching the approach of some kind of angel. Never before has he seen anything so beautiful! It's as though he's dreaming.

Then, like a flashback in time, Thomas remembers the scene described by old Engvald, and hears his words of warning. "Don't vait too long." For a moment, Thomas feels he is re-living Engvald's experience and that he must somehow break the spell of the shadow that has been cast over Engvald's life by letting life's one great opportunity slip through his hands.

Elsie approaches, unaware of the Deja vu he has just experienced.

Smiling curiously, Elsie asks, "Are you going to take a picture?"

Thomas looks up at her and answers, "I don't think a camera can even capture the images that I have of you this day. But I'm sure the memory will last forever."

Elsie, still unaware of his thoughts, reaches up and puts her hands around his neck and says with a joking tone, "I'm sure it won't last forever. I'm not your wife, you know," she says, looking into his eyes with a teasing smile.

"Do you want to be?" It is almost as if the words fall from his lips by themselves. "Did I really say that?" Thomas thinks to himself.

They both look at one another for a moment, not really sure if Thomas is asking her the big question, or just asking her thoughts. Both of them are surprised by their own words. Together, they stand speechless for a moment. Then Elsie answers softly, with a thoughtful look in her eyes, "Yes!"

Their lips meet in a long, passionate kiss, confirming the words that neither one of them had really planned to say, yet answering in the way they truly feel about one another.

It is not some dry, bended-knee speech, just two people

sharing the way they feel about one another. There is no talk of where or when. It seems as though the words just slipped out, yet in their hearts they both know that they really meant what they have just said.

"Are you ready to take the wheel?" Thomas finally asks Elsie, after their long kiss.

"Yes," says Elsie, coming back to reality.

The two finished loading their things into the truck and Thomas helps Elsie climb on.

"Remember how to start?" asks Thomas.

"Yes," says Elsie, sitting at the driver's seat of the Model T. "I advance the spark, right?"

"Yup," answers Thomas, reaching for the crank. "Are you ready?"

Elsie nods. "Ready!"

Thomas cranks the engine, but it doesn't start. "Oh-oh," he says with a puzzled look. "I'll try it again." He leans forward once more and turns the crank again, giving it a spin.

"Nothing," he says with a note of disappointment. "Did you advance the spark?"

"Yes," says Elsie, showing him how she moved the lever.

Thomas looks a bit puzzled. "It always starts," he mutters under his breath.

Walking around to the front, he tries turning the crank one

more time. Again, nothing happens. Then he stands there for a moment and grins. "Looks like we'll have to walk back to Thompson tonight."

"Oh dear," says Elsie. "It's a long ways back, and it will be dark soon. I'm sure Father and Mother will be worried. What will we do?" asks Elsie.

"Well, let's try it one more time," says Thomas with a little smile. "But this time, let's make sure the ignition switch is turned on first."

"Oh," Elsie laughs. "You knew it all the time, didn't you!"

Thomas laughs and gives the engine another crank. This time it sputters to life. Thomas runs around and jumps in, smiling sheepishly. "Do you remember what to do now?"

"Yes," says Elsie, with a look of confidence. "The spark goes here, and the throttle goes here," she says, moving the levers. "I push this pedal all the way in to go." As she pushes it down, the truck moves forward.

"Good," says Thomas, encouragingly.

"Then I let the pedal out all of the way to go faster."

"That's right," says Thomas.

Elsie lets out on the pedal, and the little truck jostles down the road more quickly. Elsie holds onto the wheel and steers with a determined look, her face beaming with pride.

"You're doing great," says Thomas.

"I can't believe I'm really driving this," says Elsie, looking as pretty as a picture behind the wheel. "Thomas! This is the most wonderful day of my life!"

"Mine too, says Thomas, moving a little closer to Elsie.

The little truck rolls along over the bumpy road through the woods on its way back to Thompson.

CHAPTER TWENTY-ONE – SECRET SISTERS

Thomas and Elsie approach the house in the automobile. Thomas is careful to have Elsie pull the Model T up far enough into the driveway that no one can see them from the front windows, to afford him them a brief moment of privacy. The vehicle comes to a halt. Elsie knows right away the reason they pulled up out of sight, and the young lovers silently embrace again for just a few moments. Sandy, the dog, approaches the Model T and greets them by jumping up onto the running board, with her front paws up on the edge of Thomas' door, distracting them for a moment.

"Sandy," Elsie exclaims through her beaming smile. "You are such a pretty dog. Did you come to greet us?"

Thomas reaches over with one hand and pats her on the head. Leaning over, he gives Elsie just one more short kiss before they walk back to the house, both stopping for a moment to pet the ever-affectionate dig. Then they make their way back into the house.

Before they get through the door, the twins both come running up to greet them, and leap into their arms. Thomas is a bit amused and surprised by Pearl's actions, as they bombard them with questions.

"Do you like each other?" one asks.

"Did you kiss?" interrupts another.

Thomas blushes a little.

"Come now, children," Barbara calls to the twins. "Did you have a nice time?" she asks, smiling, even though she already knows the answer from the look on Elsie's beaming face.

"Oh yes, it was quite nice," Elsie replies as calmly as possible, trying to conceal a part of her excitement.

"Well, do come in, Thomas, and join us," Barbara says. "We are all in here, working on Christmas wreaths."

Thomas and Elsie join in at the table.

"Well, it must have been a great day for a picnic. It sure warmed up this afternoon. Melted a lot of our snow, too." Captain Schuenemann smiles, handing them some materials for making wreaths.

Thomas and Elsie quickly busy themselves making wreaths, trying to divert the focus of attention from themselves.

"Tomorrow morning, Nelson Boushour and I are going to take the tug *Cisco* over to Manistique, and get the *Rouse Simmons*, and tow her back to Thompson, so we can start loading her with trees."

"That's great," says Thomas. "How many trees do we have so far, captain?"

"Well, it looks like we've got about fifteen thousand, but a lot of the locals will be bringing in their trees when we start loading, so it should start adding up fast over the next few days."

They all continue working on wreaths, visiting and telling stories as they work. Osbourn always has some interesting tale to tell about the Indians, or about some settler from the area.

As the evening hours grow later, Thomas gets ready to leave. "I'll see you all tomorrow."

"Thomas, I'll put you in charge of hauling the trees tomorrow, while I go and get the ship."

"Yes, sir. You can count on me, captain," says Thomas, as he grabs his coat and hat and makes his way to the door.

"All right. Have a good night, Thomas."

"Good night, Thomas," everyone tells him.

"Good night."

Elsie follows him out the door. They walk over to the Model T together.

"I've got to put some fresh carbide in the acetylene generator for my lights," he tells Elsie. Taking out a small can, he measures a couple of spoonfuls of carbide rock and places it in the generator.

"I'll run and get you some water from the pump," Elsie says, hurrying off.

"Thank you. That would be great," says Thomas.

Elsie quickly returns with a ladle full of water from the

pump and hands it to Thomas.

"It will sure be nice to have the ship so much closer, after tomorrow," says Thomas.

"Yes, you'll be able to stay longer in the evening."

"I'll like that," says Thomas, closing the lid to the acetylene generator and adjusting the flow of water.

Walking to the front of the Model T, Thomas strikes the starting flints, and the flames give off their light, shining on the brass reflectors of the lamps.

"Well, I'll see you tomorrow, Elsie," says Thomas, gently leading her to the far side of the truck, where no one would see. They embrace and kiss one more time, with the sweetness that only young love has.

"I'll see you tomorrow," Thomas says again, turning the crank on the truck.

"Good night," says Elsie, from halfway to the house, giving one last lingering wave.

Thomas drives off, down the road towards Manistique.

Back in the house, everyone is busy cleaning up after making wreaths, and getting ready for bed.

"Elsie, could you go upstairs and get the twins ready for bed, while I help Florabell tidy things up?"

"Yes, Mother," Elsie answers.

"And be sure to have them say their prayers."

"All right, Mama. Good night."

Elsie reaches over and gives her mother a big hug. Barbara holds her close for a moment, while Elsie rests her head on her shoulder. Barbara is happy now to see the sadness gone from her daughter's eyes.

"So how was your day today, Honey?"

"Oh Mama, it was the best day of my life!"

"I'm so happy for you!"

They give one another a big hug.

"Good night, honey. I love you."

"I love you, too Mama, good night." Off she goes up the stairs.

The twins are already in their nightclothes and in bed when Elsie comes up the stairs.

Elsie sits on the bed by the twins, and they both sit up anxiously.

"Tell us about your picnic today," Pearl asks.

"Yes, do tell us more," says Hazel. "Are you in love with Thomas?"

The twins want to hear the kind of inside information that only sisters can share. The expression on Elsie's face is enough to tell them that something is happening. They both are dying to know more.

"Oh, I have just had the most wonderful day of my life! It

seems as though Thomas and I have been made for each other. I just love everything about him."

"Did you kiss?" Pearl asks.

"Oh yes, we kissed."

"Was it nice?" asks Hazel.

Elsie leans back and closes her eyes. "It was more than nice. It was more than wonderful. It was…it was…just beautiful. And each time we kissed, I felt as though I wanted it to last forever. So much different from the way I felt when I was with Edward. I had always felt so awkward and uncomfortable, like I was trying to be in love. But I really wasn't.

"When Thomas and I are together, it's like we're in love, and each moment we spend together we are more in love. But it's not just when we kiss. No, it's in everything we do and say together. It's in the way we treat one another whenever we're together. We can laugh and talk together. Share our hopes and our dreams together and really just enjoy being together."

The twins are sitting up and absorbing every word that falls from Elsie's lips. To them, their sister Elsie is the epitome of what a lady should be and the twins just think the world of her. Elsie know this; so she takes this opportunity to give some sisterly advice.

"You know, kissing and romance are wonderful, but you have to be careful too," she cautions, "Because when you're young and impressionable, you can sometimes be fooled by all the romance. But later on, when the excitement wears off, you may find that the person you are with is really rather uncaring or even unkind, and the little things that were overlooked about that person because of passion really may conceal his true character. And many a girl has spent her life in misery because she was charmed by kisses."

The twins both sit wide-eyed, taking in their big sister's counsel.

"When Thomas and I are together I notice all the little things he does and the way he acts. It's not like he is trying to be helpful and kind, it's just the way he's been raised. And the way he acts when he's around others. They all enjoy his company. I think that's why father likes him so. Father has been working with him every day, and you can tell that he loves him like a son," Elsie continues. "When we are making wreaths together, he's always so patient and easy to talk to and yet he can make us all laugh. Those are things you should consider when you start seeing someone."

The twins both quietly nod.

"Something else about Thomas I like is that we can talk so openly to one another about anything, and that nothing is secret. I have told him things about myself that I haven't spoken to anyone else. It's as though we are best friends, and that's important if you're going to spend the rest of your life with someone."

"Are you going to spend the rest of your life with Thomas?" Hazel asks anxiously.

Elsie pauses thoughtfully for a moment. "I think so."

"Do you love each other?" Pearl chimes in.

A big smile sweeps across Elsie's face and she takes a deep breath. Cautiously she tries to answer without showing how excited she really feels. "Spend the rest of our lives together," she repeats, trying not to show how her emotions. "Well, that would be nice. Time will tell."

Then her emotions, like the waters of a dam can no longer be held back

"YES," Elsie exclaims, unable to contain herself any longer. "Yes! We love each other," she says, gesturing with her arms, then holding her hands to her heart trying to express her joy.

The twins both wrap their arms around her and rest their heads each on one of her shoulders in an effort to share her joy.

Then together they all hug and squeal with delight, sharing the joyous moment together as only three sisters can.

"If you marry Thomas, do we get to be bridesmaids?" Pearl asks.

"I wouldn't have it any other way," Elsie answers, wrapping her arms around them. They both respond by squeezing her even tighter. Then they all fall backwards onto the bed together in one joyous embrace.

CHAPTER TWENTY-TWO - PIRATES

The moon shines brightly that evening, occasionally obscured by low, passing clouds. Only the sound of the breeze and the lapping of waves along the lakeshore are heard. A few white snowflakes drift down through the cold night air, giving the lakeshore an almost mystical appearance.

The lights of the homes in town are all extinguished, and the inhabitants have all settled in for the night. But out on Lake Michigan, near the harbor entrance from the open lake, a twin-mast schooner cautiously steers its way through the narrow harbor entrance into the small harbor, completely unobserved by the residents of the sleeping town. The muffled sounds of the engine drones; its under-water exhaust port makes only a low gurgling sound like the deep throaty sound of a distant bullfrog along a summer shore at night.

The ship makes a full turn in the small harbor, then quietly comes to rest at the dock, facing its way back out into the open lake, from where it came. A couple of men from the ship jump to the dock and quickly tie up to the posts. Not a light can be seen aboard the ship, and the men go to their work in total darkness. Finally the gangplank is lowered   and a large, shadowy figure of a man slowly makes its way down to the dock, followed by several others, all dressed in dark clothing.

The large man, obviously the captain, gives orders in whispered tones. "Okay men, start loading those trees. Fill the cargo hold first, and then load up the deck. I want this boat to hold as many trees as possible by morning. You guys each get a dime for every tree on this ship by tomorrow, so you could make a lot of money tonight, if you work hard. Maybe as much as a couple hundred dollars apiece."

"That's a lot of money," one of the men says to the man next to him.

"Yeah, sounds good to me."

"Well, have at her, boys," the captain says, pointing at the piles of trees stacked on the dock. Then, like an army of worker ants, they each grab a tree and begin loading them onto the ship. The captain stands guard and peers cautiously off into the night. The captain is none other than Dan Seavey, the pirate of the Great Lakes.

"I'll keep an eye out for a while to make sure nobody's coming," Seavey tells them, trying to whisper. They nod and immediately begin carrying trees onto the ship.

It soon becomes quite obvious by the boldness and precision of their movements that they have carried out this kind of endeavor before. These men are veterans at what they do, well practiced in the hurried art of night shopping. Anything left on the docks that might turn a good profit on the black market is on their list, even if it means stealing Christmas trees. Their sinister work progresses into the night, and piles of Christmas trees begin to accumulate in the cargo hold of the ship.

After a while one of Seavey's men approaches him excitedly, wearing a couple of wreaths around his neck and several more on each arm.

"Hey, captain! I found a pile of wreaths, under a tarp over there. There must be a couple hundred of them," he says, with a toothless grin.

Dan Seavey looks elated. "Really! Where are they?" he asks.

"Right over there, under that tarp."

Seavey walks over and takes a look. "Here," he gestures to the others. "Take and load these first," he tells the others as they come off the ship. "This is the best Christmas I've ever had!" he laughs in a whispered voice. "They'll be calling ME Captain Santa. We'll make so much money on this one load, we'll have to donate some to the poor," Seavey snickers to the others, as he loads up each man with arm loads of wreaths.

Energized by their windfall opportunity to gain easy money, and driven by greed, the pirates work on into the night, with an almost superhuman effort to steal as many trees as they can in as little time as possible.

Back and forth they go onto the ship, sometimes carrying more than one tree, back and forth to the dock for more trees. Again and again the process is repeated. Steadily the number of trees stolen from the dock grows as each hour of the night slowly passes.

As the night wears on, the pirates become bolder. Elated by their prospects of easy money from their ill-gotten gain, their once-stealthy and whispered tone becomes louder and the sound of their laughter more becomes more obnoxious as they feel themselves becoming enriched at the expense of others.

"Hey Chester, what are you going to do with your money?" one of them asks the other.

"I'm not sure yet, but I know I won't be thirsty for quite a while," he laughs with a toothless chuckle. Then they both laugh.

"Quiet, you idiots!" Seavey sneers, "Or I'll knock your heads together." He shakes his big fist.

The two henchmen cower in an apologetic gesture, and slink off to get more booty.

Back at Osbourn's place, Sandy the dog lifts her head in her doghouse, suddenly awakened by some far-off distant sound. With her head cocked and ears slightly lifted, she listens intently. Not for usual, nighttime sounds of the call of the owl or the rustling of the wind in the tree branches, but for sounds that are somehow out of place from the normal nighttime sounds.

Out of her cozy doghouse she steps, out into the chill nighttime air. Sniffing the air and bending her ear, she's drawn toward the dock. Not sure why, Sandy pads off towards the harbor, some 250 yards from the house. Halfway to the harbor she stops and stands motionless. She senses some unusual sounds and smells in the air. Aware of something strange, she cautiously stands by. Straining her senses to discern more about these shadowy figures of men, lifting and moving Christmas trees. Not the familiar Captain Schuenemann and his men, but someone else; someone who didn't belong there.

Instinctively she lets out a low growl, 'till finally she lets out a full bellowing bark.

"Bow-wow!" The sound cuts through the night air like the cold steel of a sharp knife. Dan Seavey and his henchmen instantly freeze, remaining still and silent, wondering what will happen next.

More suspicious now than ever, Sandy lets out another barrage of barks. "Bow wow! Wow! Friend or foe?" There is still no response. By now, her hackles are up, and the hair on her back stands on end, making her look quite fierce.

"Bow-wow-wow," she continues. "Friend-or-foe, let-me-know!"

Then she continues with more barking. "Bow-wow-wow-bow-wow-wow!"

Seavey's men, now puzzled as to what to do next, look to their pirate leader for direction. But Seavey remains motionless.

Again, Sandy barks out her warning. "Bow-wow-wow! Bow-wow-wow! Friend-or-foe, let-me-know!"

Sandy continues with more barking. "Bow-wow-wow-bow-wow-wow!"

Seavey finally makes a move, announcing quietly under his breath to the others, "Let me take care of this." He quickly disappears from the deck of the ship, into the ship's cabin.

Meanwhile, Sandy continues with a barrage of questions now. "Bow- wow-wow, bow-wow-wow," she barks relentlessly.

The pirate leader emerges from his cabin onto the deck, carrying a longbow and a quiver of arrows, and quickly makes his way down the gangplank. Placing an arrow to the bowstring, Seavey steadily walks towards the barking dog, as a hunter stalking his prey.

"Good dog," Seavey calls out in a soft voice, and continues walking slowly forward.

Sandy continues barking. Cautiously she turns a bit to get ready to run if need be.

"Good dog," Seavey calls out again, slowly advancing, hoping to get close enough to take a good shot. Then raising the bow, he draws back, hesitates for just a moment then lets the arrow fly.

Sandy lets out a "Yip" and runs off into the night.

"That'll quiet him down," Seavey says triumphantly. "I know how to take care of barking dogs at night! I've taken care of lots of them. Now, get back to work, and keep it quiet. I'll keep an eye out for awhile to make sure no one is coming."

"Okay, boss," they answer, and continue loading trees.

Back at the house, Osbourn has been awakened by Sandy's barking, but it's really not so unusual to have her bark sometimes at night, so he continues lying in bed, hoping she'll stop. Not hearing any more barking, Osbourn is a bit relieved. "After all, I wouldn't want the neighbors complaining," he thinks to himself. He closes his eyes again and slowly starts to doze off.

All of a sudden, he hears scratching at the door. *Scratch, scratch, scratch.*

A bit reluctant to get out of bed, he waits for a moment. "What the heck is that dog doing now?" he wonders.

Scratch, scratch, scratch. There it is again.

"What's that dog up to tonight?" he mutters under his breath. Slipping on a robe, Osbourn reaches over to the nightstand and opens a box of matches. Striking a match, he quickly lights the wick of a candle.

Picking up the candleholder he walks through the house over to the back door. Then, opening the door, he finds the dog on the back porch, jumping around in pain, with an arrow protruding through her abdomen, twisting in pain and at the same time trying to bite at the arrow.

"Oh, my gosh! Florabell! Come quick and help me!" Osbourn yells. Kneeling down over his dog, he grabs hold of Sandy. "Hold still now, girl." A small pool of blood drips from the arrow onto the porch, giving off a wisp of steam.

"What is it, Osbourn?" Florabell comes hurrying to see what's the matter.

"Sandy's been shot with an arrow!"

"Oh my gosh!" In an instant Florabel grabs her night coat and hurries into the kitchen. Bring her in here," she says, holding the door open. "Put her on this old rug by the stove," she yells as she pulls the rug up in front of the stove.

"Come now, Sandy," Osbourn leads her to the rug.

"I'll get some more light," Florabell tells him.

Just then, Captain Schuenemann enters the kitchen in his nightshirt. "What's the matter?" he asks.

"Sandy's been shot through with an arrow. She was barking at something down by the dock, then suddenly she stopped and came scratching at the door like this!"

"Down at the dock, you say?" says Captain Schuenemann with a puzzled look on his face.

"Yes. Let me take care of Sandy, here, for a minute, then I think we should go down there and have a look around."

"I'll get Barbara and grab some clothes," says Captain Schuenemann. "Barbara, come here! We need your help."

"What is it, Herman?"

"Someone shot Sandy with an arrow, down by the dock. I'm going out there to go see what's going on. You can give a hand here taking care of the dog. I'll slip on some shoes and grab my coat," he tells her, rushing around madly.

Barbara hurries to the kitchen, where Osbourn and Florabell are tending to Sandy. "Here, let me help you," says Barbara, and bends down to hold onto Sandy's collar. "Poor thing," she sympathizes.

Flora lights the lantern on the table.

Barbara holds Sandy's hindquarters while Osbourn tries to get her to hold still. "Okay, hold on now. I'm going to break the arrow off, so I can pull it out."

"Okay, here goes." *SNAP!* Sandy yelps. The bloody arrow splinters and breaks off in Osbourn's big hands. "Hold on, now," he announces again, and he gives the arrow a tug, extracting it with one quick pull. Sandy lets out another yelp.

"Try to stop the bleeding with these rags." Florabel hands some clean rags to Osbourn.

By now Captain Schuenemann is half-dressed, and heading out the door.

"Here, wait a minute. Take this," says Osbourn, reaching

behind the door. He hands the captain a double barrel shotgun and a couple of shells. "I'll get my coat and boots on and I'll be right behind you."

Meanwhile, back at the dock, Seavey cautiously watches for trouble. Seeing lights go on at the house, he announces, "Oh-oh, I think we got trouble! Jed, get down below and start the engine. You men, prepare to cast off. Everyone else get aboard. Stand by till I give the order; they may just go back to bed.

"You men get ready to pull up the gangplank," Seavey gestures as soon as the others are on board. He walks back and takes his position at the ship's wheel and watches intently.

After about fifteen minutes of silence, Seavey yells, "Oh-oh! I just saw the door open. Looks like someone's coming outside," he announces. "Prepare to cast off!"

"Yeah, it looks like someone's headed our way. Cast off!" he yells.

The men on the deck cast their lines free.

"Full speed ahead," Seavey orders.

"Full ahead," someone repeats.

The chug-chug-chug of the engine churns up the water at the stern of the boat and slowly pushes the ship away from the dock.

Captain Schuenemann, in his coat and nightshirt, hurries towards the dock. When he notices the ship beginning to move, he begins to walk faster, then breaks into a run. The closer he gets, the more he realizes what's been happening.

Christmas trees are scattered every which-way.

By now Captain Schuenemann is running full speed towards the moving ship, past the piles of Christmas trees and lumber stacked along the dock.

Osbourn comes running from behind. "It looks like Dan Seavey's boat, the *James Hall*."

"It's Dan Seavey! They've been stealing the trees!" Osbourn shouts.

"That slippery bastard!" Captain Schuenemann shouts. "He's getting away!"

Seavey's ship is just then threading its way through the harbor entrance. Captain Schuenemann runs faster now in hot pursuit, the quickly raises the shotgun to his shoulder, takes aim, and fires. Dan Seavey can be seen at the back of the ship, standing at the steering wheel.

"POW!" A burst of flames shoots out from the end of the barrel. Seavey instantly dives for cover and hits the deck.

The sounds of breaking glass and pellets bouncing off the back of the ship ring out as Captain Schuenemann fires again. More breaking glass and pellets ricochet across the deck. The rear windows of the *James Hall* are shattered, with pieces of breaking glass splashing all around into the harbor.

Seavey rises back to his feet and starts laughing out loud as though it is all some kind of exciting game. Then he shouts, "Hoist the main sails!" The pirate ship slowly makes its way out into the open lake and off into the blackness of the night.

"Those bastards are stealing my trees!" shouts Captain Schuenemann.

The two men both stand there a moment and helplessly watch the ship disappear into the darkness.

"I think we scared them off, before they got too many," Osbourn tells the captain, trying to be encouraging.

The two of them look around in the darkness, trying to assess the damage.

"Look! That slippery devil got all our wreaths," says Captain Schuenemann with a look of disgust, holding up the piece of canvas that had covered them.

"I don't think they'll be back here any more tonight," Osbourn says. "You sure gave that pirate something to think about."

"Yeah, well, I wish I would have gotten here a few minutes earlier. I would have given him a few shotgun pellets in his behind."

"We'll get hold of the sheriff in the morning, but I guess there's nothing more we can do about it tonight, Osbourn. Let's go back and see how your dog is doing."

"Yeah, yer right." The two men turn and start walking back towards the house, trying to survey the damage of what has been stolen.

"That pirate would have taken a lot more trees, if it wasn't for Sandy. I hope she'll be all right."

"I hope so, too," says Osbourn. "She's been such a good dog." The two men walk towards the house.

Back at the house, everyone is awake and they're all huddled around Sandy. The poor dog is exhausted now from pain and loss of blood, and is lying on a rug in the corner by the wood stove, nearly too weary to lift her head, and yet still she wags her tail from time to time.

"Let her sleep now," says Barbara as Elsie and the twins try and comfort her.

Just then Osbourn and the captain come back in the door.

"Oh Herman, are you all right?" Barbara asks, her arms around him. "We heard shots!"

"Yeah, we're okay. It was that damn pirate, Dan Seavey. He was stealing our trees! The slippery devil got away, but I blew out the back windows on his ship with the shotgun just as his ship was leaving the harbor. He got all our wreaths, and I don't know how many trees, but he would have gotten a lot more, if it hadn't been for Sandy waking us up. How's she doing?"

"It's hard to say," says Elsie, who is still kneeling beside her. "We don't know how much damage is done inside her. Only time will tell, now."

"Well, I say we all go back to bed and try to get a little rest before morning," says Captain Schuenemann. "We'll be bringing the *Rouse Simmons* over here from Manistique, so we need to get a few hours rest. In the morning we'll be better able to tell how many trees are missing. So let's all go back to bed and try to get some rest."

They all agree and once again try to settle in for the night.

DAN SEAVEY THE GREAT LAKES PIRATE

Came sailing in, on a winter's storm
One cold and gray, Chicago's morn
Bootleg whiskey, black market goods
Bring a good price, like you knew they would.
But a pirates life, it ain't no good
Should have listened to mama
Like you know you should

CHORUS:
But the whiskey tasted good tonight
And the women they all were fast
But the only thing about a pirate's life
The good times just don't last

They say he was born a preacher's son
Just before the war between the states was won
He ran away when he was thirteen
A sailor's life grew up hard and mean

2nd CHORUS:
When Seavey sailed into a town
You know there'll be a fight
But he's buying us all, another round tonight.

He stole a ship, out of Frankfort they say
But the law caught up, took him away
Seavy stood trial for piracy
Of the Nellie Johnson but soon was free.

3rd CHORUS:

Said he drank the Captain and her crew
Flat on their backs you see
They sold me the ship for a gambling debt.
Seavey got off free.

We'll make you a marshal
If you work for us
One less outlaw, we have to chase
Cus a pirates life, oh it ain't no good
Should of listened to Mama
Like you knew you should.

But the whiskey tasted good tonight
And the women they all were fast
The only thing about a pirate's life
The good times just don't last

The only thing about a pirate's life
The good times just don't last.

CHAPTER TWENTY-THREE – THE SHIP AT THOMPSON HARBOR

The next morning finds Captain Schuenemann and Osbourn down at the dock talking with Nelson Boushour, the tugboat captain, and surveying the damage. Thomas arrives with some of the workmen, prepared for another day of work in the woods. They all join Captain Schuenemann, Osbourn, and Nelson Boushour standing at the dock.

Trees strewn about everywhere, the piles are noticeably smaller, and the wreaths are gone. "What happened here, captain?" Thomas asks. The rest of the men gather around to find out what happened.

"Dan Seavey paid us a visit last night," the captain informs them with a frown. "He stole all of our wreaths and maybe about 400 trees."

"Took all the wreaths," Thomas moans in disbelief.

"Yeah, and he would have gotten a lot more trees, if we hadn't chased him off! The captain here blew the back windows out of his ship with my shotgun," Osbourn reports.

"Yeah, we sent that ol' pirate on his way with something to think about," captain Schuenemann laughs.

"Yeah," says Osbourn, "But it could have been a lot worse,

if it hadn't been for my dog, Sandy. She came down here barking and raising a fuss, so one of them shot her with an arrow to try and quiet her down."

"An arrow! Is she all right," asks Thomas.

"She came running back to the house, scratching on the door, whining, and bleeding like a stuck pig. So, while I was tending to her, Captain Schuenemann came running down here with a double-barrel shotgun and gave ol' Seavey what-for just as his ship was leaving the harbor. I hope Sandy's going to be okay. She just lies there beside the stove, hardly moving. We'll know more in a couple of days if she's going to make it, I suppose."

"I should have known," says Hogie. "That night we got in a fight down at the tavern, Dan Seavey seemed awful interested in the Christmas tree business. He asked us a lot of questions. I should have known. Darn it!"

"Well, like I say, it could have been a lot worse," says the captain. "Thomas, you take the men up to the camp and get more trees, while a few of us take the tug over to get the *Rouse Simmons*. Hogie and Engvald, you come with me and give us a hand moving the ship."

"Yes sir, captain," Hogie replies. Engvald silently steps forward.

"All right, let's go make up for them missing trees," yells Thomas

"Yeah, let's go!" and they all climb into the wagon, and off they go for another day of gathering trees.

Hogie and Engvald join Captain Schuenemann and Nelson Boushour all walk over and climb onto the tug. Nelson lights a blowtorch and heats the cylinder head before trying to start the engine.

"There's no sense even trying to start this beast till I get some heat on her," he tells the captain. He soon gives the flywheel a turn, and the big old engine sputters to life. After letting her warm up a bit, they throw off the dock lines and head off to Manistique, about five miles distance by water.

Captain Boushour is a dashing young man in his mid-thirties from a family of sea captains, and it's quite obvious to see him work he knows his job and loves the lakes very much.

The little tug clears the harbor entrance then heads out into the open waters of Lake Michigan. The little tug pitches and rolls in the churning waves.

"It's a little choppy out here his morning," Captain Nelson says with a smile.

"How many years now have you been shipping trees to Chicago?" he asks.

"Over twenty years," the captain answers.

"I know you've been doing it ever since I was a kid," Boushour tells him.

"It just seems to be a tradition around here gathering Christmas trees and greens every fall. I used to earn money for my winter clothes gathering greens. Now my kids are gathering greens for you."

"You can tell them to start bringing their greens down to the dock tomorrow. I'll be buying as many greens as I can get, especially now that Seavey got all of our wreaths."

"This isn't the first run-in you've had with Dan Seavey, is it? I know Hogie, here, got in a fight with him a couple of weeks ago. Sounds like he gave him a bit of a thrashing. I guess he gave him something to think about."

"Oh yes," says Captain Schuenemann. "A few years ago I was sailing the *Mary Collins*, looking for Thompson harbor light, and we saw a light from a house at Barq Point. I mistook it for the harbor light, and I started heading in and ran aground on a shoal there.

"We all got off the ship safely, but before we could get back to do any salvage work, someone had stripped her of every piece of hardware that they could take from the ship. We don't know for sure, but we all suspect it was Seavey."

"I wouldn't doubt it," Captain Boushour sympathizes. "I wouldn't put anything past him."

"He may even have had something to do with that bright light in the upstairs window at the Point. He's known around the lakes to be a wrecker. There are stories of him even changing buoys so ships will run aground. Then he can salvage the cargo, or whatever hardware he can steal."

"Did you tell the sheriff?"

"Yeah, but he said there really isn't much he can do. Once he sails off into the lake, he pretty much disappears, and then it's out of his jurisdiction, anyway."

"That figures," Captain Boushour responds.

Amidst the drone of the engine and the rocking of the tug, the two captains swap tales of their maritime adventures. In no time, they're approaching the Manistique harbor entrance.

"The harbor sure is busy here," Captain Schuenemann points out.

"There's a lot of work going on here," Captain Boushour tells him. "The Corps of Engineers are building a lighthouse and a concrete break wall. They hope to have it all completed by next fall."

"That will be great," adds Captain Schuenemann. "Then Manistique will really be a first-class harbor."

Once inside the break wall, the waters are calmer. The dark waters of the Manistique River stand in contrast to the deep, blue-green waters of Lake Michigan.

The Manistique waterfront is a bustling place, with steamboats and sailing ships continually coming and going about thirty to forty ships of various kinds are tied up along the wharfs. Captain Boushour brings his tug in to the dock, and the men tie up just long enough for Captain Schuenemann and his men to climb aboard the *Rouse Simmons*. The men throw the towline to the tug, and untie the ship from the dock.

Engvald silently gives the tug captain the signal that they're ready, and Captain Boushour revs the engine of his little tug into action, churning up the water behind him, pulling the towline tight then giving her full throttle. Slowly, the *Rouse Simmons* responds, following closely behind.

Captain Schuenemann takes the wheel and guides the *Rouse Simmons* out of the harbor. "You men work the pumps a little while to pump out the bilge water while I steer."

The sky is blue and the sun sparkles on the water as they head out into the open lake and back to Thompson. Although the lake is rather rough, the trusty little tug faithfully carries out its mission, and soon they are nearing the Thompson Harbor entrance. The two captains carefully guide their vessels safely into the narrow harbor and tie up at the docks. The crew of the *Rouse Simmons* busily makes her ready for loading the precious cargo of Christmas trees.

The day quickly passes in mid-November. Thomas arrives back at the dock with the mother lode of trees.

Captain Schuenemann, Engvald, and Hogie Hoganson are

already loading trees onto the ship. Captain Schuenemann is cautiously optimistic.

"Well, men, it looks like we may be ready to leave in a couple more days. But we definitely could use more trees. I've gotten the word out to the locals to start bringing their trees. I'll be buying trees and greens right up to the time we're ready to sail. I've also sent Peter Anderson up to the Soo where I've made arrangements to purchase a couple of train car loads of trees to make up for the ones Seavey stole from us last night. So as it stands now, we're a little shy of the number I was hoping for, but in the next couple days, we'll be better able to tell. So you men go back and get rested up. Tomorrow's going to be a big day for us. We'll be loading trees all day."

The woodsmen climb onto the wagon, and Thomas drives off, pulling them behind. Thomas drives them all over to the boarding house.

That evening at Osbourn's place, they're all gathered around the table for supper. The conversation is mainly about the events of the night before, and the number of trees needed.

Thomas and Elsie are sitting next to each other at the table. The past few weeks have drawn them close to one another.

Captain Schuenemann recounts the events of the night before. "Well, I don't think ol' Seavey will be back tonight," he laughs.

They all agree with a smile.

"You sure gave that old pirate something to remember," Osbourn says with a grin.

"Yeah, but it might have been a different story, if it wasn't for Sandy. How is she doing?"

"It's hard to say," Florabell answers quietly. "She just lies there by the stove, asleep. Once in a while, if I'm over there tending to her she'll open her eyes and try and wag her tail. But most of the time, she just sleeps."

"She's lost a lot of blood, and who knows what kind of damage is inside of her. We'll just have to wait and see," Osbourn says with a sigh. "I hope she makes it, because we sure love that dog."

"Yes, she sure is a nice dog," they all say sadly.

"Well, animals are pretty tough. I think she'll make it," Captain Schuenemann adds, with his always-positive attitude. The others all nod, and dinner continues on with a much cheerier note.

After supper, they all prepare for making wreaths. As they begin their work, everyone pitches in and works a little harder than usual to help make up for the wreaths that were stolen.

"So, how many wreaths did Seavey get?" Barbara asks.

"Well, we still had about twenty-five here by the house, so I only think he got about a hundred," the captain replies.

"We'll make up for it, Daddy," Elsie says with a note of

determination in her voice.

"That's my girl!" Captain Schuenemann leans over and gives her a hug. "That's right, honey, we'll all make up for it!"

They all smile and work even more intently.

That night, Thomas and Elsie make plans together. Thomas invites Elsie to go out for a drive to Manistique and see a performance at the theater in Manistique.

Thomas and Elsie are more absorbed in each other's company every day, and it's obvious that they are quite happy to spend time together. Whether it is work or time alone, they not only have a budding young love, but an enjoyable friendship that makes it a pleasure to be around them.

Barbara looks over at them talking together as they work on their wreaths, then quietly looks over at the captain. He acknowledges her gaze with a warm smile and a little twinkle in his eye. They both think the world of Thomas, and they are pleased to see Elsie so happy.

In the kitchen, Florabell can be heard cooking popcorn. The smell of popcorn fills the house, and somehow gives whole house a festive mood.

Everyone talks together while they work. Barbara tells them all stories of Chicago, and all of the city's cultured events, of the fine buildings, and of the architecture, and that since being newly rebuilt after the Chicago fire, how the city has a look that would rival any city in North America, or maybe the world.

Then Osbourn tells tales of the history of the area, of local fishermen, and Indians, and loggers, and trappers.

Captain Schuenemann talks about life on the Great Lakes, the Chicago waterfront and all the marvels of the modern age.

Thomas listens with intense interest, and he dreams of adventure, and listens intently to their tales of courage and cowardice, of heroes and zeros.

But all through the evening, there's a spirit of determination to overcome any setback that comes their way, and a sense of loyalty that Captain Schuenemann is somehow able to secure from all those who associated with him.

Later that night, when the evening winds down, they all decide it's bedtime. Elsie and Thomas step outside to visit for a few moments before Thomas is ready to go back to the ship.

Thomas says good night for the evening and gets ready to leave.

"Thomas, you know that tomorrow afternoon, Mother and I will be leaving with the twins to go back to Chicago."

"Yes, I know," says Thomas

"The time here has just flown by," says Elsie. "But I'm so glad we met, Thomas. I have never met anyone so... so…" Elsie struggles to find the right words. Wonderful!" She speaks with tears welling up in her eyes. "I'm going to miss you."

They embrace, and Thomas holds her close for a while. "You know, I was thinking," Thomas pauses. "I was thinking that if I went to Chicago with your father on the ship, when I got there, I could check out the Chicago schools, and maybe with some luck, find a good photography school."

"Oh, that would be wonderful!" Elsie squeals with delight. "I'm sure Father would let you stay on the ship for a while. I mean, 'till you find a school."

"Then we could be together more, too," Thomas explains.

"Oh, that would be just wonderful," repeats Elsie, practically jumping up and down. "I could talk to my father about it. I'm sure he would let you. Oh Thomas, that is so sweet of you to think about us seeing more of each other!"

"Let me talk to him first. I think I should be the one to ask him about it. We are pretty good friends now, and I'm sure that he'll give me fair consideration to the idea. Besides, I think it would be a great adventure to be sailing from upper Michigan to Chicago on a three-masted schooner! Elsie, I have never been farther from home than I am right now, and that's only about seventy or eighty miles. And just look at all the things I have been able to do, and all of the people I've met, and all the money I've earned, in just the short time I've been away from the farm. Elsie, there's a great big world out there, and I want to see it! And I've even met you, as well. And besides that, going to Chicago would mean we would be able to see each other more often. And what a great place to learn about photography and journalism! I bet there's a dozen schools I could attend there."

"Oh, there are," encourages Elsie. "And lots of opportunities."

"My mind is made up. That's what I'm going to do."

"Oh Thomas! This is so exciting. I'm so glad you met father and decided to help him with the Christmas trees. He has so enjoyed your company, and your help, and I too am so happy we met."

"You know, it seems funny, in a way, how things happen. I mean, by the choices we make. I could have just stayed and helped at the farm this winter, and worked a few odd jobs around the neighborhood, and maybe have forgotten my dreams and just stayed there in my little world, never realizing that this great big world is out here all around me. And now, it seems for the first time in my life, I actually have the power to decide, the power to make it happen and to follow my dreams. Before I met you and your family, it seems I was just drifting along taking any path life would push me down. But since working for your father, and meeting you, I've come to realize there's more to life, and I can follow my dreams."

"Oh Thomas, that is so awesome!"

"I used to think that dreams were only fantasies that other

people wrote about in songs and books, and that a person could toy with them for a while, and then like some little children's game, you would put them away. Soon they would be forgotten. But now I see that I can really make my own choices, and actually make my dreams come true. Meeting your father was a bit by chance, but if I had chosen to stay on the farm, I would never have met him, and of course, never have met you.

"I believe God guides us through life, and I'm sure He had something to do with meeting your father, but our choices can put us in the way of God's opportunities."

"Thomas, your words to me are like the light from a falling star. When its fire catches our eye for a brief moment, we are taken away from our ordinary little world into a world that seems so much bigger! Thomas, I have to tell you something. The night before we met I was walking along the lakeshore just after dark. I was feeling quite sad and lonesome as I walked along the shore. The sky was suddenly lighted up by the brightest falling star that I have ever seen. So I made a wish that I would soon meet my true love."

"Oh really," says Thomas. "The night before we met I was out on the deck of the *Rouse Simmons*. I saw a beautiful falling star, and I too was feeling lonely. When it suddenly brightened up the night sky, I too made a wish that I would meet my true love. So it must have been the same falling star."

"That's so awesome!" says Elsie. "I don't know if that has ever happened to anyone else before."

"It is really amazing, but now that I've met you, I know that amazing things can happen," says Thomas, holding Elsie closer to him.

"Let's promise each other tonight to follow our dreams, and to take the steps, however small, that will help us to make those dreams come true. Elsie, I have never felt this way before. I can't help but feel that it's you and I together that has inspired my heart and mind to the world around me, to see the wonder of it all. Before I met you and your father, I feel that I only looked at life as if through some thick glass window from a darkened room, but now that am actually living, I am breathing in the air around me. I have now seen for myself the bright sunshine, and I am never going back to the way I was before. When I 'm with you, I feel I am in the sunshine of life itself."

"Oh, and I with you, Thomas! And I with you!"

Together they embrace, with a love born of heaven and with a sweetness rarely witnessed on this earth. Thomas and Elsie stand holding one another in one long embrace, while the freshly falling snowflakes quickly cover them with robes of white.

CHAPTER TWENTY-FOUR – A FRIEND

The next morning sun rising over the glistening waster of Lake Michigan finds the lakeshore village covered with a fresh blanket of snow. Thompson Harbor is bustling with activity; men carrying trees up onto the ship, others working up in the rigging, preparing the ship for their winter voyage. Local woodsmen are arriving with their wagonloads of trees and greens for the ship.

In the midst of this bustle, Captain Schuenemann can be seen directing the loading of the ship, while negotiating the purchases of the trees and greens. Word is out that the *Rouse Simmons* is now in the harbor, and the townspeople of Thompson and the surrounding areas converge on the ship for their opportunity to earn some extra money for the winter. Some come with wagons, others with sleighs. Others are pulling toboggans and small sleds.

The captain has a large scale set up near the dock, and is weighing bundles of evergreens to be used to decorate the city of Chicago. An Indian arrives with a dog sled filled with wreaths and greens. It is Paul Ag-Wa-Na-Be, a friend of Captain Schuenemann's and one of his regular suppliers. The captain drops what he's doing and hurries over to greet him.

"Mr. Ag-Wa-Na-Be," he says, with a beaming smile,

extending his right hand.

"Captain Schuenemann! I had heard that you were loading the ship, so I loaded my sled last night to bring my greens."

"Well, it's good to see you! And how is Mary and the family?"

"Oh, they're all fine, and the baby's not just a little papoose anymore. He's running around now, and even beginning to talk a little," he tells the captain.

Paul Ag-Wa-Na-Be is a well-educated young man of fine features; slim and tall, of noble appearance. His words are articulate, and yet, his tone and mannerisms are definitely Indian. He has adapted well to the changing times, but still seeks to live a more traditional lifestyle of his people.

The sled is loaded to the hilt with wreaths.

The two men talk together as they unload the sled. The captain holds up one of the wreaths, admiring it. "Your people sure do some fine craftsmanship. I'm going to give you a little more than I told you for your wreaths, because I can charge a little more for such beautiful work."

"Thank you, captain. I have also brought the beaded moccasins and some baskets that you ordered."

"Great," says the captain, admiring each item as Paul unloads them. "The folks in Chicago just love your work."

"I'll be bringing some from the other families tomorrow,"

Paul tells him.

"Excellent," says the captain, holding up a pair of moccasins and admiring them with wonder. "You tell your people I will buy as many of their products as they choose to make."

Captain Schuenemann pays him, counting out the money.

"Thank you, captain," says Paul. "You're a good man. I'll be back tomorrow." He nods graciously and turns towards his sled, then orders his dogs in his Indian language, and off they go, barking.

Next comes a young lad, about fourteen, pulling a sled load of greens. The captain greets him, "How are you this morning, young man?"

"Fine," he answers quietly. "I've got some bundles of greens for you, captain."

"Well, bring them right over here, and I'll weigh them," he says with a smile. "A penny a pound," he says, as he lifts the bundles, places them on the scale, and adjusting the balance beam to find the weight.

The captain looks a bit puzzled then he picks up the bundles one at a time, judging their weight.

"You've got some heavy greens here," says the captain, looking over at the lad.

"Yes, sir," the boy replies, sheepishly.

The captain holds up a bundle and shakes it sideways.

CLANG! Out drops a piece of scrap iron. "What's this?" he says with a surprised look. "There must be a lot of iron in the soil where you pick your greens," he says, shaking the next bundle. CLANG! CLANG! Two more pieces of iron drop on the dock.

The captain sets the bundles back on the scale. "Thirty cents," he says, and hands the boy three dimes. "Next time, bring the greens, but leave the iron home."

"Yes sir," says the boy quietly. Placing the iron back on his sled, he turns and walks off, pulling his sled behind him.

Just then, Thomas pulls up with another load of trees and begins unloading. Captain Schuenemann joins him, pulling a tree off of the truck.

While they're unloading the truck, Barbara arrives at the dock with the twins. "Herman, we're all packed now. Is there anything you would like me to do here?" she asks.

"Daddy!" The twins come racing to him. He gives them both a hug, one in each of his arms.

"Yes," he tells Barbara, smiling. "If you could take over her at the scale for a while, I would like to go up to the store and pick up some provisions for the trip back to Chicago."

"All right," she says, giving him a quick kiss.

"Here's some money for the greens. Thomas is going to bring me over to the store. Albert made out a list of provisions for me, so I gave it to Joe VanDyke yesterday. He said he'd have it ready for me this morning, so we'll be back in a little while."

"Okay, honey. I'll take over here."

The captain climbs into the Model T, and Thomas drives off. When they arrive at the store, Joe VanDyke is out front, hanging up a side of meat on the left side of the doorway of the front porch leading into the store, advertising the meat special of the day.

"Captain Schuenemann," Joe greets him. "Top of the morning to you."

"The same to you, Joe! This is my assistant, Thomas Berger."

"Pleased to meet you, Thomas. I heard about your automobile. Everybody in Thompson has been talking about it. Mind if I look at your automobile? Haven't seen one like this before."

"Go right ahead," says Thomas.

"Thomas here taught me to drive this thing," the captain brags. "I've even got a driver's license."

"A driver's license!" Joe repeats. "That's really amazing," he says. "Next thing you know, you'll be buying one."

Captain Schuenemann looks over at Thomas with a knowing glance, but just smiles.

"Well, I've got your order ready here," says Joe, walking back up the steps, wiping his hands on his white apron.

"Good. We'll give you a hand," the captain says, following him.

Joe leads them back to a pile of bags and boxes, and picks up a piece of paper and reads off the list of items the captain has left him, pointing out each item as he goes through the list.

"That all comes to $85.43."

"Hey Joe, could you put that on my account? You know how it is for me, this time of year. I'm always broke till after Christmas."

"Yeah, that's all right," says Joe, thoughtfully. "Just sign here, and I'll keep it till you can take care of it after Christmas. But, don't go sinking that ship, or we're both going to be sunk."

"I wouldn't think of it!" the captain smiles. "Thanks, Joe."

"You take care of yourself out there. You've gotten to be quite a regular here. I want you to keep it that way."

"So do I," says the captain, as the two shake hands.

The three of them each grab as much as they can carry, and start loading the truck.

As they start loading the truck, Joe asks, "When are you leaving?"

"I'm hoping, if the weather is good, maybe the day after tomorrow."

"Well, God bless you, captain. It was nice meeting you, Thomas. Take care of the captain for me."

"Are you sailing, too?" Joe asks.

Thomas hesitates for a moment. He looks over at the captain. "Well, maybe."

The captain looks up at him in surprise, but says nothing.

Thomas starts the truck, and they both climb in and drive off.

"Well, I've been meaning to ask you, captain, if maybe I could join you and the crew on the trip down to Chicago," says Thomas, over the chugging of the engine. I think it would be a great adventure, and to tell you the truth, I've become quite attached to the *Rouse Simmons* these past couple of weeks. I already feel like part of her crew."

The captain listens thoughtfully. Thomas continues, "Well, I thought that Chicago would be a good place for me to look for a school to go to, and I've heard so much about Chicago, I think it would be interesting to see the big city and all. I've never been any farther from home than I am right now!"

The captain listens thoughtfully, but remains silent. So Thomas continues convincingly, "And besides all that, I was thinking that, if I were to find a school there, then Elsie and I could see each other more often."

A broad smile comes across the captain's face. "Ah! So it's more than the love of the sea!" he laughs.

"Yes, sir." Thomas smiles, blushing a bit.

"Well, let me think it over a bit. I would love to have you, but the ship is going to be a bit crowded now. How about if I let you know tomorrow."

Arriving at the dock, Thomas turns and backs the truck up to the side of the ship. The captain asks Hogie to help unload the supplies. "Hogie, could you give Thomas a hand loading these supplies? I got to get back to buying greens."

"Yes sir," Hogie replies. Together, Hogie and Thomas begin carrying the supplies aboard the ship.

The captain walks back over to the scale, where Barbara seems to be having a bit of a problem with one of the customers, a woman with a sled load of greens, and Barbara is weighing them, but Barbara seems to be a bit confused about the weight.

It was a middle-aged woman, obviously rather poor, from her appearance, but rather insistent on being paid.

"Is there a problem here?" the captain says.

Barbara looks up and says, with a puzzled look, "Yes, well, these bundles seem to be awful heavy. I shook them, but nothing fell out."

"Let me take a look," sighs the captain. Cutting the bundles apart, he finds them packed with frozen mud. He loads them back on her sled and points down the road. "I'm sorry, but you can take these back to where you got them, and don't ever try that again, or we'll never buy greens from you any more."

The woman hangs her head and walks off.

The captain mutters something under his breath as she walks away. "Mud Hen Molly."

"What did you say, Herman?"

"Mud Hen Molly. That's what my brother August used to call her," he says, laughing.

Barbara begins to laugh, too. "You mean she's tried this before?"

"Oh, yes." He laughs. "So remember to keep an eye out for 'Mud Hen Molly'!"

"I will," she smiles. "I'm going back to the house now. We're all packed and ready to go, and the train leaves this afternoon at three o'clock so remember to pick us up at the house at 2:30 sharp."

"All right, honey." He reaches over and gives Barbara a hug.

"Come on, girls," she says to the twins.

"Bye, Daddy."

"All right, I'll see you at the house. Two-thirty?"

"Yes, 2:30," she answers. "Don't forget."

"I won't," says the captain, looking at his pocket watch.

Barbara and the twins walk back to the house. Captain Schuenemann continues directing the loading of the ship, periodically climbing the gangplank, to give orders how he wants the ship loaded.

CHAPTER TWENTY-FIVE – GOOD-BYE LADIES

"Stow the smaller trees and bundles of greens down in the hold, and all of those bigger trees here across the deck," says the captain as he points, motioning with his arms. "And try and keep count," he informs them, "Mark it down on this paper on top of the cabin. I've got a pencil here on a string so we can have a pretty good idea how much cargo we have on the ship. Make sure to balance the load on both sides of the ship. We don't want to be sailing all the way with the ship listing to one side."

The captain's warm smile, rosy cheeks, and broad smile have a winsome effect on all those who work for him, adding to the productivity of the crew.

More horses pulling wagons and sleighs loaded with trees, some with greens. The captain personally goes down to the dock and greets each one, eager to purchase their Christmas greens.

"This is going to be my best season ever," he tells Thomas. "It's taken years to build this business to where it is today, and I have to say I have enjoyed every minute of it, and I'm glad that you have been a part of it, Thomas."

"Oh, it has been my pleasure, captain," Thomas answers. "I have really enjoyed this whole season. "I couldn't have dreamed of finding a better job, and staying on the ship, and all. It has all been one great big adventure for me."

"And also for me," replies the captain. "You teaching me how to drive the automobile really was one of the highlights of this trip. And who would have thought that I would have learned to drive on up here, in the bush of Upper Michigan, of all places!"

They both laugh together.

"Maybe I'll teach you how to captain a ship," he says, with a twinkle in his eye.

Before they know it, it's already 2:30.

"Oh-oh, we better get over to the house and pick up the girls, or they'll be late for their train," the captain says, looking at his pocket watch.

The two of them hurry off the ship, down to the Model T. The captain turns the crank and jumps in. Thomas gives it the throttle, and they race off toward the house.

Clambering up the drive, they see the girls waiting on the porch with their bags. Florabell is there also, to see them off. As they come to a stop, the girls grab their bags and hurry towards the Model T.

"Herman Schuenemann, where have you been," says Barbara, with a hurried sound in her voice.

"Here, you and Elsie can ride up here, in front. The twins and I can ride back here, with the baggage," he tells them, looking a little sheepish that he's running late.

Thomas and the captain grab the baggage and load it in the back of the truck.

"Oh daddy, look who's here," Elsie points. It's Sandy, the dog, limping slowly towards the truck.

"Oh, good dog," Captain Schuenemann leans down and holds her head in his hands, petting her.

"She's a little slow-moving yet, but I think she's going to be all right," says Florabell.

"Oh, that's great!" the captain smiles. "Good dog, Sandy."

"Come on now, captain, we've got a train to catch," Barbara urges.

"Good bye, Flora. Thanks for everything!"

"Good bye, Flora." Elsie gives her a hug then climbs in.

"Good bye, everyone! Have a nice trip."

The captain turns the crank and climbs in back with the twins, and off they go to the railroad station.

Elsie and Thomas glance over at one another fondly as he drives to the station, trying not to openly show how strongly their affection for one another has grown, even though they have tried to be discreet about it. It's quite obvious to those around them that theirs is a budding romance, and they are all happy for them.

Arriving at the station just as the train is pulling in, the captain grabs the luggage and helps the twins down.

"Give the conductor our bags while your father and I get

our tickets," says Barbara, and together they hurry into the station. The conductor loads the baggage onto a cart and wheels it over to the train.

"Wait right here a moment, and watch for Mom and Dad. I must say good bye to Thomas, so call to me as soon as they come out."

"We'll be right here, around the corner," they assure her.

Slipping around the corner, Thomas and Elsie find a moment of privacy. Holding one another in their arms, Elsie asks, "Did you ask Father yet?"

"Yes. He told me he had to think it over 'till tomorrow. But, I want you to know that one way or another, I will see you again."

"Oh Thomas, I will be waiting for you." Their eyes close as they kiss and hold one another tight.

After a long embrace, Thomas whispers, "I've got something for you." Pulling a small package from his pocket, he gives it to Elsie.

"That is so thoughtful of you! Whatever could it be?" she says, quickly unwrapping the small package. Elsie opens the box and pulls out a silver heart-shaped locket on a necklace.

"Oh Thomas, it's the picture you took of us together at the Big Spring! However did you get it into this locket?"

"There's a photography shop in Manistique. I had them

make the picture fit into a locket." Thomas just smiles.

Elsie reaches out and gives Thomas a big hug. The both kiss and embrace.

"Elsie," the twins shout, "Here comes Mom and Dad!"

Quickly, they part, and join the twins around the corner.

As the captain and Barbara approach them, the conductor yells out, "All aboard for the train!" They all say their last goodbyes as the girls turn and make their way onto the train.

The conductor looks at his watch and signals to the engineer. A puff of black smoke belches from the stack. The engineer rings his bell, blows the whistle, and with a steady chug-chug-chug the train slowly pulls away.

Barbara and the girls all wave out the window, leaving Thomas and the captain standing at the station. The captain smiles and waves as the train disappears down the track.

"What a great bunch; my wife and kids," says Captain Schuenemann proudly.

"Yes, they are," says Thomas.

Together, the turn and walk back to the truck, climb in, and drive back to the ship.

CHAPTER TWENTY-SIX – BAD OMENS

That night, the weather changes and by morning an all-out gale is blowing off the lake. Nasty winds, gusting hard out of the northeast with a freezing rain, make everything seem more difficult. The wind blows so hard at times that the work of loading the ship nearly comes to a halt, and all the men can do is wait. And when they are able to load, it's at a snail's pace. There's a fire going in the wood stove in the main cabin aboard the ship. The men gather there to warm up around the stove.

Between the dark, gloomy weather, and the impatient hours of idleness, the crew grows restless. Even Captain Schuenemann, who is usually upbeat, seems edgy in the darkness of the ship's cabin. He repeatedly goes to the window to look out at the weather. The captain and his crew leave the cabin only when some brave soul arrives with a load of greens, and then only long enough to get them unloaded before the weather sends them retreating back into the ship's protection.

Hurrying back into the ship's cabin, the crew gathers back around the stove.

"Dang! This weather is nasty," the captain says, looking out the window. "This is the worst possible direction for a storm. This harbor entrance is already shallow, and a storm from this direction could wash in more sand, making it impossible for us to leave. If I don't get these trees to Chicago in time to sell them before Christmas, they'll be worthless."

"Don't worry, captain. We've always made it before," says Albert, the old cook. "Besides, Chesbrough has that sand sucker that he uses to keep the harbor open."

"Yeah, but that thing is as slow as molasses in January. It could take days, even weeks, to suck the sand out of the entrance. By then, we could be frozen in."

"I just wish it would shop blowing," he says, looking out the window again.

"Well, that's all we can do, is wait."

The storm continues to blow all that day, and into the next. The idleness and gloom bring on a melancholy spirit. The crew is unusually quiet. Hogie Hoganson is especially gloomy, and begins voicing doubts about the ship.

"We should have gotten the ship caulked this spring," he complains. "Now we're pumping water out of her a couple times a day. If we get caught out in the lake in a good blow like this, and start working them seams, we'll have more water in her than we know what to do with," he says, looking around.

"Besides that, this freezing rain makes them ropes so stiff they don't even want to go through the pulley blocks, making her a beast out of control. It's bad news, I tell ya. We got to be crazy, sailing this time of year."

"Yeah, you're right," Albert chimes in.

"This old boat is getting tired, but she still has a few more good years left in her," the captain responds, trying to be positive.

"I think that when the weather breaks, we'll all feel a lot better," Albert adds. "More coffee?"

"Yeah, something warm for the belly."

"It's a good soup day today, and I've got some bean and barley soup cooking. It will make you all feel a lot better, and it will be ready pretty soon."

"Yeah, you're right, Albert. I guess we're just getting more gloomy here in this dark old cabin, but there's nothing we can do but just wait it out."

That evening, on the second day, the weather begins to moderate. The skies clear, the wind dies rather suddenly. The crew resumes their work of loading the ship. Even though the sky has cleared, there's still a haze in the air, giving the evening sky a brassy appearance.

The crew talks together as they carry the trees up onto the ship.

"It's strange how the wind just stopped all of a sudden like that," Hogie tells Andrew. "It was so nasty earlier. Now it's deader than a doornail. But, I'm not complaining. It's a lot better than it was."

Captain Schuenemann is busy scurrying about the ship, directing the crew and making ready for the voyage.

Captain Nelson appears on the dock and makes his way up the gangplank to join Captain Schuenemann. Together they look things over. Captain Schuenemann speaks up.

"I think we should sail in the morning."

"What about those extra train car loads Peter Anderson is bringing down from the Sault?" Captain Nelson asks.

"Oh, I'll just have to send them down to Chicago by train. We're already loaded pretty heavy, and I guess I'm a little worried about getting out of this harbor. Another blow like we just had, and we'll never make it out of here."

Captain Nelson nods in agreement. "I think the sooner we leave, the better. The chances of one storm following so closely after another would be very unusual, so I think the weather should be good for the next few days."

"That's what I was thinking too," says Captain Schuenemann, with at decisive look. "In the morning, we'll set sail!"

CHAPTER TWENTY-SEVEN – MORE BAD OMENS

That evening, Osbourn Stanley finishes work at the Thompson Lumber Company and walks along the dock towards the ship. The air now is dead calm, so calm in fact, that there's not a ripple in the water in the harbor; a strange contrast to what it has been just a few hours or so earlier.

As he approaches the dock, he meets Hogie Hoganson coming down the gangplank for another tree to carry on board.

" Well, if it isn't the old pirate slayer himself," jokes Osbourn. "It sure calmed down quick out here, eh?"

"Yeah, too calm."

Osbourn looks at him in surprise.

"Too calm, too quick. It's a bad sign," Hogie replies. "I don't like it." Hogie grabs another tree and throws it over his shoulder. "Captain Schuenemann and Captain Nelson are on board. They've decided to set sail in the morning."

"Oh?" says Osbourn, with a bit of surprise. "I thought he was going to wait for that load of trees from the Sault that Peter Anderson's bringing down." Osbourn joins Hogie and grabs a tree, throwing it over his shoulder.

"I think the captain's worried about weight. The freezing rain the last couple of days has added a lot more weight to our deck load, so we're already overweight, and unless we get some real warm weather in the next day or so, we'll already be sailing overweight."

"Yeah, I suppose he would know," says Osbourn, following Hogie up the gangplank of the ship. The calm is so still now that it seems almost eerie as the two men climb the gangplank.

Suddenly, out of the corner of his eye, Osbourn looks up and points toward the back of the ship. "Look, rats!" he yells, pointing with his left hand. "Rats, climbing down that dock line." He points them out to Hogie.

Sure enough, two rats climb along together down the dock line from the ship to the dock. Reaching the dock, the rats quickly scamper off into some nearby stacks of lumber.

"Rats leave a sinking ship."

"What's that you say?" asks Osbourn.

Hogie looks back at Osbourn then repeats it with a hysterical look. "Rats leave a sinking ship. All the sailors will tell you that. It's a sign not to take this voyage! Mark my words, if she sets sail tomorrow, it will be her last."

The other sailors gather around as they raise their voices.

"What's the matter?" they ask.

"We just saw rats leaving the ship. It's a bad omen, I tell you," Hogie shouts.

"You don't really believe all that, do you?" says Osbourn,

trying to make light of the incident. "I've heard that before, too, but how's a rat going to know if a ship is going to sink? They probably get on and off of ships all of the time."

"Maybe so," Hogie replies, "But somehow they know. I don't like it, I tell ya," he says emphatically. "I don't like it at all!"

A couple of the other men on deck stop what they're doing and listen to Osbourn and the others. Osbourn tries to downplay the incident, in order to calm Hogie's fears. But Hogie continues more vehemently.

"You saw it with your own eyes, and ye can't deny it," he says, looking at Osbourn.

"That's true, but the more you believe in that superstition, the more it comes true. I suppose every time you see a black cat cross your path, you get all worried about that, too!"

"No, but I don't like it. Rats leave a sinking ship," he says again.

"Ah, it's just one of your sailors' superstitions," the others mock. "Don't let it spoil your trip."

"We've got two of the best captains on the lake on his boat. They're not going to let us down," says Andrew.

"There's a lot of good captains that put business ahead of right and wrong, and we all know it. The captain has gotten himself out on a limb. He's spent so much money in these trees that he'll be in debt up to his eyeballs the rest of his life if he doesn't get them to Chicago in time."

"He's got all this money invested in trees, and has hardly spent a dime on this ship! He hasn't had her caulked in ages, and her canvas looks like an old patchwork quilt! One good blow and who knows what could happen. You can say what you want about rats and superstition, but I say the rats have more common sense than we do! Yer the ones believing superstition and fairy tales, I tell you. Just because we're carrying a load of Christmas trees for the good girls and boys in Chicago, we all think the story is supposed to have a happy ending. You're all living in a fantasyland, but the reality is there's not always a happy ending. Just ask the captain's brother, August. He'll tell ya. This ain't no fairy tale, and Captain Schuenemann ain't no Santa Claus." With that, Hogie throws down his Christmas tree onto the deck of the ship and walks off the ship. Two other sailors follow him off the ship down onto the dock. Captain Schuenemann and the others stand there staring at one another in silent disbelief.

CHAPTER TWENTY-EIGHT - DECISIONS

That night there's a cold chill in the air. It's quiet in the harbor. Captain Schuenemann has a hard time sleeping, so he gets dressed and takes a walk down to the ship. The moon is rising, giving its light through the light clouds. He looks things over and slowly walks up the gangplank and wanders around the deck. Reaching into his coat pocket he pulls out a pipe and a pouch and packs the pipe with tobacco, strikes a match, cupping it with his hands to protect the flame from the wind, and lights his pipe.

Leaning over the ship's rail he looks out over the lake. The moonlight reflects on the water, leaving a shining path. Captain Schuenemann contemplates the events of the past few days, slowly puffing on his pipe. When he's done with his pipe, he takes and taps it on the rail and puts it back in his coat pocket and makes his way back towards the gangplank. He's just about to walk back down the gangplank when he hears someone open the cabin door of the ship's cabin and step out on deck.

"Oh, Thomas! What are you doing up this time of night?" the Captain asks.

"Oh, I don't know. I was just a bit restless. How about you?"

"Well, same thing. It must be the moonlight."

"Yeah, and maybe the incident this afternoon, too."

"Well, even though I've worked around the water all my life and have never been one to worry about superstition, you can't help but wonder sometimes. Most of the time, they're wrong. People tell me one thing, and more often than not, just the opposite happens. I haven't kept score, but if I had always heeded every bad kind of sign or these kind of warnings, I don't suppose I'd still be in business, So what do you do?" he says, shaking his head.

"I've pretty much just learned to just ignore them and go by what I think is right. That's why the superstitious ones usually aren't captains, because captains have to show a profit and the seamen don't," he says with a smile. "So tomorrow, if it looks good, we sail.

"I told you the other day I'd give you an answer about sailing with me, but I'll tell you now if you want to sail with me to Chicago, be ready in the morning. We'll try and leave as early as we possibly can finish loading."

"Yes, sir!" says Thomas, nearly leaping for joy.

"And while you're looking for a school down in Chicago, maybe you would like to stay on the ship."

"Oh, thank you, captain! That would be wonderful."

"But you do have to come by the house and see us once in a while."

"Oh, I will, sir. You can count on that. Thank you very

much. I'll be ready in the morning. I just have to send a letter to my father to come on the train to get the Model T. Oh, I am so happy! You don't know how excited I am. Elsie's going to be happy, too!"

"You two have become quite fond of one another since you've been here."

"Yes sir, I guess you could say that. I have never met anyone in this world quite like your daughter. She is by far the most wonderful girl I have ever met. I don't think there's anything she couldn't do, if she sets her mind to it."

"Yes," the captain agrees. "She is quite a girl. I remember when she was only five years old. Even then, she was so determined to help. That's when she made her first Christmas wreath, and she's still making them. She is quite talented. I don't think that there's anything that girl can't make.

"She makes just about all her own clothes. But Christmastime—that's her favorite time of year. You'll see, when we get down to Chicago. We'll have this ship full of ladies making wreaths, and Elsie will be right there, making sure they are all kept busy and that everything is running smoothly. But she does it in a way that everyone loves her."

"Oh, I can see that," says Thomas. "You know, when we went on our picnic together, we talked about what we wanted to do with our lives, and she told me that helping you with the Christmas tree business was what she wants most. I can see why. I have really had to work hard these past few weeks, but I must say that it's been the best month of my life. Thanks for hiring me, captain."

"Well, it's really been great to have you, Thomas, and I'm glad that you were able to meet the family. I don't think I've ever seen Elsie so happy. She's going to be pleasantly surprised when she sees you arrive in Chicago."

"Yeah, well, I can't wait!" says Thomas. "I've heard so much about Chicago from Elsie, and I'm sure that the schools there will be able to teach me all of the latest advancements in photography. To me, photography is most fascinating. It's art. It's history. It's science. It's everything!"

"Well, I'm excited too, about the automobile," says Captain Schuenemann. "You know, I have always admired them ever since I've first seen them, but I never really thought I would actually drive one, or own one myself. I guess I thought they were only for the rich--some kind of rich man's toy. But you and Henry Ford have changed my mind on that. I've decided I'm going to buy one myself, now that I know I can drive one. I can hardly wait to drive Barbara around the streets of Chicago in our own automobile. Won't that be fine," the captain laughs.

"And you'll be amazed at all the electric lights. When we tie the ship up at the Clark Street Bridge, the men take and string electric lights up in the rigging." The captain points up into the ship's rigging. "And the ship looks like a floating city. People come from all over town, some in carriages, some with automobiles, others on foot, some by rowboat, others with boats with gasoline engines, all come to buy Christmas trees, and everyone is happy.

"There's just something about buying a Christmas tree that makes people happy, so we sell them trees and wreaths, and everyone has a good time. Oh, there's other people that sell trees, too," the captain continues, "but I think we've got the best spot in town, and it's getting to be kind of a tradition to buy a Christmas tree right off the ship. You know, human beings are creatures of habit, and they like some things to be the same every year. We've been in business now there now for so many years that for a lot of people, buying Schuenemann Christmas tree is like a part of Christmas itself."

The captain continues. There's a smile on his face and a light in his eye as he recounts to Thomas all the joys of Christmas time. "Oh, and all the parties! It's a time of year Barbara and I love to have people over to our home. Some are the city fathers some are sea captains. It is always fun to invite a few people that we just meet when we're selling them trees. It's a great time. You're going to love it!"

The captain looks as though he's in vision as he speaks. "As we approach the Chicago harbor entrance, there can be as many as a hundred ships, all in sight at one time, coming and going, big steamships, passenger ships, package freighters, schooners, tug boats, all coming and going in and out of the Chicago harbor. They say it is one of the busiest ports in the world, and who would have thought it would be on the shore of a lake, at a town that was barely even on the map seventy years ago. It's a great time to be living in this land, I tell you. It is a great time to be living here in America."

"They tell me that there's street cars that run on electricity there. Is that so?" Thomas asks.

"Oh yes," Captain Schuenemann replies. "Many of the buildings the buildings are all new, having been built after the Chicago fire, so the city has a clean new look, and the architecture I'm sure will amaze you. Hopefully, by this time tomorrow, we'll be well on our way there. The weather should be all right the next few days. It is very rare for one storm to follow right after another, so I'm quite sure it's going to be good sailing.

"You look like you're half frozen, Thomas."

"Yeah, I am starting to shiver. I better go back to my bunk."

"Yeah, we both better get some sleep. It will be busy in the morning. So good night, Thomas."

"Good night, Captain Schuenemann."

The captain slowly makes his way down the gangplank, and

Thomas goes below into the ship's cabin. The captain walks back along the road to Osbourn's house. But as he climbs the steps up onto the porch, he looks up at the moon one last time before opening the door.

"H-m-m-m, that's strange," he mutters to himself, "a ring around the moon." He waits and ponders for a moment, then enters the house for the night.

CHAPTER TWENTY-NINE – SETTING SAIL

The morning light finds the harbor a blur of activity. The rising sun gives the distant cloud cover a reddish hue. The captain and crew are busy loading trees onto the ship. The ship's flag is flapping with a steady breeze of about 15-20 knots out of the northwest. Captain Nelson and Captain Schuenemann are at the dock discussing the weather when one of the sailors points out the red sky.

"Cap'n Nelson, what do you make of that red sky this morning at sunrise?"

"Yeah, it was a bit red, wasn't it. Captain Schuenemann and I were just discussing that we figure that it's going to blow out of the northwest today, but I don't expect any kind of storm because of the way it's been storming the last couple of days out of the northeast. It would be very rare for one storm to follow another, so even if it gets a little sloppy out there this afternoon, we'll be on a following sea, and that will be a perfect direction for sailing down the lake to Chicago.

"After all," Captain Schuenemann chimes in, "It *is* a sailing ship. A little wind can be a good thing."

"Ya, that's true," says Captain Nelson. "But handling that rigging in a nor'wester this late in the season is a lot different than in the summer. We could start icing up."

"Well, the way it is now, I think it could be a nice, fast sail down the lake, and if any weather is coming in behind this wind, we'll be far enough ahead of it that we won't have to worry. And if things start looking nasty, we can pull into port someplace and wait it out.

"I just don't want to stay here any longer. You know how shallow this harbor is, and any kind of storm would wash in enough sand to block the entrance. Fully loaded like this, we might never get out of here."

"Ya, yer right about that," Captain Nelson agrees. "That last blow may have washed in enough sand to give us trouble."

"Nelson Boushour is coming down to the harbor this morning. I told him we're loaded pretty heavy, and we may need a tow from his tug to get out of the harbor. The way the wind is blowing, we should be able to sail right out of here," says Captain Nelson. "And you're right about this harbor. Another good blow, and we could be stuck here for a while. And then, we've got to worry about freezing in. I say we at least get to a deeper harbor."

"That's my call, too," agrees Captain Schuenemann. "I think we should get out while we have the chance. If we get out into a blow, we can anchor behind one of the islands, or in some other port, and wait it out."

Just then Thomas comes walking over to the dock, carrying his stuff.

"Thomas, how are you this morning?"

"Oh, just fine. I just sent word to my father that I'm sailing with you, and that I'm leaving the truck at Osbourn's place, so I'm all ready to sail."

"Good. We're just about ready to get under way here. A couple of the men are going to hoist a tree up to the top of the mast. If you like, you could give them a hand there. It's a tradition to tie the last tree to the top of the mast, letting everyone know that this is the Christmas tree ship."

"Yes, sir," says Thomas eagerly. He joins Jack Pitt and Andrew, who are already tying a rope to the tree.

"I think you young guys should climb up there and tie it." Andrew looks at Thomas. "Are you up to it?"

"Yeah, why not."

"Here are some smaller pieces of rope. Use these to tie it to the top of the mast, and tie it good and tight. Nothing looks worse than a crooked tree at the top of yer mast. We don't want people saying 'Here comes the crooked Christmas tree ship'," the captain laughs. "They'll all be mistaking us for Seavey's boat!"

The crew all laughs heartily.

Thomas and Andrew take off up the gangplank. When they get on deck, Jack throws Andrew the end of the rope.

"Here, let me tie it around your waist," says Andrew. "That way you'll have both hands free to climb the rigging."

Together, they begin the long climb up to the top of the

mast. Thomas has the rope tied around his waist. Higher and higher they climb, till they finally reach the top.

"This is a long way up," says Thomas.

"This ain't bad," scoffs Andrew. "Wait till you have to do it sometime when we're under way and we're in a heavy sea, then you'll know what yer made of. Are you scared?"

"Nah. I used to climb a lot of tall trees when I was younger. It never bothered me," he said, finding a place to hang on to at the very top. "I remember one time I took the neighbor boy on a climb with me to the very top of the tallest spruce tree around, and when we got to the top, he just froze there and I couldn't get him to climb back down. Well, after a while I had to go and tell his father where he was, and his father had to climb up there and help him get down."

"Was the dad mad at you for bringing him up there?"

"Yeah, I don't think he was too happy about it. But the kid was a year older than me, so I figured he could do anything that I could do."

Finding a good place to hang on, Andrew says, "Are you ready down there?"

"Yeah, heave away!"

"Okay, let's start pulling it up."

Together they start pulling, and the tree begins to rise higher and higher. Jack guides the tree up as high as he can reach, assisting till it's out of his reach. "It's all yours!" he hollers.

"Okay!" Andrew yells back.

Finally they are able to grab onto it.

"Whew! This is harder than I thought," says Thomas warily.

"Just take your time," Andrew tells him in a steady voice.

Together, they secure the tree as high on the mast top as they can.

"Lash her down good now. We don't want to have to climb back up here and do it again. Last year it stayed up here till spring. No one felt like taking it down," Andrew laughs nervously. "Give me that other piece of rope. I'll do everything twice, just to make sure."

Thomas hands him the rope.

"That should do it," says Andrew, tightening the last knot. "You never know what kind of blow we're going to get into and it's bad luck to lose yer tree from the mast, so I wouldn't want to be the one to blame for that. All right, let's go back down."

"Whew!" Andrew pauses a minute to catch his breath. Just then a sudden gust of wind hits, blowing his hat off.

"Hang on!" yells Thomas.

"Dang that wind," grumbles Andrew. "It's starting to blow pretty good. Let's get down."

Together they slowly descend from the rigging down to the

deck of the ship.

In the meantime, the other sailors are making their last preparations before getting ready to sail. A small group of locals gathers at the dock to see them off. Osbourn comes from the mill. He meets with the men on the dock.

"Osbourn, how are you this morning?"

"Good. So are you leaving this morning?"

"Yes. We should be ready to go shortly. I just thought I'd tell you the barometer in the mill is quite low, and still falling."

"Yes, I know. But we're not likely to have much bad weather because one storm doesn't usually follow another. And besides that, Captain Nelson and I are concerned that if there is another blow, the waves could bring in more sand at the harbor entrance, making it impossible to get out of here fully loaded," Captain Schuenemann explains.

"Well, yer right about that," says Osbourn.

"I'm concerned that that blow we had the past few days brought in a lot of sand. I've asked Nelson Boushour to be ready on his tug. I see he's over there now, starting the engine."

The two men stroll over to the tug.

"Morning, Nelson."

"Morning, Captain Schuenemann."

"I'll be ready in just a few minutes. Are you all set to go?"

"Yes, I see the deckhand is getting the tow line ready there right now."

"That wind seems to be picking up quite a bit. Are you sure you want to leave now?"

"Yeah, we better get the ship out of here now. You know how shallow it gets out here when it storms."

"Yeah, yer right about that. It looks like that blow we had the past few days has washed some sand in. I hope we can get you out of here.

"That's what I'm afraid of," says Captain Schuenemann. "Let's give it a whirl."

Nelson climbs into the pilothouse of the *Cisco* and revs the engine. Osbourn unhooks his front dock line, and Captain Schuenemann unhooks the rear line, and they give him the all-clear signal.

Nelson skilfully pulls the tug away from the dock and around to the front of the ship. The deck hand throws him the towline, and Nelson attaches it to the tug.

The two men walk towards the ship. The deck hands have already untied the ship and are hurrying up the gangplank.

Captain Schuenemann turns toward Osbourn. "Thanks for everything, Osbourn. You've really made us feel right at home here."

"It's been a pleasure having you, captain. You be careful out there. I want to see you back here next year."

"All right. Good luck!" the captain shakes his hand. "I'll square up on the rest of the money we owe you as soon as we sell some of these trees. Thanks again, Osbourn, and tell Flora she is a wonderful hostess."

The captain climbs the gangplank and up into the ship. Several friends are down on the dock, and wave to the captain and crew. Thomas waves to Osbourn.

As the ship slowly moves from the dock, the little tug chugs into action. A puff of black smoke shoots up with a roar of the engine as the tug churns up water behind it.

Captain Nelson is at the wheel, while Captain Schuenemann walks toward the front of the ship to get a better look.

All of the sailors are climbing about the ship, each one readying the ship to set sail. Captain Nelson guides the ship from the dock toward the harbor entrance. All is going well, but as they are about to clear the harbor, the ship slows to a crawl.

Captain Schuenemann has a concerned look on his face. "We're dragging bottom!" he yells to Captain Nelson. "Keep her a little more to starboard. It looks a little deeper."

He walks over to the starboard rail and leans over for a closer look. By now, the ship is barely moving, and the tug is churning up the water, but the ship comes to a halt.

"Damn. This is what I was afraid of," the captain mutters.

Thomas and the woodsmen that are standing on deck look on helplessly as the little tug churns up a rooster tail of water. Nelson Boushour, realizing the ship is stuck, begins working the tug back and forth to try and free the ship.

He does succeed in turning the nose of the ship from side to side. The ship inches ahead, but progress is slow.

"Hoist the main sail on the mizzen!" orders Captain Schuenemann, walking back to talk with Captain Nelson. "When the tug moves the front of the ship from starboard to port, we'll jibe the sail back and forth. That should roll the ship back and forth, and maybe break us loose."

Captain Nelson nods in agreement.

The wind catches in the sail, causing the ship to lean to starboard. The ship moves ahead a few feet, but stops again.

Captain Schuenemann goes back to the front of the ship and points for Nelson to pull the bow of the ship to the port side.

"Prepare to jibe!" Captain Nelson orders. When the bow of the ship swings to port, the ship jibes back across with such force the whole ship shakes from the shock, but as the ship heels to the other side, it again moves slowly forward.

Again and again the process is repeated. Closer and closer the ship is pulled toward the open waters of Lake Michigan. Again and again the sail is jibed back and forth, each time pounding the ropes and pulleys with a sickening thud, repeatedly straining them to their limits.

Finally, after what seems like hours, the ship breaks free. The men on the ship all let out a cheer.

The tug captain tows the *Rouse Simmons* out into deeper water, then throws the tow line free, signals and waves an "all clear", and climbs back into the pilot house and turns the tug back in to port.

Captain Schuenemann orders the crew to put up more sail, and they busy themselves at the task.

Captain Nelson yells up to Captain Schuenemann, "I don't think we're going to need any topsails today. It's blowing pretty hard."

"Yeah, that wind has really picked up. It's a good thing we got the ship out of there when we did. Some more rough weather, and for sure we wouldn't make it out of there at all."

The captain looks out at the color of the water. As the ship enters the dark green water, the captain is sure it's deep enough.

"Lower the centerboards! We're in deep water."

Two of the crewmen respond immediately. The ship is alive with action. Everyone aboard is busy hoisting sails, securing lines, and making sure the deck cargo of Christmas trees are all secure.

"Batten down the hatches," Captain Schuenemann orders. "It looks like it's going to be a fast ride to Chicago."

Just then, a strong puff of wind catches Captain Schuenemann's hat, almost pulling it off before he catches it, pulling it tighter on his head.

"It sure is blowing pretty hard out here, isn't it?" he says, looking over at Thomas. Buttoning up his coat around his neck, he makes his way to the back of the ship.

Captain Nelson is busy at the helm, keeping the ship on a steady course.

"It sure has gotten nasty all of a sudden," says Captain Nelson, peering out at the white froth blowing off the top of the waves.

"Well, hopefully we can stay ahead of it. It's just about as perfect a direction as we could ask for. Just as long as it doesn't get too much stronger, we're all right," says Captain Schuenemann.

"Yeah, it's going to be a fast ride to Chicago. Take the wheel, captain. I'm going below to get my oilskins on. I need something to cut that wind. You'd best do the same."

Captain Schuenemann takes the wheel while Captain Nelson goes below.

Thomas comes back to see Captain Schuenemann. "How's it going, captain?"

"Well, it could be better, but I'm just glad we finally made it out of that harbor. I just hope we aren't biting off more than we can chew. We've got plenty of wind, though, and that's one thing we need to move this ship. We can take a lot of wind from this direction, so it should be a fast sail to Chicago. It's a good thing we're not trying to sail into this stuff. We'd really be taking a pounding."

"Here comes another ship headed our way," Thomas says, pointing out over the lake.

"Yeah, it looks like it's sailing for Thompson," says Captain Schuenemann, "That ship is staying awfully close to shore, there. Probably trying to stay in close to shore to block the effects of this wind. He better swing out a little wider going around Wiggins Point, or he'll tear the bottom out of his ship if he gets in too close. A fishing tug from Thompson got in too close last year and bottomed out in the waves. Nelson Boushour spotted them and was able to rescue them, but one of them died later from exposure to the cold.

"That ship is really taking a pounding, heading into the waves. This isn't good weather for sailing up wind. It looks like they're having quite a time of it. I think Nelson Boushour sees him, 'cuz it looks like the tug is coming back out of the harbor to meet him to tow him in."

"I've never understood that, how a ship could sail into the wind," Thomas says.

"Well actually, they can't sail directly into the wind," the captain explains. "The best you can do is about tack 45 degrees into the wind, and then come about and tack in the other direction, like risers on stair steps. Eventually you reach your destination. But sailing into the wind in a gale can be much more difficult, and sometimes you just have to turn and run with it.

"That must be the *Butcher Boy*. She's supposed to be sailing into Thompson for another load of lumber. That's Captain August Hansen. He sails out of Thompson quite often. I wouldn't want to be beating up wind today, that's for sure."

Eventually the two ships approach one another. "I've got to give him wide berth," says Captain Schuenemann. "He doesn't have as much room to steer as we do, going down wind."

The two ships pass within about a quarter-mile of each other. They give each other a sailors' wave. The captain of the *Butcher Boy* looks out across the waves at the approaching ship.

"It looks like the *Rouse Simmons*," he says to his crew. "What are they doing, sailing out of port in this kind of weather?"

"Looks like they're overloaded, too," points out one of the crew.

"Yeah, with a deck load of Christmas trees, heading for Chicago," says Captain Hansen. "I wouldn't be leaving port in this kind of weather. I'll be surprised if those boys don't end up on the bottom of the lake!"

The two men look at one another in disbelief. Then they watch as the ship sails by.

CHAPTER THIRTY – A TERRIBLE NIGHT

Leaving Thompson Harbor in the distance, the *Rouse Simmons* plows ahead, with waves foaming under her bow. The sky is partly sunny, but wind-driven clouds are quickly covering the sky, and like leaves before the autumn wind, the *Rouse Simmons* is driven furiously ahead. Dark clouds appear on the horizon, painting an ugly picture of what is to come. Rainsqualls start pelting the ship with driving rain mixed with sleet. All that afternoon and evening, the *Rouse Simmons* is driven by high winds. Captain Nelson and Captain Schuenemann take turns at the wheel.

"I wish we would have gotten out of there first thing in the morning, like we planned. Now, with it getting dark, we'll be running blind."

"We'll just have to keep a steady course."

Captain Schuenemann gives the wheel back over to Captain Nelson. "It looks like we're not going to have a pleasant ride down there."

"No, but as long as it doesn't get any worse, I think we can ride it out. If we stay on this course, it should put us somewhere near Sturgeon Bay, Wisconsin. We could pull into port along there, if need be."

The crew huddles near the wood stove in the cabin, taking turns manning the sails. The entire crew is dressed in their oilskins, but the woodsmen and Thomas don't have oilskins, so they just try and stay out of the way. By now, several of the woodsmen have become seasick, and sit covered with blankets, huddled in the corners. Occasionally, one of them moves only enough to vomit in a bucket. The dreary light of a kerosene lamp is all the light in the cabin now, as darkness shrouds the already struggling ship. Thomas too, sits covered with a blanket, sicker than a dog.

Jack Pitt comes in from up on deck, and huddles in closer to the fire. "Damn, that wind is nasty," he curses, as he rubs his hands together. "How are you doing over there, Thomas?" he asks in a concerned tone.

"Not so good," he answers in a loathsome voice. "If it wasn't so nasty, you could stay out on deck and get some fresh air."

"Well, there's not much we can do about it now. Just hang on, and try and ride it out."

Up on deck things are going from bad to worse. The two captains struggle to keep their Christmastree laden vessel on course. The temperature is dropping dangerously, bringing with it a blinding snowstorm.

Down below, Albert, the cook, is handing out cups of

coffee to the crew as they come in.

"Here's some coffee, Jack." He comes staggering over to him, trying to keep his balance. "To tell you the truth, I'm having a hard time keeping things nailed down in here. If it gets any rougher, I'm not sure I'll even be able to make coffee for ye," he says, handing him the cup.

Jack takes the cup and sips it. "No coffee? That would be bad!"

"Now that it's dark, about all we can do is ride it out till morning, and if it doesn't settle down at all," Captain Nelson says, "we'll pull in to a port somewhere along the Door Peninsula. The trouble is now, that in the dark like this, we can't even see to pull in behind one of the islands. If we could see, that's what we'd do, but running blind like this, we're safer to just ride it out, out here in deeper water, or we might end up on some shoal. Then we'd really have a mess! About all we can do is just hang on and hope it doesn't get any worse."

Then, BANG! The sound of some metal pots clanging rings out as they come falling to the floor.

Captain Schuenemann sticks his head in the cabin door. "Make sure you've got everything that's loose down there as secure as you can get it. It seems to be getting worse out here. The rain is turning to snow, and it's getting colder. I think the storm is catching up with us." He pulls his head back out and closes the door.

"Catching up with us," Jack mutters under his breath.

By now every timber on the ship is making creaking and moaning noises as though in agony.

"That doesn't sound good. Try and secure everything you can--everything that's not nailed down," announces Jack to the crew.

They all grope around, trying to keep their balance, stashing whatever loose items they can. Captain Nelson hurries through the door, closing it as quickly as he can behind him. He staggers his way over to the wood stove.

"The weather is getting worse. It's snowing cats and dogs out there now, and blowing even worse." He reaches his hands out to the stove. "I'm concerned about our deck load icing up out there. All this snow and ice could cause the ship to get too top-heavy, and cause us to turn over. I need a few of you men out on deck. We're going to have to get rid of some of our deck load. Jack, Andrew, Frank, Gilbert, start throwing some of those trees overboard! Engvald and Steve go out and try and secure the yawl, or we might lose it. Bring some rope with you."

After warming himself, Albert hands Captain Nelson a cup of coffee. Captain Nelson sips on it. Several of the men hurry toward the door up on deck. The deck is now covered with snow and ice.

"It's very slippery," Captain Nelson warns them as they head out the door. "Be careful."

"I better get out there and relieve Captain Schuenemann. It's going to be a long night," he says, handing his cup back to the cook.

A few minutes later, Captain Schuenemann comes stumbling in the door, covered with snow, icicles hanging from his mustache. He huddles near the stove.

"It's turning into a real blizzard out there. The men are having a hard time out there on deck. Those trees are frozen together, and they're having a hell of a time trying to cut them loose. They may have to start chopping them loose, one at a time."

Just then, the ship is hit by a terrible wave. BANG! Water sprays over the rail and washes over the deck.

"What was that!" The captain looks up in surprise. Hurrying up to deck, he struggles through the door and up onto the deck. Jack Pitt struggles to the back of the ship.

"What was that noise?" yells Captain Schuenemann.

"I don't know," yells Jack over the noise of the storm. "But I think the yawl tore loose!"

Struggling along the rail to get a closer look, Jack points. "It's gone! The yawl is gone!"

"Steve and Engvald were trying to secure the yawl," yells the captain. "They're gone, too!"

Immediately Captain Schuenemann yells back to Captain Nelson, "Man overboard! Engvald and Steve are gone overboard!"

Captain Nelson just shakes his head and holds onto the wheel. "I can't turn the ship around. I can't turn it around in this wind. It's impossible! God help them, they're lost!" He hangs his head for a moment. "There's nothing we can do," he yells. "I'm sorry. I'm so sorry!"

Captain Schuenemann and Jack struggle to the back of the ship, clinging to the rail, straining to see through the driving snowstorm.

"There's the yawl!" Jack yells over the screeching wind. "I don't see anyone in it!"

"God help them, they're lost!" Captain Schuenemann says, lowering his head. "They're lost!"

"Everyone on a line!" he yells. "Everyone on a line. We just lost two men! There's no turning the ship in this storm, so make sure you're on a line."

Several of the woodsmen join the others up on deck carrying axes. Together with the crew, they struggle to lighten the deck load of trees from the ship.

The wind whips them mercilessly, pelting them with the freezing spray as they desperately try to remove the ice-encrusted mass of evergreens.

With every wave, the ship shudders, often knocking the

freezing men to the deck with the savage blows of a prizefighter. The storm hammers them continually through the night like a vicious opponent hoping to deliver a knockout punch, but each time, they somehow struggle back to their feet in what has become an unending battle with death.

Together, the woodsmen and crew work tirelessly through the long night, hoping against hope that they will see the dawn. Just when it seems it can't get any worse, one of the crew comes from down below with more bad news.

"Captain Schuenemann, there's water rising in the hold!"

The captain nods and answers, "I want two men on the pumps continually, and find two others to relieve them. Just keep pumping steady."

"Yes, sir, captain, I'll get right on it."

With almost super-human effort, the men work through the night. Hour after hour they endure continual torture of the cruel storm, with nowhere to escape. The battle rages on.

Later that night, one of the men working the pumps reports back. "Captain, we're taking on more water than the pumps can handle. The water is rising."

"Get everyone left below to start bailing! Use every pail, every bucket that you can find. Tell Albert we need his pots and pans, washtubs, everything. Form a bucket brigade and just keep bailing. We've got to keep this thing afloat until daylight. It's our only hope."

"Yes, sir," he answers. Then, going below, he repeats the captain's orders.

The buckets and pails, some of which the seasick men have been using for catching their own vomit, are now pressed into service for saving the ship. Albert provides others with washbasins, pots, and pans.

Together they all pitch in, and soon a human chain of buckets, pails, pots, and pans of water are being poured out the window in a steady effort to fight back the rising tide of water in the ship's hull.

They are all united now in a desperate battle to win back the ship, even though they're so sick it pains them to move.

After what seems like hours, the water level appears to be going back down. Albert announces to them, "It's going down." And they let out a cheer, but they continue bailing into the night.

CHAPTER THIRTY-ONE – MORNING HOPE

All through the dark and terrible night, they struggle on-- Captain Schuenemann and Captain Nelson at the wheel, the sailors, the woodsmen, Thomas, and the cook all working desperately to keep the ship afloat.

The storm continues to punish the ship and her bedraggled crew. But as the day dawns, their hopes of survival again grow brighter, giving the men renewed vigor and determination to continue their fight with nature, and even though they are cold and weary, they re-double their efforts to keep the ship afloat.

"Put up the distress flag," orders Captain Schuenemann. "We may be spotted by a passing ship, now that we've got some daylight."

"Yes sir," Jack Pitt answers, and he quickly disappears below, returning momentarily with the flag. Jack and Captain Schuenemann work together to run the colors up, with the stars and stripes upside down to half-mast. Every movement is an effort in the screaming wind. The flag flaps wildly in the captain's hands as he attaches it to the halyard.

"All right, now. Raise it up to half-mast!" he yells over the gale.

Jack pulls on the halyard to raise the flag, but the frozen

rope and pulleys don't want to work. Jack jerks on the rope. "It's stuck! I can't get it to raise!"

Frozen ropes make even this simple task take every bit of effort they can muster.

Captain Schuenemann grabs one end of the rope, and Jack pulls on the other, and after working the pulley back and forth a while, the ice on the pulley breaks free, finally allowing them to raise the flag.

Then Jack and Captain Schuenemann duck back into the cabin. Inside, there are several of the men huddled around the wood stove. Others are handling pans and buckets, continuing their efforts to bail the ship.

Captain Schuenemann speaks up. "We should be somewhere near the Door Peninsula, so I'm hoping that we can nurse the ship into one of the ports along the shore there. Hopefully, we'll get in close enough that one of the harbor tugs will come out and tow us into port."

Just then, Andrew enters the cabin. "Captain, I just spotted land. It looks like we're about five miles from shore."

The captain looks up. "Thank God. I'll go take a look." He makes his way out on deck. Captain Nelson is holding the wheel.

"We just spotted the shore about five miles off the starboard side. I can't see it right now. It looked like the mainland, but I can't turn the ship in to shore, the way this storm is driving us. All I can do is nurse her in a little at a time. That's all we can do, is hold her on this course."

He shows Captain Schuenemann the compass heading. Captain Schuenemann nods. "I'll take the wheel for a while," he says, struggling to keep his balance. "You try and warm up. I'll keep nursing her in toward shore as much as I can."

All throughout the morning, the gallant crew struggles to survive. The men all take turns manning the pumps, and bailing continually throughout the morning.

Inside, Captain Nelson goes below and huddles near the stove in the cabin with several others trying to warm up.

"How's the water in the hold?" he asks.

"Not good," answers one of the others. "It's coming in now, faster than we can get rid of it."

"Our seams are opening up," says Captain Nelson gravely. "We can't last. This old ship is taking too much of a pounding. If we don't get help soon, we'll be in trouble."

"How long do you think we can last?" asks Jack.

"I don't know," Captain Nelson answers. "But I know we'll never make it through another night."

"Can't we turn her in to shore and run it aground?" asks one of the woodsmen.

"Not the way the ship is iced up and the winds like this.

All we can do is try and nurse her in towards shore a little at a time, and hope that someone sees us. We're in God's hands now. I think that if yer a praying man, now's the time for it."

"Yes, sir," he answers quietly.

CHAPTER THIRTY-TWO - RESCUE

All through the morning and into the day, the sailors and woodsmen work desperately to bail the ship to stay afloat, but now it seems the lake is winning the battle, and time is running out. All the men can do now is pray and bail, and hope against hope for some form of rescue.

Later that day Captain Nelson goes back on deck to relieve Captain Schuenemann. The wind whips him in the face as he opens the cabin door.

"How are we doing?" Captain Nelson asks.

"It looks like we're getting in closer to shore now. I'd say we're about two or three miles out. Maybe close enough in that someone will spot us. How much daylight do we have left?" asks Captain Schuenemann.

"About four and a half hours. Maybe five!" Captain Nelson shouts over the noise of the wind. "I hope someone sees us before dark. We'll never make through another night."

Captain Nelson takes the wheel and looks out ahead. Captain Schuenemann is about to duck into the cabin door when Captain Nelson yells out, "A ship! Dead ahead!"

Captain Schuenemann quickly steps back out on deck. "Where?"

"Look over there," Captain Nelson points. "Just off the port bow."

"I see it now!" he says excitedly. "It looks like it's coming our way!"

Together they watch intently.

"I'd say he's coming closer. I hope he gets close enough to see our distress flag. I'll go below and find something to make a flag to wave and try to get their attention."

Captain Schuenemann goes below. "We can see a ship!" he tells the others excitedly. "Albert! Get me a broom. I want to make a flag to wave, to get their attention and let them know we need help."

"Here you go, captain," Albert quickly stumbles over, trying to keep his balance, and hands him the broom.

"I'll tie this old shirt on here, so I can wave it back and forth. That way, they're more likely to notice we need help. A couple of you men find something you can wave, and come out on deck, but be careful. We don't want to lose anyone else."

Several of the men grab whatever they can find and follow the captain out on deck, their hearts beating with the hope that they'll be rescued.

"Do you still see it?" Captain Schuenemann asks Captain Nelson.

"Yeah, it's coming closer. Looks like a steamer. Should

pass close enough to see us."

Climbing up on the icy roof of the ship's cabin, the weary crew struggles to hold on and wave their flags in a desperate attempt to be rescued.

At the wheel in the pilothouse of the steamship, the captain guides his ship *Ann Arbor No. 5* a ferry of rail cars headed for Kewanee. He drives his ship on through the storm.

The mate enters the pilothouse. "Captain, there's a schooner over there, on our port bow. Looks like we'll pass within about a half-mile of them."

"Yeah, I see them," he says. "What the hell are they doing out of port in weather like this?"

"It looks like she could be in trouble, sir," the mate adds.

"They probably are," he answers with a cynical tone. "They were probably in trouble before they left port," he adds with a note of disgust.

"I can't tell for sure, but it looks like they might be flying a distress flag. Her sails are torn and she looks to have quite a list."

"Yeah, you're right. It does look to be in sad shape," he says with an unconcerned voice. "Listing, torn sails, ice on her deck and rigging. I don't even know why they let them old things sail anymore."

"What's that?" the mate asks.

"Those old sailing schooners. I don't know why they let

them sail anymore," he repeats more emphatically. "They're just a hazard to navigation," he says with a sneer. "None of them can make enough money to keep their boats in half-way decent shape, and then they sail them this time of year, when they know they'll freeze up in a blow."

"Captain, I do believe I see a distress flag now for sure!"

"Well, as far as I'm concerned, they're all in distress. Every damn one of them!"

"Are we going to go to their aid, captain?" the mate asks.

"Naw. They look like they're holding their own. They're probably not having much fun over there, but I'm sure they'll make it in."

"But captain, what if they're in serious trouble?"

"Serious trouble?" the captain sneers. "Them old schooners. Every time it gets rough enough that a sailor gets a little seasick, they got their distress flags out. I've towed them into port before, and they never really appreciate it. The next time it blows, they're out there doing the same thing. Leave them out there for a while. Maybe they'll learn a lesson. Maybe the next time it blows, they'll be smart enough to stay in port. There's so many of them leaky old schooners, if I was to stop and help all of them, I'd be better off to be in the tugboat business. But this is a rail ferry, and we've got a schedule to keep. If we stop and tow in every old wreck out there, we'd be out of business."

"Well, don't you think we should at least take a closer look?"

"Naw. Then we'll really be in trouble. If we stay this far off, we can say we didn't see their distress flags, and we didn't know for sure if they needed assistance. We'll be into port soon. We'll report that we saw a vessel in trouble to the lifesaving station in Kewanee. It's their job to rescue ships. We've got a schedule to keep.

"So, that's what we'll do. When we get to shore, we'll call 'em and tell 'em we seen this schooner having a hard time of it. But no distress flag. Ya hear me? And if anyone asks you, that's what you tell them, or you may be looking for a new job, if you know what I mean."

The mate nods reluctantly.

"We'll leave it to the life savers. That's their job, not ours." He turns his head and looks off ahead and slowly steams past the stricken schooner.

Inside the ship, the hopes of the bedraggled crew turn from desperation to elation. Looking out the window, the men inside stop bailing.

"It's coming closer!" yells Albert. "I think they're close enough to see our distress flag. I'm sure they can see the Captain and the others waving to them. The steamer must only be about a half-mile from us now. I'm sure they'll see us now and come and help us!"

Captain Schuenemann and the crew are frantically waving their makeshift flags in one last desperate attempt to get the steamer's attention.

"He must see us, damn it! Please, please stop and help us!"

But the ship slowly steams on past, as though nothing is wrong.

The crew of the *Rouse Simmons* looks on in utter disbelief as their would-be rescuers slowly fade into the distance.

Captain Schuenemann and the others come back down into the cabin, nearly frozen and even more discouraged. Their chances of rescue had been so high, and now their hopes are dashed to pieces, leaving them all with a terrible feeling of despair.

CHAPTER THIRTY-THREE - LIFESAVERS

Meanwhile, on shore at the lifesaving station at Kewanee, Wisconsin, keeping watch in the station's watchtower, a lone surf man keeps a steady vigil, scanning the storm-swept waters, watching for ships in distress.

The lifesaving service has been formed by an act of Congress on June 20, 1874, in an effort to aid in the great number of shipping disasters. These storm warriors, as they came to be known, saved thousands of lives from coastal shipwrecks along the Great Lakes shores.

Standing in the watch tower overlooking the angry waters, a lone surf man continues his faithful watch even more diligently on a day like today than other days because he knows from experience that the kind of gale that is now blowing is the very kind of storm that brings trouble out on the lakes; the kind of trouble that makes his job as a lifesaver even more important on a day like today.

After standing his watch, he hears another surf man coming up the watchtower steps to relieve him. The two men talk together briefly as they're about to exchange duties.

"How's it look out there?" the newcomer asks.

"Looks pretty nasty."

"Seen anything?"

"Well, I saw a steamer go by about an hour ago. Looked like the *Ann Arbor No. 5*. Having a time of it out there too, but making good progress."

"Anything else?"

"No," he says hesitantly, his eyes still scanning the horizon. "No, nothing else."

"You can go now. I'll take over."

"If you don't mind, I'll stay and stand watch with you for a little while."

"Yeah, that's okay," his buddy tells him. The two men sit and watch for a while. "Hey, is something bothering you?"

"No," the surf man says hesitantly. "Well, yeah, there is."

"What is it? Woman troubles," the other jokes.

"Well, no. Last night I had the strangest dream. I woke up in a cold sweat with my heart pounding, and couldn't get back to sleep.

"What was your dream about?"

"In my dream, I was looking out over the water. It was all so real. It was storming terribly. I was on beach patrol, walking along the shore, when suddenly a man appeared, as though he was walking up out of the pounding surf. He looked like a sea captain, dressed in a dark pea coat and a leather-billed captain's hat. He had a thick mustache and a distant look in his eyes that went right through me. He came out of the water onto the beach right in front of me and stood pointing out into the lake. He seemed to be saying something, but I couldn't make out what he said. He just stood there, for a moment, pointing out over the water, then disappeared back into the waves. Then the water appeared to be covered with some kind of green like seaweed covering the surface of the water and washing up on the shore. Then I woke up suddenly in a cold sweat. It all seemed so real!

"I couldn't go back to sleep or get the dream out of my mind. I don't know for sure what it means, but mark my words, there's going to be a shipwreck before this storm is over." He looks over at the other surf man's response.

"I think maybe you ate something that didn't agree with you last night," his friend jokes.

"No, it was so real. Mark my words, there's going to be word of a wreck out there before this day is through."

"Okay, take it easy. I think maybe you need to take a little break. You've been staring out over the water too long."

"Yeah, maybe you're right. I'm going to try and get a little rest before supper. I'll see you later."

He starts making his way down the tower steps, but before he makes it halfway down, his buddy's voice calls out, "Hey, Mark! Come here. I think I see something!"

Mark quickly hurries back up into the tower.

"Look, over there! It's quite a ways out, but I see a schooner out there," he says, pointing.

"Oh yeah, I see it! I wonder why I didn't see it before?"

"Well, there are a lot of snow squalls out there. It may have been in a snow squall. See if you can find them in the telescope."

Mark carefully turns the telescope then stops.

"I've got them in the telescope. It looks like a schooner, having a hard time of it. It's hard to tell, but it looks to me like it's flying a distress flag. Here, you take a look." The surf man hands Mark the telescope. He stands behind the telescope and peers through it intently.

"Yeah, I think they're in distress all right. I'm pretty sure that they've got their distress flag flying. I better tell the captain!"

"All right! I'll keep watching it."

Mark hurries off down the steps and into the station.

Captain Craite, the lifesaving captain, is busy at his desk, scattered with papers. He scribbles something then crunches the paper roughly. Several surf men are working in the kitchen. The captain voices his frustration.

"Ah, the government and their damn paperwork," he says with a heavy Irish accent. "They hire me as a lifesaving captain to save drowning people, and then they try and drown me in paperwork," he complains to the others in a frustrated tone, looking for their sympathy.

The others just laugh. "That's why they pay you the big bucks!"

"Yeah, right. When I die, I might have enough money left for ye to bury me, if they don't bury me first in this damn paperwork."

They all laugh.

The door opens and the surf man hurries in.

"Captain! We spotted a schooner about five miles out. Looks to be in distress, and we think it's flying a distress flag."

The captain jumps up from his desk. "Let's go take a look!" he says, heading for the door.

Quickly the captain shouts out orders as he opens the door. "Round up the others and tell them to stand by till I see what's happening. I'll go up and take a look."

Instantly the station crew leaps into action. In a moment, Captain Craite grabs his coat and hat and quickly bounds up the steps into the observation tower.

"Captain, I still can see it. It looks like a three-master, having quite a time of it out there," the other surf man says, standing back from the telescope and pointing out the direction to look.

"How far out would you say?"

"I'd say about four miles."

"Four miles," the captain mutters under his breath, and leans closer to the telescope. He stands gazing out at the troubled ship for a moment, his mind racing as to how best handle the situation, voicing his thoughts as he weighs his options.

"If we row out to them in our surf boat it could take us a couple of hours to reach them in this gale, and then we could rescue only five or six people. The speed they're moving, they'd be about halfway to Two Rivers by the time we reached them. He pauses a moment. I think they're too far out to row out to them, especially this late in the day, and with the gale blowing like this.

"Mark, you and a couple of the others hurry to the dock and see if we can secure a tug. Maybe we can tow them in. While you're doing that, I'll telephone Captain Sogge down at the Two Rivers station. They just got a big power launch that will get to them about the same time we would, and it can hold a lot more people. So go to it!"

"Yes, sir," Mark snaps a salute and is off to the harbor.

"Fred, you keep a lookout on that ship as long as possible, and don't let them out of your sight. I want you to estimate weather, speed, and position."

"Yes, sir," he replies.

"I'll telephone Captain Sogge, the lifesaving captain." He hurries down from the tower into the station. Reaching for the telephone, he picks up the receiver and gives the phone a crank.

"Operator, this is an emergency. This is Captain Craite, of the US Lifesaving Service. I need you to connect me with the US Lifesaving Station at Two Rivers."

"Yes sir, captain. I'll connect you right away."

There's a brief pause, then a ring, and a voice is heard on the other end.

"Hello, this is a long-distance call for the Two Rivers Life Saving Station.

"Hello. This is Captain Sogge."

Captain Sogge, this is Captain Craite. We've just spotted a three-masted schooner about four miles offshore, displaying a distress signal. They're moving at about six or eight knots, so they'd be halfway there to Two Rivers before I could row out to them. Is your power launch operational?"

"Yes, it is. I can have her ready in a few minutes."

"All right. Prepare to launch. My men are trying to secure a tug, but there's no guarantee we can secure one. If we are able to find one, we'll see you out there on the lake."

"All right," Captain Sogge answers. "We'll be leaving the station here shortly."

"Okay, Captain. I'll keep in touch. Thank you! Good luck, and God bless."

"Same to you," Captain Sogge replies.

Meanwhile, back on the struggling ship, things are going

from bad to worse.

"Captain! The water level is rising faster than we can get it pumped out or bailed."

The men continue to fight valiantly. The raging storm takes its toll on the old wooden ship, but the weary crew continues to battle on in hopes of staying afloat long enough to be rescued, or to try and work the ship closer to shore. The ship creaks and shudders continually, while the wind in the rigging makes a low moaning noise like the sounds of a sick calf.

Captain Nelson struggles back on deck to relieve Captain Schuenemann at the wheel. "Any sign of rescue?" Captain Nelson asks.

"I don't see anything out there. We should be passing Kewanee. Maybe the Lifesaving Station there will spot us."

"Let's hope so," he responds gloomily. "It could be our last chance before dark. We'll never make it through another night. All we can do is hang on and pray that they see us."

"I wrote a note and put it in a bottle," Captain Nelson says, pulling the bottle out of his pocket. "If we start going down, I'll throw it adrift. You'd best do the same."

Captain Schuenemann nods and answers, "The water is rising in the cabin. We're all going to have to come up on deck soon. The rest of the men are all tying themselves to a line. We'll stay below as long as we can, but we're all getting ready to come up on deck together."

Then Captain Nelson grabs him by the arm and looks into his eyes. "Maybe you could lead them in a prayer."

Captain Schuenemann nods solemnly, opens the cabin door, and goes below.

The men are all huddled together, tying a rope around their waists. Captain Schuenemann comes in, covered with snow, icicles hanging from his mustache, and shivering from the cold. He addresses the men in a low voice.

"Listen up, all of you." There's a solemn silence in the cabin as he gives his address. "As you all know, things are not looking good for us. I would first like to say what a fine group of men you are, and that I am deeply sorry that it has come to this. Our only hope left is that the lifesavers have seen us and are planning a rescue. But other than that, there's not much hope, so we all should prepare for the worst. I'd like to lead us all in a prayer."

They all bow their heads.

"Dear God, I pray that you will be with us in this time of great need. If rescuers are on their way, give them Godspeed, and if we are to meet our end, I pray that you will forgive us of our sins, prepare us for your kingdom, and be with our loved ones. In the name of Jesus, our Savior, we pray. Amen."

"Amen," the men repeat.

Then the captain leads them all in reciting the Lord's Prayer. The men all join in.

"Our father, who art in heaven, hallowed be thy name. They kingdom come..."

CRASH! The ship shudders and water comes dripping in. They continue on undeterred until they finish.

"For thine is the kingdom and the power and the glory forever, Amen."

Just then Thomas steps forward and speaks up. "Captain, I just want to tell you it's been a pleasure knowing you, and I want to say this in honor of Engvald, God rest his soul. He told me that he waited too long and missed his chance to marry. I just want to say that if we were to make it to Chicago, I was going to ask you if I could marry your daughter Elsie."

The captain is speechless for a moment. Then, like the sun breaking through the clouds, that old familiar smile breaks across his face, and he reaches out and embraces Thomas.

"If we had made it to Chicago, and you had asked me, I would have said yes."

The crew lets out a cheer, and they all huddle together and embrace, with tears of both sorrow and joy running down their faces.

CHAPTER THIRTY-FOUR – EVERYBODY GOOD-BYE

The Lifesaving Station at Two Rivers is soon a beehive of activity. Within minutes, Captain Sogge and his Lifesaving crew have readied the lifeboat and lowered it down the launch rails into the water. Clad in their foul weather gear, the lifesavers climb into their power launch and head out of the harbor entrance.

Huge waves smash over the break wall, sending their white spray far into the air. The storm lashes out with a stunning display of force, as if to try and discourage the would-be rescuers from their mission of mercy.

The Captain Sogge and his lifesaving crew never so much as flinch. Faithfully they continue on out of the harbor entrance and out into the full fury of the open lake.

"We have to go out, but we don't have to come back" was the motto of the Lifesaving service, the code that each man in that storm-tossed boat lived by. Realizing that the lifesaving crew intends to continue on, the storm unleashes its wrath upon them now with unfettered cruelty, sending wall after wall of mountainous waves crashing down upon them.

But the stout lifeboat plows through each and every wave, the bow rising higher and higher with each wave, until it seems the boat is about to fall backwards. But just as the boat seems to reach the point of no return, and the engine seems strained to its very limit, the lifeboat pushes the bow over the wave, and is sent plummeting down the other side of the huge wave with a renewed burst of energy.

Captain Sogge skillfully handles the wheel, twisting it endlessly from left to right each time the tiny ship rises and falls, guiding the sturdy craft on a steady course through the constantly surging waters.

Again and again the lifeboat is pounded. Again and again they continue ahead.

Captain Sogge speaks up over the storm. "When we round the point, we should be able to see them, so hang on and keep your eyes open."

The crewmen nod.

Back on the ship, the water in the cabin is rising through the floorboards. Lashed together on a line, the men are ready to make their way up on deck. Groping for handholds and footholds, they work threir way to mid-ship and climb on top of the hatch. Green waves wash over the deck, threatening to wash them all overboard.

"I'll tie myself to the wheel," Captain Nelson yells to them. "I'll stay here and steer as long as I can."

All of a sudden, there's a terrible snapping noise, and the rear mizzen boom of the ship breaks loose, swinging wildly right down toward Captain Nelson.

"Look out!" Captain Schuenemann shouts. Just as the boom is about to strike like a giant battering ram, Captain Nelson dives to the deck. The massive wooden boom strikes with deadly force in the exact place where has been standing. With tremendous force, the boom smashes off part of the cabin roof, sending the ship's wheel crashing over the side of the ship, with the terrible smashing sound of splintering wood, the huge boom swings back wildly, as the ship rolls in the storm, sending another telling blow. Again the huge boom smashes the top of the cabin.

"He's gone," yells one of the men. "He's gone!"

They all look on in horror to see the ship's wheel gone, and no sign of Captain Nelson.

But then, through the snow and spray, Captain Nelson can be seen crawling hand over hand along the windward rail towards the others. After a long struggle, he reaches the rest of the men. Captain Schuenemann helps him to his feet. They all huddle together near the main mast.

Captain Nelson grabs hold of Captain Schuenemann and pulls the bottle with the note from the pocket on his oilskins and looks him in the face and shouts. "I was still hoping I wouldn't come to this," he says with a raspy voice.

"Yeah, me too," says Captain Schuenemann, pulling a bottle with a note out of his own pocket. Together, they toss them over the side of the ship, just as a giant wave slams over the ship.

CHRISTMAS SHIP

A sailing ship, on a winter sea
A sailing ship, a load of Christmas trees
For 15 years we've been counting on you
Chicago's Shores are waiting for you
And those evergreens

So Christmas Ship set your sails
Christmas Ship We'll tell your tales
But remember oh remember
Those November gales

The northwest wind was starting to blow
The Captain said we gotta go
Don't hesitate cause we're running late
Lash them trees out across the deck
We gotta go

They made ready to sail out of Manistique
We'll be back home in a couple of weeks
Then he kissed his wife and kids good-bye
Then he said with a tear in his eye, good-bye

So Christmas Ship set your sails
Christmas Ship We'll tell your tales
But remember oh remember
Those November gales

A winter storm and a blinding gale
Crashing waves and frozen sails
The Captain and crew did all they could do
Tons of ice building on her decks

And those evergreens
A note in a bottle was all they ever found
The Captain said, "We're going down"
Two men overboard and the lifeboat is gone
Then he said God help us now, good-bye

So Christmas Ship set your sails
Christmas Ship We'll tell your tales
But remember oh remember
Those November gales

CHAPTER THIRTY-FIVE – NO SHIP

Meanwhile, Captain Sogge and his men continue their planned rendezvous towards the distressed ship. Wave by wave they continue ahead on their urgent mission, fighting a pitched battle against the angry seas.

Captain Sogge and his crew round the stormy point where they expect to see the troubled ship.

"All right, everyone keep your eyes open. We should be able to see them now."

Desperately they continue on. Though stormy seas and blinding snow squalls hamper visibility, still they continue on.

"I don't see anything out there. Maybe we should turn back," one of the surfmen says wearily.

Just then someone says, "Captain, I think I see them. Over there!" He points off into the distance.

Captain Sogge turns the wheel in the direction the crewman points out. Just then, a violent snow squall erupts, pelting them with blinding snow. "Do you still see them?" he asks.

"No, I don't see them now! I just saw them for a moment, but now I can't see them through the squall. Keep going that way." He points into the white abyss.

The snow squall continues for about fifteen minutes,

pelting them with blinding snow. When visibility finally improves a little, the crewman announces, "I don't see it anymore!"

"I'll keep going that direction for a while. Maybe we'll come up on them. They could be in a hidden squall now. We're practically sailing blind." He curses under his breath. "Damn! I wish we could see them. It's starting to get dark! Are you sure you saw them over this way?"

"Well, I'm not really sure. I thought I caught a glimpse of a ship for just a moment."

On and on Captain Sogge and his lifesaving crew press on, over one mountainous wave after another, then through into the trough, each wave grabbing at them like the arms of some angry giant reaching out to stop them. Each towering wave momentarily blocks their view, making it even more difficult to see ahead of them.

Up, then down. Up, then down. Each time they reach the top of a wave, all they see is the bow raised toward the sky, blocking their sight.

The only time they are able to see around them is when they ride over the crest of each wind-driven swell. On and on they search. All that evening, and into the night, the search continues. Only when darkness completely envelopes the determined crew does Captain Sogge consider turning back.

"Captain Sogge, we've used nearly half of our fuel," one of

the surf men announces.

Captain Sogge acknowledges with a flip of his head and a wave. "All right. We've got to turn back now. I hope Captain Craite was able to find a tug and tow them in. If not, God help them in this mess." And with a booming voice, Captain Sogge announces his intentions.

"We're returning to the station," he yells, turning the wheel around. "We did our best. God help them!"

Slowly, the boat changes course and turns back towards Two Rivers with only a compass to guide them through the darkness. The lifesavers guide their craft back over the icy waves toward the safety of the harbor. But even now, the half-frozen lifesavers keep an eye out for the ship.

Later that evening, Captain Sogge and his weary crew guide the launch back to the station and tie up at the dock. The frustrated men, shivering from the cold, make their way back to the station. When they arrive there they peel off their frozen oilskins.

Captain Sogge immediately telephones back to the Kewanee station and talks with Captain Craite.

"This is Captain Sogge. We took the power launch out around the point and searched for hours, but there was no sign of them. One of my men thought for a moment that he may have caught a glimpse of a schooner, but visibility at times was quite poor. I was hoping you had found a tug and towed them in?"

"No, I wasn't able to find one," he answers.

"I didn't think so, or I would have seen you towing them in. Do you have any idea what ship it was?" asks Captain Sogge.

"We couldn't tell, but we got a report from the captain of the steamer *Ann Arbor No. 5* that they saw a schooner about 2:00 this afternoon having a hard time of it, but they said there was no distress signal out, so they kept going, thinking they would be able to make it into port. He said they weren't close enough to read the name of it, but that there was a tree tied to her top mast."

"A tree tied to her top mast, you say?" asks Captain Sogge.

"Yeah. So it could be the *Rouse Simmons,* coming down from Upper Michigan."

"I'll make some telephone inquires to try and find out."

"All right. If you hear anything, keep us posted. We're going to get some rest, and try it again in the morning."

"I hope they are all right out there. I wouldn't want to be out there all night. God help them! We'll search again at daybreak."

"I was sure we would see them when we got around the point," Captain Sogge says in a discouraged tone.

"You did your best!" Captain Craite assures him. "All you can do now is pray that they make it through the night, and see what the morning brings. You get some rest, and I'll try and find out more, and let you know."

"All right. Good-bye." Captain Sogge slowly hangs up the phone and slowly shakes his head. "We tried," he says to himself quietly, resting his face in his hands. "We tried."

"So Christmas Ship set your sails
Christmas Ship We'll tell your tales
But remember oh remember
Those November gales…"

CHAPTER THIRTY-SIX – BAD NEWS IN CHICAGO

The following day in Chicago, Barbara looks out of her upstairs window toward Lake Michigan. The treetops sway back and forth in the wind, and the sky looks angry and dark out over the lake. It has never easy for the wife of a sea captain on days like this, but it had always been that way for her. In over twenty years of her marriage to Captain Schuenemann, Barbara had always waited for him to return, and he always had. Sometimes he had stories of his wild encounters with storms out on the lake, but he had always returned.

Busying herself with her duties, Barbara tries not to think about the way the wind rattles the shutters and blows light wisps of snow through the air past her window. But she finds she can't stop thinking of him, and in her thoughts she drifts back and to all the wonderful times they have spent together, and even though times weren't always easy, and at times the future seemed uncertain, sharing one another's love had always been enough to carry them through.

Her mind drifts back to that first winter together with her dashing young sea captain. Just his presence made her feel as if she breathed the very air of heaven, and even though they were so poor that they had to spend the winter living in the cabin of a ship, they were only too happy just to be together.

Walking down the stairs, Barbara finds Elsie and the twins in the kitchen, making muffins.

"How are you girls doing in here?" she asks, entering the room.

"I'm just helping the girls make muffins. The muffins are still in the oven, but they should be done pretty soon."

"Mmmm, well they sure smell good," Barbara compliments.

"They're Daddy's favorites, so we're making a double batch. I do hope he'll be home soon," says Hazel.

"Me too," says Pearl, with a pout.

"Well, don't be too anxious. The way this weather looks outside, he may be a bit delayed."

"I suppose," they say, looking a bit downcast.

Just then there's a knock on the door.

Barbara opens the door. It is Captain Holmes, of the schooner *Onida*, standing quietly, holding his hat.

"Why, Captain Holmes! How are you?"

He stands there speechless for a moment, fumbling with his hat.

"Do come in, Captain," says Barbara.

"Thank you." He nods and steps inside the door. At first a bit hesitant to speak, Captain Holmes finally speaks up. "Barbara,

I received some rather disturbing news this morning at the Mariners' Hall. I received a telephone call from Captain Sogge of the Two Rivers Lifesaving Station. He was inquiring if we had any schooners due in their routes. He also told how the Kewanee Lifesaving Station had called him and asked for assistance, because they had seen a schooner about four or five miles offshore of their station flying a distress flag, moving at about five or six knots to the south. Because the Two Rivers station had a power launch, they had requested their assistance. Captain Sogge said they went out to meet the vessel, but when they rounded the Kewanee Point that they didn't find the ship, nor any sign of it. The aren't sure of the identity of the ship, but it did have a tree attached to the top mast."

Captain Holmes pauses for a moment. "Captain Sogge told me that they searched the area till after dark, but no sign of the vessel or any debris was found. He also informed me that this morning a search was made of the area, but again, nothing was found. So I made a long-distance phone call to the Thompson Lumber Company, and they informed me that the *Rouse Simmons* had left there about one o'clock the day before the ship was seen. The schooner was spotted by the railcar ferry *Ann Arbor No. 5* about an hour earlier than it was seen by the Kewanee Station. It flew no distress flag then, but it fit the description of the *Rouse Simmons*. That's all that I can tell you now, Barbara."

Barbara nods in acknowledgment. Elsie and the twins listen intently from the kitchen, and come hurrying out to join them.

"So they're not sure where the ship is, then?" Elsie asks with a worried look.

"No, Ma'am," he says quietly. "All we can do now is wait for any more word."

There's a solemn silence for a moment, then Captain Holmes says, "Perhaps I could lead us in a word of prayer?"

"Yes," says Barbara. Elsie draws close to her mother, and Barbara puts her arm around Elsie and the twins.

Captain Holmes places his hand on Barbara's shoulder and together they bow their heads in prayer.

"Dear Heavenly Father, we do pray today for the safety of our family and friends of the *Rouse Simmons*. We pray and hope that they will return to us safely. And I do pray that you will give us all patience and strength in this time of need. We ask these things in the holy name of Jesus. Amen."

He gives them all a reassuring hug. "That's all we know right now, so I'll keep you informed of the latest word, if I hear any more news."

"Thank you so much for stopping by, Captain Holmes. I do hope that they are found safe in some harbor."

"I hope so, too. God be with you," he adds, and slowly

turns and steps out of the door.

As the door closes, Barbara and Elsie give one another a long embrace then try to go back to their daily routine. But they often find themselves wondering about the fate of the ship.

Later, Elsie confides to her mother, "I do hope Father and Thomas are safe. I am so worried, Mother."

"Thomas?" Barbara says in a puzzled tone.

"Well, I don't know for sure if Thomas is with Father, but we talked together the night before we left Thompson to come home on the train, and Thomas said that he wanted to come to Chicago to see what kind of opportunities there were for a school of photography. I assured him that I was sure that if anywhere, Chicago would be have some of the finest schools. Thomas also told me he would ask father if he could sail with him when he returned with the trees."

"So you don't know if Thomas is with father then?"

"No, I don't," says Elsie, wiping a tear from the corner of her eye.

"You and Thomas are quite in love, aren't you?"

"Oh, yes, Mother!" she says, bursting into tears again. "I have never loved anyone like this before. I could just spend every moment of my life with him, and never get tired of it. It's like I'm in awe the whole time we're together, and we laugh and talk so. It's as though we've been best friends all our life. I just cherish every moment we're together."

"Your father and I were so like that, too," Barbara recounts. "No matter where we went or whatever we did together, we had a ball! And even though we spent that first winter together on the ship, we couldn't have been happier. I do hope that we hear from them soon!"

"I hope so too, Mama." They embrace again.

Over the next few days, Captain Holmes stops by several times with mixed reports, some indicating that the ship was lost with all hands, some that the ship was safely in this port or that. Other reports indicate that the ship was sighted in other parts of the lake, perhaps blown off course by the winter storms. On several occasions, two or three Chicago newspapers give conflicting reports on the same day, with the newsboy on one corner yelling, "Christmas Tree Ship is lost." The newsboy on the next corner yelling, "Christmas Tree Ship found safe!" But one thing was certain, the more time that passes without word from Captain Schuenemann and his crew, the more doubtful are the chances of their safe return.

All the conflicting reports have the Schuenemann family on an emotional roller coaster. With one report their hopes soar, only to have them dashed to despair by the next report. After days of conflicting reports Barbara has become so troubled emotionally from all of the stress that she has become ill, staying in her room and refusing to see anyone.

Joining the family at this time of need is Rose Schuenemann, Barbara's sister-in-law, who had lost her husband August, fourteen years earlier on an ill-fated voyage of the *S. Thal* to Chicago with a cargo of Christmas trees. She has borne the sorrow of the loss of her husband, and now comes to comfort and help her sister-in-law through this difficult time.

The days that follow bring friends and relatives offering their aid and support, and news reporters also stop by their home. It seems there is always someone at the door and today will be no different.

Knock, knock, knock.

Aunt Rose answers the door. "Yes?"

"Is this the Schuenemann residence?" a middle-aged man asks.

"Yes, it is," answers Aunt Rose.

"My name is Charles Davidson, and I work for the *Chicago Inter Ocean,* and I was wondering if I could ask Mrs. Schuenemann a few questions about her husband and the missing schooner."

"I'm sorry, she won't be feeling up to it today, but Elsie, the Captain's daughter, is here. Perhaps she will see you."

"That would be fine, Ma'am. Thank you," he says, tipping his hat. The door closes.

In a moment, Elsie appears at the door. "Yes? Can I help you?" Elsie asks.

"Yes. I'm Charles Davidson, with the *Chicago Inter Ocean*. I would like to speak with you for a moment. I just wanted to inform you and your family that the newspaper has started a relief fund for the families of the missing crew members from the *Rouse Simmons*, and that if there is any way we can assist you and your mother and the children, please let us know!"

"That's very gracious of you, Mr. Davidson. I'm sure that the families of the missing crew could use some assistance. Mother and I are doing just fine, and I would like to say that we fully expect to hear word of my father's ship being found, perhaps near one of the islands. The revenue cutter *Tuscarora* is making a thorough search of all the islands in hopes of finding them, and when they're found we fully expect to repay every penny that the kind people of this city have given."

The reporter is writing on his pad as quickly as he can. He realizes now that Elsie is in total denial that her father's ship and crew probably won't be returning. So after a few short questions he thanks her and leaves.

Elsie closes the door, but she stands by the door for a moment to cry. After putting on a brave face, she now breaks down and weeps in despair, but as she does, another knock comes on the door. Hurriedly Elsie wipes her tears then opens the door.

There stands a smiling old gentleman, holding his hat.

"Mr. Anderson!" Elsie says with surprise, rushing toward him. She gives him such a hug that it startles the shy old Swedish man. "What are you doing here?" Elsie asks.

"I chust arrifed vit da two train car loats of Christmas trees," he answers in his heavily Swedish brogue.

"Christmas trees!" exclaims Elsie.

"Yes. Your father sent me up nort to buy more trees, but ven I arrif pack at Thompson, ta ship vas alreaty con. So your father left vord for me to pring dem by train to Chicago. So, I chust arrifed."

"Oh Peter, I must tell you there's been some terrible news. Father's ship has been missing now for nearly a week, and we are afraid something has happened to them," says Elsie, bursting into tears.

"Oh my gott," says Peter, holding Elsie closer to him, trying to comfort her.

"What are we going to do?" Elsie lets out a sob.

Peter now just stands there holding Elsie in his arms, and for the first time, Elsie begins to accept that her father and the others may not return. Elsie weeps in his arms for a good long while. Peter weeps with her, resting his head on hers.

Finally, Elsie regains a bit of her composure, and Peter hands her his handkerchief to dry her tears and wipe her nose.

"Do come inside now, Peter. You must be tired after such a long trip. Mother is up in her room. She's not taking things too well right now, but Aunt Rose is here helping, and the girls will be happy to see you."

They walk into the kitchen together. Elsie announces to the others that Peter has arrived.

"Aunt Rose, Pearl, Hazel! Look who's arrived! It's Peter Anderson, from up north. He's just arrived with some train cars of Christmas trees."

They all greet him. "Hello Peter," says Aunt Rose, giving him a hug.

Then Pearl and Hazel do the same.

"Come sit down here in the kitchen and rest for a while, and I'll get you something to eat. Pearl, Hazel, could you get Mr. Anderson a bowl of soup and some of that delicious bread that you just made?"

"Peter hadn't heard that Father's ship has been missing," Elsie tells them. "Father had sent him up to Sault Ste. Marie to acquire more trees. When he arrived back at Thompson, the ship had already gone and Father had left word to bring the trees here to Chicago."

Peter nods in agreement as Elsie relates the story.

While the others serve him some food, Aunt Rose sets a hot cup of tea out for him. Peter slowly eats his meal and listens quietly while Elsie and Aunt Rose take turns sharing all of the news that they have been hearing about the ship and how conflicting some of the reports have been.

Peter quietly listens, nodding now and then, taking it all in and trying to make sense of it all. When he has finished with his lunch he sits quietly for a moment and listens to them for a while longer. Then he looks up and asks, "So vat do you vant me to do vit the Christmas trees?"

Elsie ponders his words for a moment. There's a moment of silence. Elsie looks at Peter, then at Aunt Rose, and for the first time she realizes that if anything is to be done, that it is up to her.

CHAPTER THIRTY-SEVEN – A BRAVE GIRL

After asking about what should be done with the Christmas trees there is a moment of silence. Seeing Elsie deep in thought, Peter and Aunt Rose quietly wait for an answer. Neither of them has even a suggestion of what to do next.

"Oh," Elsie says, holding her hand up to her chin and thinking for a moment. "I have an idea," she says with a bright new look in her eyes. "Peter, you just take and relax and have another cup of coffee. I'm going to get myself ready, and we'll see about taking care of those trees," she says with a knowing look. "I'll be back in a few minutes."

When Elsie returns she is smartly dressed and her hair all in place, carrying her best coat and hat.

By this time Mr. Anderson has finished eating and is looking a bit more refreshed.

"Are you ready, Mr. Anderson?"

"Yes." He nods.

"I'm not sure how long I'll be," Elsie tells Aunt rose, "so don't worry. I will see you later."

Elsie and Peter put on their hats and coats and leave the house. Elsie strolls down the street confidently. "We'll go down to the Mariners' Hall."

It's just down the street from the Clark Street Bridge, and Elsie and Peter hurry their way along through the busy water front district to the Mariners' Hall.

The Mariners' Hall is a hub of activity for all those doing business in the maritime shipping trade. Farmers, merchants, and manufacturers desiring to ship their products make contact here to find available transportation to and from other ports.

Sea captains and sailors would gather at the Hall, the captains to find cargoes for their ships, and the sailors to find work as crewmembers on those vessels.

Elsie and Peter step inside. It's a busy place. Several men are standing near the front desk, talking. Some are dressed as sea captains, others are in regular mariners' garb, but all are surprised to see this beautiful, golden-haired young lady step through the door.

They all stop and turn their attention. Some of them recognize Elsie as Captain Schuenemann's daughter. Among them is Captain Holmes, the one who has been keeping the family informed about the latest word on their father's ship. There are also other close friends of her father and the crew of the *Rouse Simmons.*

"Elsie, what a surprise! What can we do for you?" says Captain Holmes.

A small group of men gathers around. "This is Peter

Anderson," Elsie says, introducing him to Captain Holmes and the others. "Mr. Anderson has just arrived with two train car loads of Christmas trees down at the rail yard. He has been traveling for several days to get here. He hadn't heard that my father's ship has been missing. So now we have these trees that need to be taken care of, and I was wondering if any of you men could help."

They all quickly look at one another and immediately pledge their support. They all respond together, "Of course! Whatever we can do to help."

Elsie looks at them meekly and with a pleading look in her lovely blue eyes. "I," she hesitates as though afraid she may be requesting too much. By now they all are desperate to hear what request will come from those beautiful lips.

"I was wondering, if any of you have a schooner that is not in use, if we could use it for selling Christmas trees at the Clark Street Bridge.

Immediately there's a flood of offers, with several captains offering their ships, including Captain Holmes. "You could use the *Onida,* if you like."

"Oh Captain Holmes, that would be so kind of you! Thank you," she says. Rushing to embrace him, she closes her eyes and rests her head against his big chest. Tears begin to stream down her cheeks. Captain Holmes comforts her a while and wipes a tear from his own eye. Even though many of the men are hardy seamen, every one of them is moved as they witness the touching scene.

Captain Holmes offers Elsie his handkerchief, and when Elsie has dried her eye a bit he asks her, "Is there anything else we can do?"

"Yes," says Elsie, wiping her eyes, "If you could bring the ship to the dock down by the rail yard, Peter and I could sure use some help loading the trees from the rail cars onto the ship."

"I can help," one of the sailors offers.

"I can help," offers another.

"I'll help." "I'll help." Until it seems that everyone joins in.

"I'll get together a bunch of us," says another eagerly.

"Well then!" says Captain Holmes with a look of surprised satisfaction. "I can start getting the ship ready right away. I'll arrange to have it over there yet this evening, so it will be ready to start loading in the morning."

They all nod in agreement.

"Oh, that would be wonderful!" says Elsie, wiping a tear from her cheek. "You are all so kind. I want to thank all of you for offering your help"

The sight of this beautiful young woman wiping away tears of gratitude is too much for them to take, and even though they are all rugged and hearty sailors, many of them are wiping tears from their own eyes.

At that moment if Elsie had asked them for the moon and stars, somehow they would have gotten them for her.

"It's settled, then!" Captain Holmes announces out loud to the whole hall. "I'll have the *Onida* down at the rail yard dock, and anyone who can help, I want you to be there first thing in the morning!"

The whole hall lets out a cheer. "All right!"

Peter Anderson wipes tears from his eye, too then together, Elsie and Peter walk out of the hall and slowly make their way back down the street.

"That was so kind of them," says Elsie.

"I vill go pack to ta rail yard," Peter tells Elsie, "Ten I vill make sure tat da rail cars are at ta dock in ta morning."

"Oh, thank you, Peter. You have been so helpful. Do you have a place to stay tonight?"

"Ya. I got a room at ta poarding house town ta street."

"Could I invite you to the house for breakfast in the morning?"

"Ya, dat voot be alright."

"Good!" says Elsie. "Then we can walk to the rail yard together. And Peter, I want to thank you again for all your help. I really appreciate all that you have done." She gives him another big hug.

"You're velcome, Elsie," he says warmly, hugging her

back.

Peter slowly turns to leave.

Elsie turns to leave also and begins to walk the other way, then she turns back. "Oh, Peter, one other thing."

Peter turns to listen.

"Do you know if Thomas went with Father on the ship?"

"You mean tat young man vit da automobile?" asks Peter.

"Yes," answers Elsie.

"I think so," answers Peter. "'Cuz I saw ta automobile sitting in ta yard at Osbourn's, and he told me tat he left it dere for his father to get it.

A distant look comes across Elsie's face. " Thank you, Peter."

She slowly turns and walks away down the street, grasping the locket around her neck with the picture Thomas had given her in her hand. She bursts into tears and rushes back to the house crying.

CHAPTER THIRTY-EIGHT – A GRAIN OF MUSTARD SEED

That evening, back at the Schuenemann home, Elsie is rather quiet, sitting by the stove. Aunt Rose and the twins are working together on some sewing projects when she asks, "Elsie, could you fix a tray with a bowl of soup and some bread and butter for your mother? She hasn't eaten anything all day, and I am worried. She's not eating enough. Maybe you can encourage her to eat something."

"All right, Aunt Rose. I'll try."

Taking a bowl from the cupboard, she takes it over to the stove and fills it with the warm soup and sets it on a tray, then cuts some bread and places it on a plate next to the soup. Setting them on a tray, Elsie carefully carries them to her mother's room and opens the door.

"Mother, I brought you some soup," says Elsie, as cheerfully as she can.

"Thank you, dear. Come in and just set it right here," she points to the nightstand.

Elsie places the tray on the table and leans over her mother's bed. Then, kneeling by the bed, she leans over and puts her arms around her and just holds her. Barbara reaches up and holds Elsie too, and they embrace for a long while.

"How are you feeling, Mother?"

"Oh, I'm still feeling rather weak," she says quietly. "How about you?" she asks, looking up at Elsie.

"Not much better," she answers. "But you know, a strange thing happened today."

"What's that honey?"

"Peter Anderson showed up at the door. He said that he had just arrived with two train car loads of Christmas trees."

"Oh really?" Barbara sits up a bit, giving Elsie her full attention.

"Yes, and he knew nothing about father's ship being missing, so I told him all about it, and he was really quite disturbed. He was also quite weary from all of the travel, so I brought him in and fed him some soup and bread, and when he finished, he asked me what I wanted to do with the trees."

"So what did you tell him?" By now, Barbara is sitting straight up in bed.

"Well, at first I was quite taken back, then I had an idea. Peter and I went down to the Mariners' Hall and asked some of the captains there if they had a ship that wasn't being used, if we could tie up and sell the trees from the ship at our usual place by the Clark Street Bridge. They thought it was an excellent idea, and Captain Holmes offered the use of the *Onida*, and said that he would arrange for it to be brought to the rail yard dock this evening. In the morning, it will be ready to load."

"Who's going to help load it?" Barbara asks.

"Just about everyone in the Mariners' Hall said they would help, and it sounded like they would bring others, too. So if they all show up, I think the work should go rather quickly. So you better eat, because you're going to need your strength. I'm not going to be able to sell all of those trees by myself!"

"You are a dear girl," says Barbara, leaning over and giving Elsie a hug.

"So, it looks like we're still in the Christmas tree business, then, Mama."

"Yes, it does," answers Barbara. "Yes, it does."

There's long pause, then Elsie continues. "I also asked Mr. Anderson if he knew if Thomas had joined Father on the ship." She looks at her mother, and then her lip begins to quiver. "He said he was quite sure that he had!" She breaks into a sob.

Elsie falls into her mother's arms, and for a good long while they both weep together in each other's arms.

CHAPTER THIRTY-NINE – THE O'MALLEY'S PRAYER

That night, in another part of town in a small apartment, a poor Irish immigrant mother and father--the O'Malleys--are getting their children ready for bed. Mrs. O'Malley and her husband are discussing the news of the Christmas ship.

"You know that Captain Schuenemann and his ship are still missing," the father tells the others. "They're quite certain the ship has been lost with all hands."

"Oh, that must be terrible for his family!" says Mother. "Annie and Jimmy loved the captain, too. He was so kind. He took us up on his ship and even gave us a Christmas tree."

"Yeah, and we promised him we would go back to the Christmas ship again this year for a tree," says little Jimmy sadly. "I miss the Christmas ship and the captain. He's my friend."

"So do I," says Mother. "Come now, children, it's getting very late, so let's get ready for bed, and let's not forget to say our prayers."

The children kneel by their bed in the crowded little apartment. Father joins them.

"Mother," says Annie, "I think we should pray that the Christmas Tree Ship will return."

"Yeah!" Jimmy pipes up. "Let's pray that the Christmas

Ship comes back!"

Mother looks over at Mr. O'Malley and he shakes his head slowly.

"I'm afraid they're quite certain the ship has been lost and won't ever be coming back," father explains sadly.

"But Mother!" Annie protests. "Didn't you tell us that Jesus said if we have the faith of a mustard seed that God can do the greatest things and answer our prayers?"

"Yes," says Mother cautiously.

"I'm sorry, children, but I think there's some prayers that even God cannot answer," says Father, trying not to discourage their little hearts.

"Can we pray that the Christmas Ship returns?" asks Annie. "I just know that somehow God can answer our prayer. I just know it!"

"I want to pray for the Christmas Ship to come back, too," says Jimmy. "I think if we all pray together, don't you think our faith would be as big as a mustard seed?"

Father and mother look at one another, a bit puzzled at what to say next.

"All right then, children," says mother. "If you want to pray for the Christmas ship you can, because we never want to discourage your prayers. But don't be too disappointed if the Christmas Ship doesn't come this year, okay?"

"All right, Mama," says Annie.

"Let's say our prayer now, children."

Annie folds her hands and bows her head. "Dear Jesus in heaven, I know there's lots of prayers to answer up there, but please remember all of the families that won't have a Christmas tree if the Christmas Ship doesn't come. So Jesus, I believe You could somehow answer our prayers and all of the prayers of the other children praying tonight who want the Christmas Ship to come again, too. Please think about our prayers while we all sleep tonight. Amen."

Next it's little Jimmy's turn to pray. He kneels by the bed with his eyes closed and hands folded. He talks to God as though he knows Him personally. "Dear God, my sister and me are still pretty small, but our faith is pretty big. I betcha if you put both our faith together it's way bigger than a mustard seed, and this year we have enough money to buy us a Christmas tree, so if you know about seeds, we'll be sure happy when we see the Christmas Ship tomorrow."

"All right, children. Time for bed," says mother.

"Good night, mother. Good night, father."

"Good night, children." They kiss them both and tuck them in.

CHAPTER FORTY – THE MIRACLE OF THE CHRISTMAS SHIP

The next morning back at the Schuenemann home finds Elsie up early. Aunt Rose is up, too, helping the twins get ready for school and preparing breakfast. Soon there's a knock at the door.

Aunt Rose goes to the door. It's Peter Anderson. She invites him in and shows him to the kitchen. By now, Elsie and the twins are ready, and join him at the table.

"Good morning, Peter," says Elsie.

"Good morning, Peter," the twins repeat.

"Goot morning," Peter responds with a smile.

Aunt Rose serves them each a large bowl of oatmeal. "There's honey here for the oatmeal, or maple syrup. Barbara and the girls brought it back from their trip up north," she adds.

"Elsie, did you know that your Uncle August and I stayed with Peter and his wife one year when we were up north gathering trees?"

"No, I didn't know that," says Elsie, with a surprised look.

"Yes, and I must say, we had a wonderful time there! I do miss going up north for those couple of weeks. Peter's wife, Eva, still writes to me now and then."

They sit down together while Aunt Rose waits on them. "I have some toast warming in the oven, too. Let me get it for you," she says, reaching into the oven and grabbing the plate with the hot pads. She sets it on the table.

"Pearl and Hazel made this bread. They're getting to be quite the home makers."

The twins both smile proudly.

"I think it is so nice of Captain Holmes to let us use his ship to sell the Christmas trees, and all of the others who offered to help. I do hope that quite a few show up. Then it won't take too long to load the ship. I do hope Mother will be well enough to join us today. She told me last night she may come there and help."

"I'll try and encourage her when I bring her some breakfast," says Aunt Rose.

Peter pours some maple syrup in his oatmeal and stirs it in.

"Da men at ta rail yard moved ta rail cars town to da dock yesterday afternoon. Captain Holmes brought da ship along da dock just as it vas getting dark, so ve can start loading ta ship as soon as ve get dere."

"Can we go and help?" asks Hazel.

"No, you have to get to school," Elsie tells the twins. "But after school you'll be able to help, and by then we should have the ship at the dock right where we always do. So do come and help me. I think Father would be very proud of all of us!"

"All right," they both say, looking a little sad.

"I think that your father and your uncle would both be very proud of you," smiles Aunt Rose. "After all, what would Christmas be like in Chicago without a Schuenemann Christmas tree?"

"That's true," says Elsie. "The Schuenemanns have always brought the trees at Christmas time, and if it's up to me, as long as there's a Schuenemann, there will always be Schuenemann Christmas trees in Chicago!"

After breakfast, Elsie and Peter put on their coats and hats and hurry off down the busy street to the railroad dock. When they arrive, they find Captain Holmes already waiting. Several of his crew there also.

"Elsie, Peter! Good morning!"

"Good morning, Captain."

"It looks like it's going to be a beautiful day today, and I was able to get together most of my crew to help, and some more of the men from the Mariners' Hall are supposed to be here, too. So I say we get started!"

Together they walk over to the rail cars.

"I think that if we have two of you men, one on each end of the rail car, handing them down to us, that it should go pretty good," says Elsie, pointing at the ends of the rail cars.

"All right." Four men climb up on the rail car and start untying.

"Here comes some of the others now," says Captain Holmes.

"Oh, good," says Elsie. "You're just in time! The men on top are going to hand them down, one at a time, for you to carry them up onto the ship. Then I'll show you how I want them arranged on the deck."

Captain Holmes and Peter look at one another, a bit amused at how Elsie is taking charge. Then they both hurry off to catch the first trees handed down from the men on the rail car. After being joined by the others, there's a steady stream of Christmas trees being carried up onto the ship.

Elsie directs the men where she wants the trees and how she wants them arranged on the deck. Her winsome smile and kind attention soon wins the heart of everyone around her and although the work is hard, Elsie's presence seems to somehow give them a positive energy that makes their work seem more enjoyable, and in no time, she has the whole operation running as smoothly as a Swiss watch.

Elsie is somehow able to bring out the best in all of them. Her presence seems to make their work so enjoyable that even the huge task of unloading two train carloads of Christmas trees goes rather quickly.

By mid-morning both the rail cars are unloaded, and the last tree is about to be carried aboard the ship.

"We made quick work of that," says Captain Holmes, his face beaming as the last tree is being carried up the gangplank.

They all stand proudly on the deck for a moment, feeling good about how smoothly the job was completed.

"Could I ask just one more favor of you gentlemen," Elsie asks sweetly, her bright blue eyes dancing in the morning sun. "My father always had a tradition that the last tree onto the ship should be tied up there onto the top of the tallest mast," Elsie says, pointing to the top of the highest mast.

Before Elsie can say another word, Captain Holmes pipes up. "If that's what your father did, then that's what you shall have, too." The others all nod in agreement. "Do I have any volunteers?"

Before he even finishes asking, several eager hands go up. "I will!" "I will!" "I will!"

"Well, I wish they were all that eager when they were working for me," Captain Holmes jokes, looking over at Elsie's smile.

"Well, I guess she's got something you don't," says one of his men, beaming from ear to ear. They all laugh.

"Well, hop to it, boys," he tells them.

In seconds, they are climbing to the top of the rigging, towards the top of the mast, and soon they are tying the last tree to the very top of the mast. The others all let out a cheer. Elsie watches with a look of satisfaction as they tie it fast to the mast top.

Just then, a familiar gentleman appears at the dock. "Permission to come aboard," he yells and he comes walking up the gangplank carrying his camera on a tripod over his shoulder. It's Charlie Davidson, the reporter from the *Chicago Inter Ocean.* "Permission granted," says Captain Holmes.

Captain Holmes looks over at Elsie, and says with a mischievous smile, "I hope you don't mind, but I told the newspaper about your new ship. I thought a little publicity might help your tree sales, too."

"Oh Captain Holmes, you have been so helpful!" Elsie reaches up and gives him a big hug and a kiss on his cheek. All the men cheer again.

The newspaper reporter, Charles Davidson, joins the others on board the ship. "Is this Captain Elsie?" he asks cheerfully.

"That's her," says Holmes proudly.

"Good to see you, Mr. Davidson," says Elsie.

"Elsie! Good to see you, and in command of your own ship! I think first of all we should get a photograph of you at the wheel of the ship. What do you say?"

They all escort Elsie back to the ship's wheel.

"There now," Mr. Davidson tells her, "strike a pose that will show us what a brave captain you are." He readies the camera.

Elsie places her hand on the ship's wheel and points off into the distance, as though braving some approaching storm.

Click, click goes the camera shutter.

"Okay, good. Let's get one more." *Click, click.* "Good. Now Elsie, what would you like to say?" He takes his pen and notebook in hand.

"I would first like to thank everyone for their help and support in this time of need, and for all of your gifts to my family and the families of all sailors. We hope some of their needs can be met. I also want to say that we fully intend to repay all of our debts, and most important of all, that as long as there are Schuenemanns, there will be Schuenemann Christmas trees in Chicago!"

They all clap and cheer.

"Thank you very much, Elsie. You too, Captain."

"Thank you Mr. Davidson. You have been so kind."

"I hate to rush off, but if I hurry, I can still get this story in this evening's news." Gathering his camera, Mr. Davidson hurries off. "Good bye, everyone!"

"And merry Christmas to you too, Mr. Davidson," says Elsie, waving to him as he walks down the gangplank.

"Let's get this ship under way!" says Captain Holmes. "You know," he says with a look of wonder in his eyes, "the way the wind is blowing, I think we just might be able to sail over to the Clark Street Bridge." His eyes look out over the flag blowing in the wind. Then he wets his finger and holds it up into the wind, an old sailor's method for testing the wind direction. He yells out "Prepare to set sail!"

Others repeat him.

There's an air of excitement on the ship, and sailors are everywhere, scrambling to make the ship ready to sail.

Just then, a voice is heard calling from the dock. "Elsie!"

"Mother! Pearl! Hazel! I'm so glad you've come! The ship is all loaded already. Come up here. We're going to sail the ship over by the Clark Street Bridge. Come up and join me!"

Barbara and the girls hurrie up to the top of the gangplank. Elsie and Captain Holmes are there to greet them. Elsie reaches out and they all give one another a big embrace.

"Mother, I'm so glad you came!"

"I wouldn't miss this for the world. There'll be Schuenemann Christmas trees in Chicago this season," she announces graciously.

All the sailors give a cheer and greet them.

"Welcome aboard! Welcome aboard, Mrs. Schuenemann," Captain Holmes smiles. He tips his hat and escorts the women to the ship's wheel. Pointing to the wheel, he says, "I want you ladies to steer the ship. I'll guide you," he winks.

"Do you know how to use a steering wheel?" asks Holmes.

"Herman has let us steer the ship many times," Barbara tells him. The twins nod in agreement.

"Yes, and I know how to drive an automobile," says Elsie, stepping up and placing her hands on the wheel.

Captain Holmes looks a bit surprised. "You know how to drive an automobile?" Stepping back, Captain Holmes lets Elsie take the wheel.

"Father let me steer the ship many times, too," she adds confidently.

"It's in your hands now, ladies."

Captain Holmes shouts out orders. "Shove off, men! Gang way!"

The sailors throw off the dock lines and scurry up the gangplank.

"Hoist the main sail," orders Captain Holmes. "We've got Christmas trees to deliver!"

Slowly the ship pulls away from the dock, like some giant leviathan stirring after a long nap.

The ship begins to make its way along the busy riverfront. Captain Holmes watches Elsie. "You're doing great," he tells her. "Take her right straight up the river."

The Christmas Tree Ship slowly moves ahead up the river, past busy streets and buildings all along the water front. People stop and watch. Some point, and others wave and cheer. They recognize the tree on top of the mast.

"Look, it's the Christmas Tree Ship! And that's Barbara and Elsie Schuenemann at the wheel of the ship."

Just up the busy Chicago street from the Clark Street Bridge, a young Irish immigrant couple and their two children, Jimmy and Annie O'Malley, hurry down the busy street to where the bridge crosses the river.

"Mother, father, can we go and see if the Christmas Tree Ship came in yet? Mother, father, hurry up! We do want to see if God answered our prayers last night and sent the Christmas Tree Ship!"

"You can run ahead, children. We'll catch up to you. But don't be too disappointed if it's not there."

"All right," they answer, anxiously running up ahead.

Annie and Jimmy soon reach the river's edge, where the Christmas Tree Ship has always been docked. Hurrying up to the spot, the children look around to find that the ship is not there.

"See, it's not there!" says Annie, with a look of disappointment. "Maybe father and mother are right. Maybe the Christmas Ship won't come again."

Little Jimmy looks around for a moment in disbelief then he yells out at the top of his voice, "Look! It's the Christmas Tree Ship!" He points up the river. Sure enough, sailing up the river here comes a ship with a Christmas tree tied to the top of the mast.

"Father, mother, look. Come here quick! The Christmas Tree Ship is coming!"

Father and mother look at one another in surprise and disbelief then they both come running. They can hardly believe their eyes.

"The Christmas Tree Ship is coming," the children shout again and again. "The Christmas Tree Ship is coming!"

The children are soon joined by more people as word spreads like wildfire up and down the street from one group to the next. Children with their moms and dads can be seen running to the Clark Street Bridge to get a better look at the ship with the Christmas trees spread out all across the deck.

And there, waving from the deck of the ship, is the Captain's wife, Barbara, with her twin daughters Pearl and Hazel, and at the steering wheel, guiding the ship up to the dock, is the brave and beautiful golden-haired girl, Elsie Schuenemann.

The ship pulls up at the dock, and Elsie begins to sing the familiar words of the song, *Oh Tannenbaum*. Soon all the sailors on the ship join in. "Oh Tannenbaum, oh Tannenbaum, ve troy sind din ich battern."

By now, quite a crowd has gathered, and they all cheer and join in the singing, first in German and then in English, "Oh Christmas tree, Oh Christmas tree, how lovely are your branches.

Oh Christmas tree."

Over and over the refrain is repeated, then joined by others. The numbers quickly grow, till it seems the whole city is joining in. *Oh Christmas tree, oh Christmas tree, how lovely are thy branches...*

THE END

EPILOG:

Captain Schuenemann's wife Barbara and his three daughters, Elsie, Pearl and Hazel continued the family business of supplying Christmas trees to Chicago for another 21 years.

Hogie Hoganson died several years later in a barroom brawl.

Dan Seavey was made a U.S. marshal after he quit pirating and before he died a penniless death in a Peshtigo, Wisconsin nursing home in 1949.

The Legend of the Christmas Ship - A Novel Based on a True Story or Historical Fiction

What is Real and what is not?

Many of the details about Captain Schueneman, his ship, and his family are true and really did take place.

Most of the main characters in the story are real, only Thomas Berger and William Harkness are imaginary. Although I did once meet an old farmer by the name of Clarence Berger, who told me a story of how my great grandfather, Charlie Behrend, came out to their farm and sold his father a Model T. His story helped inspire the character of Thomas Berger.

Captain Bundy was a real person and actually sailed the Great Lakes as a missionary preacher. Although he did often stop at Manistique and Captain Schueneman and his crew probably knew him, the scene in the book was only what I imagine would take place at one of his meetings. His ministry had actually ended a couple of years earlier, but like I say, the Captain and his crew most likely knew him.

Dan Seavey "The Great Lakes Pirate" was truly a notorious character and all of the stories that refer to involving him are from old newspaper accounts I have read about him.

The scene where he steals the trees off the dock in Thompson was my imagination, but it could have really happened because Seavey was known to slip into a port at night and help himself to whatever cargo was on the docks.

The fight scene at Ekburgs Tavern with Dan Seavey was again the kind of situation I would imagine him to be involved in. Seavey was known around the lake as the "Fighting Pirate."

The fight scene really did occur, though not in 1912 but in 1971. When I was 16 years old I got in a fight at the Harbor Bar, formerly Ekbergs Tavern, with two bullies. I used all of the actual events exactly as I remembered them substituting Hogie Hoganson for myself. Recreating the scene was easy because it was my own experience.

The love affair between Elsie and Thomas was my fabrication. But hey, what would a beautiful 20-year-old girl be doing anyway!

The story about Ki-Chi-Ti-Kipi, which Elsie tells to Thomas, was taken from the book *A History of Thompson, Michigan, and the People Who Lived It.* This book is listed in the Bibliography.

Engvald Newhouse was the name of a crewmember on the *Rouse Simmons*. Very little is known about him but when I was 18 years old I had been a deck hand on the Charles C West and there was a sad old bachelor named "Einer" who once told me a story of the girl he wished he had married. Einer's character became Engvald who added nicely to the story.

The story about the dream involving the ship's captain in distress was based on an experience of a lifesaver from Grand Marais.

All of the other scenes and characters I have tried to glean from history and I could only imagine what they would say and do.

I hope you enjoyed the story.

Carl Behrend

Bibliography

Lumberjack: Inside an Era in the Upper Peninsula of Michigan: 50th Anniversary Edition: By William S. Crowe, Lynn McGlothlin Emerick (Editor) and Ann McGlothlin Weller (Editor). North Country Publishing (MI); Third edition (August 1, 2002). Photo Credits

The Historic Christmas Tree Ship: By Rochelle Pennington. Pathways Press Inc. (September, 2004)

Our Heritage: Garden Peninsula, Delta County, Michigan, 1840-1980: Published by The Garden Peninsula Historical Society, (1982), First Edition.

A History of Thompson, Michigan, and the People Who Lived It: By Florence "Alex" Meron, (April 13, 2003).

About the Author: Carl Behrend is an author and singer-songwriter available for lectures, photo slide shows and musical performances about the Great Lakes. Behrend, who was born in Escanaba, Michigan, has released four CDs, his latest is a compilation of his Great Lakes tunes. Prior to that, he released *More Legends of the Great Lakes*, following a theme established on his first two releases, *Ballad of Seul Choix* (1997) and *Legends of the Great Lakes* (1998), that of creating euphonious folk music versions of local maritime tales. Behrend is also the author of *Adventure Bound: Father and Daughter Circumnavigate the Greatest Lake in the World,* the true story of Behrend's journey around Lake Superior, first published in 2003. He lives in Alger County in Michigan's Upper Peninsula.

Contact Carl Behrend, or order more of his books and CDs at: *www.greatlakeslegends.com.*

About the Cover Artist: Born in Germany, Dietmar Krumrey immigrated to America with his family at the age of three. After living in the Chicago area, they moved to the Upper Peninsula of Michigan where Dietmar developed his deep affection and respect for wildlife so evident in his art. After training at the American Academy of Art in Chicago, he was employed as an artist for Hallmark in Kansas City before leaving to freelance. Dietmar returned to the Upper Peninsula to live and paint near the forest and lakes, which inspire his work. Extensively known for his realist approach, exactness for detail and feeling for the actual essence of life, Dietmar captures the very heart of wildlife art. His works are included in many private collections across the country and he has exhibited in such prestigious shows as the Leigh Yawkey Woodson Show, the Smithsonian Institute, the National Wildlife Art Exhibit in Kansas City, the Wildlife Festival in Tulsa and the Southeastern Wildlife Exposition in Charleston and the Waterfowl Festival in Easton, Maryland.

Visit *www.wildernessart.com* to view more of Dietmar's work.